every breath you take

With many thanks !

TRAVIS THRASHER

every breath
you take

Copyright © 2009 by Travis Thrasher

Lucas Lane Publishers
Mars Hill, North Carolina

Printed in the United States of America

First Edition
10 9 8 7 6 5 4 3 2 1

Library of Congress Cataloging-in-Publication Data
Thrasher, Travis, 1971-
Every Breath You Take/Travis Thrasher.—1st ed.
p. cm.
ISBN 978-0-615-33488-2

every breath you take

a novel

TRAVIS THRASHER

For my beautiful little girl

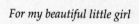

Heaven is that remote music that we are born remembering.
—C. S. Lewis

Oh, take me back to the start.
—"The Scientist" by Coldplay

I'll be watching you....
—"Every Breath You Take" by The Police

You don't remember when we used to dance together, but I do. . . .

▶ Clair de Lune (1982)

The apartment trembles against the wind. It's half an hour before midnight, before the year turns into another. The world outside is wintry and wearisome, but inside it's warm. A father holds his baby daughter in his arms, the rocking chair moving without a creak. He can't keep his eyes off her.

Her head is just starting to show a cap of hair, tiny with little blonde fuzz forming, especially in the back. Every minute or so he kisses the top of her head.

As he rocks her gently, he can feel the little breaths against his own. At times it sounds hoarse, her little body nursing a cold that he worried was something worse. But a doctor he couldn't afford told him there wasn't anything wrong, that colds just took awhile to shake, that she was fine.

The man wonders how long the cold will last, then thinks about something else.

He wonders how much time he has with her.

His daughter fidgets, jerking, raising her arms for a second like a preacher shouting hallelujah. Then she's out again.

Her skin is so soft, so delicate.

Everybody he's ever talked to tells him the same thing—to enjoy the moment. That he'll blink and she will be an adult, moving out and moving on.

He dreams about what she will look like when she is grown. He knows she will be beautiful. He hopes that she is looked after, just like now.

She is bundled, protected, helpless, so fragile.

Ten minutes before the new year she starts to cough, her breathing becoming more gravelly. He stands, rocks from side to side. Mildly bouncing, shushing her, soothing her.

The rest of the world frolics and celebrates and laughs and toasts. He used to feel melancholy when he saw the parties and found himself not a part of them. *New Year's in Rio de Janeiro* or *Countdown in the Big Apple.* They were all the same: overdone and overrated. But tonight he's glad that he's right here, in this little room, holding onto this little love.

He thought he understood love before, but he never had, not like now.

She breathes against him and he holds her. Then he walks to the small cassette player and presses *play*.

Three minutes left.

Three minutes until the new year.

Van Cliburn begins to play "Clair de Lune." The soft piano is a favorite of his, often played to get her to sleep. And as it glides softly along, he does the same with his daughter in his arms, drifting toward sleep.

With the rest of the world so far away, a father dances gently with his baby girl.

And two-minutes-till turns into one. And the man holding his daughter against his chest dances with her, watching the clock turn to midnight.

"I will always love you, Kayla," he whispers in her ear. "I will always be your father. And I will never let you go."

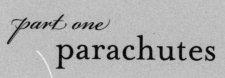

part one
parachutes

On the last day of my life, I remember one thing the most.

I remember singing to you.

I'd like to think that somewhere, deep down in the time and space of your memory, you can still hear me feebly trying to keep up with Stevie Wonder. We listened to him a lot the first two years of your life, because his music summed up how I felt. Not just the immortal and obvious "Isn't She Lovely," but all of his albums from the seventies. You had been walking for some time now—you were two years old, and you could dance better than I could. Your chubby little legs would wiggle and show an amazing sense of rhythm.

Heaven is a lot like those records and those moments.

I always imagined the day to come when I would sway with you gently, a father giving his only daughter away, dancing one final dance on her big day. For some reason, ever since you were born, this event signified the moment when I'd finally have to say good-bye. I thought of it again on that final day I breathed life on this earth.

I've carried that day with me like a snapshot softly pressed against my heart. I can still see your blue eyes peering over the railing of your crib as I opened the door to the nursery that morning. I can still hear your laugh as I tickled your belly button and changed your diaper. I can still smell that baby scent as I carried you into the family room of our small apartment.

Nothing different from any other day. But it turned out to be different because it was the last time I was able to appreciate these pleasures, to appreciate you.

Moments of that day are still as visible and vibrant in my mind as they were when I was living them. And when the sun set, and I found myself rocking you to sleep as always, the love I felt was a fraction of the love I feel today.

The sun doesn't set in Heaven, Kayla. It doesn't need to.

I used to feel overwhelmed by the limited hours in a day, confined in the little box of my own making. But now I feel calm, free, and happy.

I feel at peace.

To say this, yet to not be at your side . . . understand the power in those words. They are not false hope. They are simply true.

There are many things I need to tell you, many blanks I long to fill in. But before I do, let me start with the obvious.

I love you.

And yes, I know you. Time is different in Heaven, but I know you are twenty-six years old. Two and a half decades without a father. It's remarkable how strong you are.

But I would've guessed that even when you were only two and still in my arms.

I know you.

I saw your first tooth fall out, your first broken bone, your first wobbling bicycle ride, your first time behind the wheel of a car. Again, it's impossible to explain. I was there, in the best sense of that word, all throughout your life. I cannot read minds, nor can I see dreams, but I can see you. It's almost more like feeling you. I know you, and I'm proud.

I love the young woman you've become.

So this is my way—my attempt—to tell you what you need to know.

And if this is all you'll ever hear—that I know you, that I love you, and that I'm proud of you—that's enough.

The rest you can figure out on your own. Just as you've always done.

A distant chime wakes him.

Where am I?

Thomas feels confined, uncomfortable, a bit light-headed. The first thing he sees is the back of someone's head.

Then he glances out the window next to him and sees nothing but blue.

"Better put on your seat belt," a voice says.

He turns his head and sees a man sitting close to him. A friendly face smiles at him.

"That was the seat belt sign going on," the stranger says, pointing upwards.

Thomas feels his stomach drop as the plane dips. He no longer wonders where he is. He wonders what he's doing here.

As his hands find the belt, he stares at them in shock.

"Everything okay?"

"Not exactly," Thomas says, buckling up and taking in the scene surrounding him.

"I can imagine you're a bit puzzled."

"I'm a little more than puzzled."

The man next to him grins and extends his hand. "My name is James. And you're Thomas Rowe."

Thomas doesn't ask how the man knows. He already has an idea who James might be.

Why they're sitting on a plane is the pertinent question.

Along with how he suddenly grew wrinkles and age spots on his hands.

"Where are we?"

"I'd say somewhere between New York and Chicago."

"What am I—what is this?"

"It's okay. That's why I'm here, to explain everything."

Thomas sees an airline attendant pass by, then stares at James again. "I was just sitting by a lake, watching the sun hovering in the sky. I fell asleep in my chair."

"Amazing how that works, isn't it?" James lets out the sort of laugh that is hard not to join.

"Why am I here?"

"Well, it's certainly not for the frequent flyer miles, right?"

Thomas glances at his hands again, rubbing them together, not smiling at the joke.

"It's your daughter, Thomas. Something's wrong."

For a moment he can't breathe. And something he hasn't felt in a long time fills him.

Fear.

"What happened? Is Kayla okay? What am I doing here if she's hurt—"

"She's not hurt, nor is she in any physical danger. That's not what this is about."

"Then what?" Thomas feels disjointed, dizzy.

The man studies him for a few moments. When another attendant passes by, James asks for some water. He waits for it, then gives the cup to Thomas.

"Do you remember what you used to long for? Something you wished could one day happen with Kayla?"

Thomas stares at the affable face, but is still confused.

Fear, doubt, anxiety. How quickly they come back.

"I used to wish for a lot of things," he tells the man.

"What about when you used to hold Kayla in your arms and rock her to sleep?"

It only takes Thomas a moment to respond. "To dance with her on her wedding day."

James nods.

"And what? That's why—?"

James nods again. And for a second time, Thomas momentarily can't breathe, like a little boy so focused on opening a Christmas present he forgets to do anything else.

"Your wish has been answered."

The tears forming in his eyes are also new, something he hasn't felt in a long time. Thomas can't help but shiver, his mind thinking of ten thousand different things. "I still don't understand."

"Do you know that a week ago was Kayla's birthday?"

"No," he says, feeling a wave of sadness. "It's been some time since I've been able to see her. I haven't understood why."

"There's a reason behind that."

"How old is she?"

"Twenty-six."

"So it's been . . ."

"Almost twenty-four years," James says. "Twenty-four years since you took your last breath."

Thomas can't say anything.

"Her birthday was a big day."

"Why's that?"

"Kayla got engaged."

"And that's why. . . I don't get it. You said that something's wrong. Is she with some creep?"

"No. On the contrary, she's engaged to a wonderful man."

"Then what can be wrong?"

"There are some things you need to know before your journey begins."

Thomas shifts in his seat. "Like what?"

"Like where Kayla is at in her life, and who Billy is."

"Billy's her fiancé?"

"No. And that, Thomas, is where you come in. Let me explain." James smiles as Thomas takes a sip of his water and shudders.

2. Don't Panic

When do you get to the age when the distant whispers of childhood dreams must once and for all be drowned out?

Kayla Rowe glanced at the bird poop on her car window. It had been there for a week. Every morning as she parked the SUV, the summer sun seemed to put a spotlight on the white blotch.

Just the way birthdays did to dreams.

The door opened, and the sun spilled all over her.

She climbed out of the Chevy and faced the building. The final scene of *One Flew Over The Cuckoo's Nest* played out in her mind, and a slight smile formed on her lips.

Am I really going to break out once and for all?

For nearly four years she had gone through this routine. Waking up around six, swinging by Starbucks on the half-hour drive to work, walking into the five-story corporate building with the big H & G logo on the side. Forty-five months she'd worked at Hart & Graaf Pharmaceuticals, receiving three promotions, putting money in her 401K, working fifty to sixty hours a week.

But in nearly four years the building had never glowed like this, nor had the ground below her felt so soft, nor had her excitement been this intense. Today was a special day.

And it had nothing to do with the fact that it was her twenty-sixth birthday.

~

"I've decided it's time to leave."

She'd already been talking ten minutes. Ten minutes to say something that should have taken ten seconds. Kayla wasn't normally one to not speak her mind, but this was different.

She hated to disappoint anyone.

The faces stared at her blankly.

"You need time off?" Manager X asked.

"No. I'm leaving. Quitting."

"Where are you going?" Manager Y said.

"I don't know yet."

"You don't have another job lined up?" asked Manager X.

"Nope."

"This is a surprise," said Manager Y.

"I know."

"Have you been thinking about this for a while?"

"Yes, but no. I just recently made my decision."

"And when was that?" Manager X asked.

"About an hour ago."

"Do you want some time to think about it?" asked Y.

"No."

"Kayla—it's quite difficult getting a job in today's climate," said X.

"I know."

The faces just looked at her.

This was her moment.

She had the stage and wanted to share with them so they would understand. So they would understand and applaud her actions.

"It's just . . . for some time now, I've done the same thing day after day. Different clients and different tasks, but all falling in the same category. It's not that I don't like this company or value both of you or all the people we work with. I know having a job—*any* job— is a valuable thing these days. But I woke up today wondering if I'm going to have these same feelings inside of me next year, five years from now, even ten. And I just want to take these feelings—these dreams inside of me, ones I might not even recognize—and try to do something with them. You know?"

Two blank slates stared back at her. Unmoved and unimpressed.

"It's just . . . something I have to do."

She waited for a reaction, a word, a movement, a pulse.

Nothing.

And just like that, her four-year career in the marketing and publicity department at H & G was over.

But Kayla knew this one fact.

If she lived to be a hundred years old, she wouldn't think about H & G and what could have been. She doubted that she would even remember what the initials stood for by then . . . maybe not even by next year.

All she knew was that she needed a break. She needed to stop running—stop hoarding and climbing and rushing—and start exploring and searching. Inside and out.

That's what this was about.

It was something that X and Y would never understand.

She didn't ever want to become an X or a Y.

⤳

"Wow," Ryan said.

"Yeah, I know." Kayla moved the stack of files on her desk that stood between her phone and her workout bag.

"Are you serious?"

"This time, yes."

"What happened? What did you say to them?"

"Later. It's pretty busy around here." Kayla didn't have to remind him that she was sitting in her cubicle, where everybody within a four-foot radius could hear her talk.

"Maybe you should've gotten them to give you an office." Ryan's voice sounded pleasant as always, unruffled and unfazed.

"I'm not looking for a door to shut, Ry. I'm looking for one to open."

"Happy birthday, by the way."

"Thanks for the text this morning."

"Didn't want to wake you."

Kayla glanced at the framed picture close to her phone. It was her favorite shot of the two of them, taken at his parents' lake house in Michigan last summer. It reminded her of so many good things, summertime and family and fun.

It reminded her that she was a part of something special.

"So why quit today?" Ryan asked. "Why not tomorrow?"

"I told you I was thinking about it."

"I hope you give me a little more advance warning if you decide to dump me," he teased.

"I'll just text you," she said. "Look, it'll be fine."

"Lots of people out there desperately wanting a job."

"You still taking me out tonight?"

"You're changing the subject," he said.

"And you're paying, right?"

Ryan laughed. She could always get him to laugh.

"I'll tell you more of my thought process at dinner," Kayla said.

"Wait, there's a process?"

"Very funny."

"Did you give them two weeks?"

"Yes," she said. *Not long enough to wipe the stunned looks off their* faces.

"Well, I'll hear about it later. You still having drinks with Shannen after work?"

"Yep. Happy birthday to me."

"Have fun. And, hey—I love you, Kayla."

"Love you too," she said as she hung up the phone.

~

Quitting had been easier and gone better than she expected.

Telling Aunt Cynthia would be another story.

On the drive home, with her sunroof open and the May sun mirroring her mood, Kayla heard her phone ring and saw her aunt's name pop up—for the third time today.

"Happy birthday. Where've you been all day?" Aunt Cynthia asked.

"It's been a crazy day," Kayla said.

"But a good one?"

"The best."

She didn't want to spoil the mood by telling Aunt Cynthia. Not today. Not yet. She knew her aunt well enough to know that she'd worry and wonder and give her ten reasons why she shouldn't have done it. And Kayla would listen and probably start to believe in half of them, but for now she wanted to savor the moment, knowing that she was finished with one part of her life and on to the next.

Whatever that next part would be.

"Where's Ryan taking you tonight?"

"He said it was going to be a surprise."

"And you let him get away with it? You hate surprises."

"I know. But what could I do."

"Any birthday cake left?"

The two of them had celebrated her birthday on Sunday after

church. Aunt Cynthia had spoiled her as usual, baking a chocolate cake and surprising her with a new iPod.

"Not as much as there should be. I've eaten way too much of it."

"You can afford it," Aunt Cynthia said. "Unlike me."

"Oh, stop. The problem is you're too good a cook. What happened to me?"

"You're too impatient to learn."

"Maybe. Or I just know all I have to do is come home and you'll whip up something amazing."

"Coming by Wednesday?"

Kayla thought again of telling her.

But just not now.

"Yeah, I'll be there."

"Have fun tonight."

~

Kayla turned on the car radio and flipped through the stations. For a few seconds, a song that she hadn't heard for years filled the car. *Their* song.

She changed it quickly. A tremble coursed through her body, surprising her.

The next station was playing something she didn't know and didn't even care for, but it was loud. She turned it up and focused on the road in front of her. She rolled down the rest of the windows and let the wind beat her long hair and take her mind off the brief reminder.

And it almost worked.

3. We Never Change

"Do you want the good news or the bad news first?"

This was a horrible way to start a day. It was nine in the morning and Billy had gotten home just six hours earlier and could still feel the beer in his pores. That was the downside of working at a brewery and enjoying the product he served. Now he was wiping his groggy eyes and looking at Reuben, who stood at the foot of his bed wearing nothing but his boxers. Not the most pleasant sight in the world.

"Man, I was sorta sleeping."

"Chad's gone."

"Gone where?" Billy asked.

"Like gone gone."

"Like he died or something?"

His roommate scratched his beard, which had just about as much hair as he did on his cropped and balding head. "No, like he's out of the group gone. Packed up his things and took off."

Billy sat up in bed. He wanted to go back to sleep. He'd been dreaming about having ten tables, and all of them were waiting impatiently on him to take their order. Or maybe he was just reliving last night.

He cleared his voice to try and revive it. "Took off where?"

"Nobody knows."

"When was this?"

"Last night. We tried calling you. I texted you a hundred times."

"My phone disappeared."

"Where to?"

"If I knew that, I'd have it now." Billy ran his hand through his hair. "You talk to Gus?"

Gus was the bassist for the band. The short guy in front of him, Reuben, was the drum player. And Chad, the missing Chad, the same Chad who once decided to spend Christmas break in Alaska for reasons none of them understood, was the guitarist.

"He just called. You know Gus—laid-back as usual."

"Chad will show up," Billy said.

He got up and searched for some shorts, figuring sleep was a lost cause. In another couple hours, he'd be starting his double shift at the brewery.

"I don't think so," Reuben said. "He's pissed at you."

"He's been pissed before."

"He left a note."

"He's left them before."

"Not like this one."

Billy glanced at his dresser. He couldn't remember much of last night, including how much he'd made in tips or how much of that he'd spent.

A clump of cash lay there, along with his Brewtown card, an iPod, and his set of keys including the one to the Volkswagen he was seriously thinking of selling. The VW Jetta was a remnant of his brief career days, when he was trying to live out someone else's dreams in someone else's shoes.

"What's it say?" Billy asked.

"A lot of stuff about you moping around and needing to get over it. And something weird about you needing the shaved gorilla. What's that mean?"

Billy sighed. "I'll give him a call."

"Is that a joke or something?"

"You could say it's a joke. Yeah, pretty much."

"A shaved gorilla? I don't get it."

"You had to be there."

Billy was going to take a shower, but he knew that his roommate had something else to tell him. Reuben looked like a kid with a big secret that he was bursting to tell. Or, scratch that; he looked like a hobbit with a secret.

"What is it?"

"I told you I have good news too. That's why I was trying to call you all last night. I was even going to come to the restaurant, but we were celebrating a little too much."

"Celebrating what?"

A mischievous grin filled his face. "Lollapalooza."

One word said it all.

One word that Billy knew could have more impact on his musical career than anything had in his twenty-six years.

He sat back down on the bed and chuckled in disbelief.

They were finally—finally—going to get their big chance. Playing at the venue in Grant Park. Attendance of around 75,000 people each day. Dozens of rock groups from all over the world.

"You're not kidding me, are you?"

Reuben shook his head, still grinning a delirious smile. "They had an opening, and guess whose name came up?"

And suddenly Billy had an urge to call Kayla, even though it had been a year and a half since they'd spoken.

Some things never changed.

▶ 4. Sparks

It was a perfect afternoon for a margarita.

"Cheers," Shannen announced to the entire restaurant as she toasted Kayla.

Kayla took a sip and smiled—at Shannen's enthusiasm, and at the fact that her friend's strawberry margarita exactly matched her hair.

This was Shannen's birthday present, taking her for happy hour to Pablo's. The music in the background of the small hole-in-the-wall restaurant always put Kayla in a good mood. It felt like she was here on vacation, in a small place hidden away in some town south of the border. The margarita was perfect, served only on the rocks with a mix that tasted smooth as lemonade but that kicked your butt if you had too much.

Kayla had always had a secret desire to sell fruit in a stand on a beach somewhere. Anywhere the sand was soft and the water was clear and tropical music played in the background.

Maybe I'll get my wish now.

Of course, she wasn't going to tell anybody about this idea, one of the many she silenced throughout any given day. She was careful about appearing foolish and flighty, even to people as close to her as Shannen.

You did tell one person, though, didn't you?

Kayla pictured Billy, his sad smile, his melancholy soul. She saw him laughing, joking, arguing, staring.

"So what's the big news?" Shannen asked, thankfully breaking her train of thought.

"I quit."

Shannen waited for more. Kayla simply nodded.

"Shut up."

"I'm serious," Kayla said. "Gave my two weeks' notice to the Twins today."

That was her private name for her managers because they shared similar traits, including no personality and no character. Other than that they were great to work for.

"What happened?"

"I don't know. Just felt right."

"Do you have something else lined up?"

Kayla grinned and shook her head.

"K—what are you thinking?"

"It's about time."

"About time for what? Do you know how many people would kill for a job like yours?"

"Well, it'll be opening up then. I'm doing the world a favor."

"Was it that bad, working there?" Shannen asked.

"It just wasn't that good." She wanted to explain it, but it would be impossible to try. "I've been there for four years. I need a break."

"A break from benefits? A break from a check every other week?"

"I'm not getting any younger," Kayla said.

"You're supposed to have a midlife crisis when you're forty, not twenty-six."

Shannen laughed at her own comment, displaying a full set of teeth. They always reminded Kayla, in a silly way that she would never in a million years tell her friend, of a set of horse's teeth.

"So what did Ryan say?"

"He was surprised. But he didn't say much."

"What about your aunt?"

"She doesn't know."

"Oh boy."

Kayla touched the rim of salt on the edge of her glass. "Do you ever worry that you've gotten to a point in life where you're just settling? Where you have to trade in your dreams for something else?"

"What's that?"

"*Responsibilities*," Kayla said in ominous tone.

"You're talking to someone who can't get a second date with a guy. Dreams? What are those?"

"But you know what I mean?"

"I'm looking for a way to combine my two lame jobs into one good one."

"Maybe you should apply for mine," Kayla said.

"I would if I didn't already know I wouldn't get it. So—what are you going to do?"

"I have lots of ideas. Lots."

Shannen's eyes look like they were about to pop. "This could be scary. Or fun. Just promise me something. This doesn't have anything to do with you-know-who?"

"Not sure who you're talking about."

"Uh huh," Shannen said. "Of course not."

"I quit my job. Doesn't mean I'm breaking up with Ryan too."

"Just checking. Anytime you start talking about dreams and childhood and all that, you get a look in your eyes. A look I used to see a lot."

A waiter interrupted Shannen's lecture with a plate of chicken quesadillas. Kayla suddenly didn't feel hungry. Instead, her stomach felt like it was onboard a fishing boat in stormy waters.

She thought of telling Shannen how Billy came to mind today, but she couldn't.

It was stupid, and it was all because of a song. Or at least that's what she kept telling herself.

A year and a half is a long time.

But it felt like yesterday.

Kayla wondered if it always would.

As quickly as those thoughts came, they evaporated with the sun and the warmth and the magic of the afternoon.

Happy hour certainly did its job. When the knock came later on her apartment door, it didn't look like the magic would go away anytime soon.

"Hello, lovely lady," Ryan said as he gave her a white rose.

"Jeans, huh?" she said with a smile. "No suit for our big dinner?"

"It's your birthday. I know what you like."

"Casual."

"You don't look casual to me," Ryan said. "You might be many things, but you're not casual."

"Oh, really?"

"You look breathtaking," he told her, and wrapped his broad arms and shoulders around her. "Happy birthday."

"Nothing overboard tonight, okay?" she said. "I already got my present."

"Quitting your job?"

"No. Getting a night out with my guy."

"It's nice when you have such low expectations."

"Isn't it?" Kayla asked. "So when's the limo coming to pick us up?"

Ryan played football in college, but was smart enough to know that he wasn't cut out for the NFL. He had the looks of a tight end, and still followed his teams vigorously. Love for sports, and football in particular, was something that Kayla was still working on, under his tutelage.

She thought about this as she glanced at Ryan behind the wheel of his car. He'd told her of his lifelong dream of being a quarterback. Yet he was better at catching the ball and blocking people. He was too big and not fast enough to be a wide receiver and, as he told Kayla, not talented enough to go beyond college. He played for Michigan, though, which in itself was an amazing feat.

What happens when your dreams end before you're thirty?

Ryan didn't carry his football dreams around like some shiny high school trophy, didn't lament all the could-have-beens. He'd taken his experience and determination over into networking and fallen into the job he had now, a financial adviser who helped people (many of them athletes) plan for retirement. He focused on one day at a time, planning for tomorrow but making sure he was firmly planted in today.

"What are you thinking about?" he asked, breaking the silence.

"Do you ever miss football?" Kayla asked.

"What? Playing?"

"Yeah."

"I get together with the boys once a week."

"No, I mean playing for real."

Ryan laughed. "If you watched us play, you'd say it was for real."

"Okay, then, playing professionally."

"Never think about it."

"Never?"

"No. But now that you've asked me to . . ." He paused for a moment, appeared to be lost in thought. "Well, now that I'm thinking about it, I'm devastated."

She hit his arm. "Shut up."

"I could've tried. Some of my buddies did. Most didn't make it. It's a hard route."

"But if that's your love . . ."

"You thinking of trying out for a team or something?"

"I was just—with quitting work and stuff, it got me thinking."

"I'm hoping it got you thinking," he said with a chuckle. "I'm hoping you were thinking some before you told them."

"Yeah, well. . ."

She wanted to explain, but wasn't sure how.

Some strange thing inside of her told her that Ryan wouldn't understand.

Nobody would understand except two people who aren't here.

But of course she knew this wasn't true.

Why wouldn't Ryan understand something that Billy understood? Or something she believed her father would have understood?

I'm just making that up. He died when I was two years old.

"What?" Ryan asked her after waiting for a moment.

"Shouldn't your twenties be about exploring things? About trying to figure out what you want to do the rest of your life?"

Ryan nodded, then glanced at her. "Sure. Unless you've already figured out exactly what you want to do. And who you want to be with."

He reached over and held her hand.

Kayla knew she could tell him anything.

But that didn't mean she would.

~

One of the things she loved about Ryan was that he gave her his undivided attention. They were never at a restaurant with him scrolling through the e-mails on his Blackberry. He never interrupted their time together to take "important calls." Even though he worked long hours, work never made an appearance when they were together unless Kayla asked about it.

They sat in a booth at The Grease Pit as Kayla finished her shake.

"I know you don't love this place."

"But you do," he said. "I'd go for something that didn't have napkin holders on the table, but I know it adds to the charm."

"Did you get enough to eat?"

"Of course."

"Their burgers aren't the biggest."

"They're fine. They fit well with the name."

"I gain about ten pounds every time I come here. That's why it's splurging for me."

"The shake was good," Ryan admitted. "Though I may need to go walk it off."

Ryan had two basic expressions. One was his regular look, which was friendly and affable. The other was his smile, which was friendly and affable. Even when he was angry, something she could hardly remember ever seeing, he looked easygoing and at peace with the world.

"So, you were shocked by my news, weren't you?" she asked.

"You never stop surprising me."

"Was this a good surprise?"

"Of course. I'm curious to see what happens next."

"Me too," she said, prompting laughter from both of them.

"So when do you want your birthday present?"

"You mean it's not just dinner?"

"I went overboard this time."

"Now or later, it's up to you. Did you wanna go for a walk?"

Ryan nodded, then shifted his large frame in the booth. "Sounds like I'm a dog."

"I'll let you walk without a leash."

"What a treat."

"Seriously, Ry, thanks."

"For what?"

"For coming here. For not making things so—birthday!—you know?"

He looked at his watch, then appeared to be upset.

"What?" Kayla asked.

"Well, I've got the clowns coming in about five minutes."

"Shut up."

He put a twenty on the table. "Come on, let's at least go see if we can find some."

"I know a company that's full of them."

"Life's full of them, K. The people that head up companies are the ones who are best at dealing with the clowns out there."

"So you're going to be the next Donald Trump?"

"Would that be a bad thing?"

Kayla smiled. "No. Just—if you start going bald, let it go, okay?"

"Deal."

The Grease Pit was only a short drive from parking at the lake-front. This was enough of a present, Kayla thought, simply walking along Lake Michigan amidst joggers and bikers. The evening was warm and still and satisfying. Ryan slipped his hand into hers. It felt natural. It felt right.

The sun dipped under the city skyline next to them, its orange glow still smoldering like embers in a fire. There was a slight wind. The temperature felt warm, but not sticky.

For a moment, Kayla wasn't thinking about her job or her career or what came next. She simply thought about this evening and the water peppered with boats.

They sat on a bench that looked out on both the lake and the city beside it.

"What a gorgeous evening," Kayla said. "I love nights like this."

"You see yourself staying here in Chicago?"

"If I don't get that job I just applied for in Alaska, then yeah, sure."

"You know what I love about Chicago? Its unpredictability."

"What do you mean? It's predictably sweltering in the summer and predictably miserable in the winter."

"Sure, but then it surprises you. You'll have an occasional warm day in February. Or a cool day in the middle of summer."

"That's not unpredictable, it's schizophrenic."

"It kind of reminds me of something else. Of *someone* else."

Kayla looked at him. "What? You're saying I'm schizophrenic?"

"I'm saying that every now and then, you surprise me. Like to-day, quitting your job."

"And?" she asked, not sure where this was leading.

"And I love it. Just one of many things I love about you."

"Probably because it's so different from you. Mr. Let's-Plan-It-a-Year-in-Advance Man."

"I'm not always like that." He put his arm around her and drew her closer. "Do you know that I think I fell in love with you the first time I heard that feisty voice of yours? Arguing with Shannen about the party you wanted to leave."

"She dragged me there."

"It's wasn't all bad, was it?"

Kayla smiled. "I met you there, so no, it turned out to be a very special party."

"You've heard me say this a hundred times. I've always known I needed someone strong in my life. And I believe you've needed someone strong in yours."

"Why? To be able to deal with me?"

"To be able to deal with each other," Ryan said.

He pulled his arm back and turned to face her. He seemed oblivious to the strangers passing and to the orange turning into pink sky above them.

"Do you have any idea how incredibly beautiful you are? I'm not just talking about those perfect blue eyes or that wavy, wind-blown hair. I'm talking about the way you hold yourself and the way you see life and the way you love it. That's what I love about you."

"Well, thank you," she said with a nervous laugh.

He took both of her hands in his and seemed to wrap himself up in her eyes. "I don't know how you've done it."

"Stop," she said, knowing where this was going.

I don't want to hear it, not now, not again.

"No. Because it's true. I have two parents who still love each other, along with two younger brothers. You're so strong, so smart. And I think—I often think what you'd be like had your father lived. Or if your mother hadn't been so, well—"

"Flaky?"

"Kayla, you're a remarkable woman. I've known this for some time now, but I just—well, you know me. Everything is part of the plan. The right time, the right moment, the right decision. But I knew that *you* were right the first time I saw you. The first time you told me no when I asked you out. The first time you didn't let me kiss you."

Kayla laughed. She was hooked. There was no going back.

"I always had some big planned-out ridiculous thing in mind when I was going to do this—but now, for you, I wanted it to be simple. Simple and a surprise."

Kayla waited.

"This ring has been burning a hole in my pocket, and if I don't ask you now I'll probably die of impatience."

"Ryan . . ."

He took out a box and opened it, revealing a beautiful and perfect and glowing ring that seemed to hover in the air for a moment.

"Happy birthday, Kayla. I know that it's something we've talked about—not the ring, but *us*. About a life together. I don't want to wait any longer. I want you in my life, a part of my life. I want to grow old with you. I want to see what tomorrow will bring and how you'll surprise me next. I want to be the constant thing you don't have to wonder about, the thing that's not going to surprise you."

She could feel the tears in her eyes, streaming down her cheeks. Everything crowding her mind for the past day and week and month and year disappeared.

"I know that this is more of a gift for me than it is for you, but would you grant a guy a dream come true and marry me?"

She looked into those eyes that weren't going to let her down, weren't going to leave her. Then she glanced at the ring and saw it shimmer in the evening light.

I love this man. He's solid and he's stable and he's sweet and he's everything I want and need.

The day had started with a surprise.

It fits and it's right and I don't need any time to think about it.

Kayla put her arms around Ryan and whispered a simple *yes* in his ear.

And staring upwards with tears in her eyes, she hoped that the setting sun wasn't the only thing watching over them with a beaming smile.

5. Yellow

Some songs followed him like a stalker. If only he could call the cops and be rid of them. But the only thing the authorities would tell him would be to get a shrink. Or, as Chad told him time and time again, "Get over her."

Billy was wiping down a table full of nacho remnants when the song came on. And all he could do was curse and shake his head, then laugh.

He couldn't turn off the music here. Usually it was one of the best parts of working at Brewtown Restaurant and Brewery in Chicago. Even when he was on his feet twelve hours sweating the day and night away, he could appreciate some decent tunes in the background. Sometimes the restaurant got so loud on busy nights that the blaring background music could barely be heard. But on this late Sunday night, with only about half an hour left before the kitchen closed, he could hear the music fine.

This was symbolic of the day he was having.

First off, he was only supposed to work lunch, but someone called in sick for dinner and his manager was in a bind. And when someone needed something around here, Billy was the guy they asked. He could never say no, especially to Sam, the general manager, who should have been a drill sergeant.

He'd been here for a year now, but every now and then he had off nights when it seemed like everything went wrong: the kitchen made a mistake, he typed in the incorrect dish, he forgot to bring the five-year-old kid who'd changed his mind ten times another chocolate milk, and his tips averaged 10 percent instead of 20.

Half an hour ago he had broken a bottle of vinegar in the back. He had also spilled half a cup of the Mexican taco beef soup down his leg. And just a few minutes ago, while taking a stack of plates back to the kitchen, he got soupy sour cream all over his shirt. Even after wiping it, he looked like someone had thrown up all over him, not to mention probably smelling fabulous.

But the night wasn't over.

"You just got sat," Erika, who was working the cocktail section of the bar, told him as she passed by.

The song, the smell, the night that never seemed to end.

Sunday nights could be busy or could be dead. After working here for a little under a year, Billy still couldn't figure out what drove people to have food this late at night other than some midnight showing of a gargantuan movie. The worst scenario was thinking he was finished only to have to serve another table, which might or might not stick around for another couple of hours.

Just like now.

He acknowledged Erika's comment with a nod, wiped his eyes and stifled a yawn and headed toward his section.

As he walked toward the booth, another server sprinted toward him.

"Total hot chick in 45," Vince, cut an hour ago but still working on side work, said. "And of course it's your table."

"She alone?"

"Nah. It's a couple."

"Awesome," Billy joked. "Means I'm not going anywhere anytime soon."

Walking toward table number 45, Billy saw the wavy blonde hair that he'd have recognized from a mile away.

Then he got closer, saw the full lips and the blue eyes that stared at him with as much amazement as his mirrored back.

Was it just him, or did his feet seem to slow the closer he got?

Was it just him, or did he miss the head of the guy facing her, the guy with the square head and the square jaw and the broad shoulders?

Was it just him, or had life just stopped?

"Good evening," he uttered without thinking, then added an awkward "Or night, or whenever it is."

"Hi, Billy."

For a moment he tried to say something. Perhaps something about ordering a beer or the soup of the day or the fact that Brewtown made great quesadillas. But the words felt glued to the back of his tongue.

The guy at the table gave him a puzzled look.

"Have you worked here long?" Kayla asked, nonchalant.

"Yeah, uh, just about a year or so."

The last time they had spoken, he had been interviewing for an entry-level job at a design firm downtown. He didn't need to tell her that he didn't get the job.

"Billy, this is Ryan."

"What's up," Billy said, trying to act cool but knowing he was doing a bad job at it. He could feel the blush rise to his face.

Ryan just nodded, his eyes disappearing back into the menu as if Billy was not and could never have been the absolute most meaningful love of Kayla Rowe's life.

"Can I get you guys anything to drink?"

"I'll take a wheat beer," Ryan said. "You want a glass of wine?"

"No, not especially."

"Come on. Just have one. Get her a glass of Riesling. And two waters."

Billy nodded and then noticed something. Kayla's hands rested on the menu, and in a split second—a split second that stopped everything—he spotted the ring. It was pretty impossible to miss.

He looked again to make sure it was really there, then glanced briefly at Kayla.

She gave no hint of what was going on in her mind. But Billy knew she had a great poker face.

"We'll order some food later," Ryan said. "But we'll take those drinks now. Thanks."

Which really meant, *Thanks and please leave us alone.*

On the way back to the bar, Billy tore around a corner and slammed against Erika, who was holding a tray of drinks. Two pints of beer and a martini glass crashed against his chest, then onto the concrete floor, making a crash that everyone in the restaurant heard.

"My bad," he said as he picked up her tray and gave it back to her. "I wasn't paying attention."

Erika's wide eyes seemed more humored than irritated. "To me?"

"To anything."

"You okay?" she asked.

"Not anymore," he said, and went to find a broom.

He was more composed by the time he brought Kayla and her fiancé their drinks.

Her fiancé.

In the flurry of cleaning up the broken glass and wiping himself down, Billy hadn't had much time to think about this reality. For now he had to grin and bear it; he'd deal with the aftershocks later.

When he returned and placed their drinks on the table, he knew that Kayla must have told Ryan something. He could tell the way both of them were silent, the way both of them watched him. Ryan especially, though he still appeared friendly.

And then, instead of just taking an order and putting it through and letting things be, Billy suddenly felt compelled to say something.

"This is probably what some might call awkward," he said.

Kayla smiled. It was a sincere and warm smile.

"Not at all," Ryan said, extending his hand to Billy. "Nice to meet you."

Ryan's grip was tough and strong and rugged. Billy's grip probably smelled like onions.

"So you guys knew each other in college, huh?"

"Yeah," Billy said. So that was what she told him? That they "knew each other"?

Kayla didn't look embarrassed or bothered. In fact, she didn't *look* like anything.

She's gone. The Kayla I remember is gone.

"Can I take your order?" he forced himself to say with a forced smile and forced breathing and forced everything.

They ordered an appetizer just like any other couple might. And Billy wrote it down just like any other server might. He tried not to show his slightly trembling hand.

As he walked away from the table to take the menus back up to the front of the restaurant, Billy thought about not stopping, just heading through those doors and getting into his car and driving far, far away.

Like to California. Or scratch that—to New York City. And staying far away for a long time.

But he had tried that once. And look how far he'd gone.

⌣

The song came on just as he put the plate of spinach dip on their table.

It was the second time it had played during his shift.

It wasn't just a song. Not for someone who wrote and performed them and dreamt of doing that for a living. Not for someone who loved music almost as much as he loved the girl he was setting the plate in front of. Songs were as essential as oxygen. And the ones that stood out, that served as the soundtrack to his life, meant even more.

And this particular song wasn't just a favorite selection in the jukebox. It was perhaps one of a dozen tracks on their personal playlist, the Billy-and-Kayla soundtrack.

He hadn't heard it in at least two years. And for the second time that night, Billy realized he couldn't turn it off.

"Spinach dip," he said, then couldn't contain a chuckle.

Ryan glanced at him, then at the appetizer to see if that was what was funny.

But as the song grew louder, the lyrics more clear, Billy knew that Kayla was thinking the same thing.

And then he saw it.

That look. A knowing glance.

A slight connection.

Tell me you love me, come back and haunt me. . . .

Kayla gave him a smile that said *I know* and *I remember* and *I know this is somewhat horribly awkward.*

"Enjoy," he forced himself to say, leaving the table.

Echoes of the love song followed him into the restroom, where he glanced at himself in the mirror. If it were possible, he would slap the face of the guy he was staring at.

Instead he turned on the faucet and doused cold water over his face.

And the music just kept playing.

It always did.

An hour and a half later, the grill closed and the bar nearly shut down, Billy sat on a stool wearing his stained black pants and a T-shirt. They didn't allow the servers to stay around wearing Brewtown shirts. He was drinking a pint of pale ale and thinking of what had happened tonight.

He replayed the good-bye.

Ryan heading out to the front to get the car, Kayla making some excuse to stick behind, finally seeing Billy and apologizing, saying she didn't know he worked here, that she was sorry that it was awkward, then touching his hand ever so briefly, her eyes connecting with his, her lips telling him that she still loved him and still wanted him.

In his imagination.

Nothing like that had actually happened. He checked on them two more times, then they asked for the bill and he brought it and told them to have a good night.

He should have added "and a good life."

The one connection he had seen—and he knew he had seen it—was brief. That was all he would get. Kayla tightened her lips and said good night. No see you later. No happily ever after.

It was almost as unsatisfying as their actual farewell a couple of years ago.

Then again, nothing could top that in the tragic history of love stories gone awry. At least in his mind.

"You need another," the bartender said, putting a pint on the bar.

The bar lights lit up Izzy's freckles. It was impossible not to smile back at her.

"You don't know how much I need this."

"Bad night?"

"Yeah," he sighed. "Bad night. Bad life. Can I start over again?"

Izzy didn't bother asking him for more. In this world, the Brewtown world, people didn't ask for more. It wasn't a touchy-feely world. Mostly you kept your mouth shut and your emotions to yourself and you drank up.

And as last call neared, and some love song played in the background, and Billy thought of the ring on Kayla's finger and the ketchup stains on his, he decided to take Izzy up on last call.

"I want some shots."

The glint in Izzy's playful eyes lit up. "Celebrating something?"

"Yeah. Freedom."

Around two in the morning, after several pints and shots, closing down Brewtown with Izzy and Erika and then heading to a nearby bar for more, Billy found freedom in the form of blinking lights and a cranky police officer who asked him to get out of the car. And when he asked why, trying his best to fake it even though it was almost impossible, the officer told him he was driving the wrong way down a one-way street.

"You got that right," Billy said with a giddy laugh.

Turned out the officer didn't share his sense of humor.

6. Trouble

There it was.

The song again.

The song she had heard on her way home the day she gave her two weeks' notice and got engaged.

The song she heard as Billy served them appetizers just a few days later.

The song that was six years old and seemed to have come out of hiding.

Once was unusual. Twice was freaky. But three times?

Was somebody trying to tell her something?

Kayla brushed the thought away. She had given up trying to read signs into everything.

And now, on the way to Aunt Cynthia's house in the suburbs, the expressway lanes mostly clear at this time of night, she breathed in and felt the wind swirling down through her open sunroof.

It was just a coincidence.

But still. Why did it have to be *that* song?

This time she listened to it. All of it.

And she stared at the ring on her finger.

The melody caught her in its tide and began to pull her down.

Kayla felt afraid.

She thought of the other night and could still see him. And as much as she might not like to admit it, Billy had looked pitiful. Not because he was serving tables, not at all. But because he didn't know and had been caught surprised.

She might as well have come to the restaurant and slapped him in the face, then maybe kneed him in the groin.

There was something else she didn't want to admit.

She knew that love wasn't something one could quit. A job was one thing, and so was a relationship.

But love either existed or didn't.

And she still didn't have an answer for how to stop loving him.

⌐

The still darkness of her old room greeted her. Aunt Cynthia had gone to bed an hour ago, urging Kayla to spend the night since it was so late. She'd obliged, knowing she didn't have anywhere to be tomorrow morning. She walked into her bedroom and turned on the light.

On her dresser was a picture of her with her aunt on graduation day from Columbia College, another recent shot of her with Ryan, and a picture of her with her father. The last was one of the few she had with the man who passed away before her third birthday.

Thomas Rowe was twenty-six years old when he died.

She sat on the edge of her bed, taking off her shoes and stretching out her arms and legs. For a moment, she looked at the ring on her finger. She couldn't help looking at it, studying it, making sure it was still there, seeing how it looked in every shade of light She could still see Ryan's perfect smile when he gave it to her, could smell his cologne, could see his high-spirited smile and hungry eyes.

She let out a sigh. Then she got on her knees and reached under the bed. Her hand found a plastic container, neatly organized like everything else in the room. She carefully slid it out.

Don't do this, Kayla, not now, not tonight.

But she needed to. It felt . . . it just felt right.

This was her box of mementos from college, which included her diploma and her cap and gown and photos of her roommates and selected papers and notebooks—

Who are you kidding? This container contains memories of another life, another love, another happily-ever-after only imagined in your dreams.

She spotted a photo of him. His disheveled hair, his green eyes, his wry mouth.

There were pictures of the two of them. Concert stubs, including the memorable Coldplay concert at the UIC Pavilion. Letters. Mix CDs. Small mementos.

What am I still doing with all of this?

This box wasn't about college, as she liked to kid herself. It was all and only about Billy.

Sticking out of a corner underneath a notebook, she saw the edge of something. She took the round plastic piece in her hand.

It was a planisphere, a device that had two disks that rotated, allowing the user to recognize the stars and the constellations.

Seeing it again . . . holding it after so many years . . .

Her hands trembled, and she started to cry.

7. Everything's Not Lost

As James finishes telling about the proposal and the other guy, named Billy, Thomas drains the last of his coffee. For a moment he's lost in thought.

"I know I'm probably being a bit dense, but I still don't see the problem. Why'd you spend so much time talking about this Billy character? What's going on with Kayla?"

"The problem *is* Billy. And that's part of the reason why you're being allowed to go back."

"To keep him away from Kayla?"

James lets go with a lighthearted chuckle. The glance he gives Thomas is strange—almost the sort a father might give to his son.

This only makes Thomas more impatient.

"No, Thomas. Billy plays a key role in this."

"I don't get it. How—what—"

"You'll be able to attend your daughter's wedding and do what you've always wanted to do—dance with her on her big day. But you must understand this—she won't know it's you, and you cannot tell her. That's one thing that you're forbidden to do."

"She won't recognize me?"

"No. You'll appear as you would have if you were still living—now over fifty years old. But she won't know it's you. No one will."

"So how will I end up dancing with her?"

"As I told you, she just quit her job. She's trying to find meaning, to answer some of those voices and questions that are haunting her. She also wants to give back, to help others. And that's where she'll meet you."

"And where's that?" Thomas asks.

"At a volunteer program helping out elderly men and women."

"Am I one of them?" he asks, half joking and half fearing the answer.

James simply smiles and shakes his head, then hands Thomas a folder.

"There's more information on the program in here. The only thing you need to worry about is Kayla."

"But why?"

"Because if things continue on the way they are going, Kayla is going to end up with the wrong guy."

"What—she's meant to be with Billy? The DUI Billy? Are you kidding me?"

James doesn't answer, but his face says it all.

"But Ryan—he sounds like a good guy. I don't get it. I don't understand—"

"It's okay. That's why we're sitting on this plane—to give me a little time to help you understand better."

"But Ryan is perfect for her."

"Is he?" James asks.

"Billy's not—he's completely wrong for my little girl."

"Your 'little girl' is twenty-six," James reminds him.

"Yeah, I know, but she's still my little girl."

"Do you believe in soul mates, Thomas?"

Thomas shakes his head. "That's crazy. They're not soul mates. They can't be."

"Your task is to make sure Kayla marries the man she's meant to be with. That is the only way you can be allowed to go back."

Thomas lets out a sigh. "I'm not only confused now. I'm overwhelmed."

"Tell me something. Would you like to be a part of Kayla's love story?"

"Of course."

"Then let me start at the beginning and tell you how Kayla and Billy met."

"But why is that important?"

"Sometimes the circumstances in people's lives prevent them from moving on and finding happiness. And that's exactly what happened with Kayla."

"But why—what happened? What circumstances are you talking about?"

"You, Thomas. The circumstance I'm talking about is you."

part two

a rush of blood
to the head

Like many fathers, I was guilty of trying too hard. I think I believed that if I let you listen to enough music for the first two years of your life, then you'd turn out better than I did. That you would succeed where I had failed. That you would become someone.

But music isn't something you teach. Melodies come from the soul. And even without all the songs I played for you, I knew that you had music inside of you, just as I did.

It wasn't that I wanted you to follow in my footsteps—with visions of grandeur, of performing at Madison Square Garden, of making my personal Joshua Tree. It was that I wanted you to understand why your father did what he did, why he loved music almost as much as he loved you, why he needed to sing and write songs just as he needed to eat and breathe.

I didn't realize that you would grow up and understand this in your own way and in your own time.

We're so impatient on this earth.

Oh, if you could only know what it's like to sing in a patient and perfect place.

And to sing not out of need but out of joy.

The only thing comparable were those brief

moments I shared with you, when a father would sing to his little baby girl and she would look at him with bold eyes that couldn't hold back their love.

I shouldn't be here.

Surrounding Kayla were a dozen students standing in small clusters. The four freshman girls she'd ridden with, who were giggling about something that wasn't that funny. Two braniacs in long trench coats. A love-struck couple. Three jocks who looked as though they might be bodyguards for the petite girl they flanked.

And Kayla.

Professor Hart got everybody's attention. "Okay, before everybody disperses, I want you to think about something, not only today, but for this entire interim."

They stood in the great hall of the Museum of Science and Industry near the main entrance, tickets and maps in their hands. Tall ceilings towered above them, the escalators nearby.

The thirty-something professor held up a map. "On the cover of this are three words: *imagine, invent,* and *inspire.* These sum up what I want this interim to be about. I want you to learn about a Chicago you might not know even though you live down here. Naturally, I want you to have fun. But more than anything else, I want you to be inspired. I want you to spend—"

Just then a figure bolted into the hall, his dark hair windblown and his eyes frantically scanning the area for their group.

"Ah, Billy, you made it," Dr. Hart called. "Thanks so much for joining us."

The newcomer flashed a charming smile as he walked over to join them.

Get over yourself, Kayla thought.

"Sleep in, did we?" Dr. Hart asked.

"I wish."

"As I was saying, I don't want you to view this interim simply as a chance to skip studying and not have to think. I want you to really, truly take another look at this city, even if you're already very familiar with it. Spend these next couple of weeks using your imagination. Don't just breeze by the sights. Swallow them. Embrace them. See yourself in them."

A few of the students looked slightly confused, another few seemed unimpressed.

Kayla glanced at the newcomer and knew she recognized him from somewhere. Billy caught her glance and raised his eyebrows, smiling. She looked away.

"One more thing. On the last day of interim, I'm going to ask you to present to the class one thing that sums up this interim—that sums up Chicago. And, ultimately, that sums up you. It can be anything, but give it thought. And Billy, I don't want to see a shot glass from the Sears Tower."

"Aw, come on," Billy said, getting the group to laugh.

Obviously the professor knew Billy well, as did some of the other students.

Where do I know him from?

It didn't matter. What mattered was making the most of this interim, the one she had signed up for with Justin.

The same Justin she broke up with a week before Christmas.

Sitting in the small movie theatre, waiting for the Safari adventure film to begin, she couldn't help staring at the figure a couple rows in front of her. He wore his 3-D glasses proudly, and just before the film started he looked back at her and grinned again.

What's he so happy about?

At least she wasn't the only "group of one" in this class.

As the film played and some deep, somber voice narrated, Kayla felt her phone vibrate. She slipped it out of her pants pocket and read the text from Lisa, one of her roommates.

Having fun?

It took her a second to type back. 3D Lions.

Sounds like a blast!

What are you doing?

Just woke up. My class isn't until this afternoon.

Kayla rolled her eyes and quickly typed back. Must be nice.

How's the museum?

Exhilarating. Kayla thought for a moment, then added to her

last text. Do you know a guy named Billy? Junior or senior? Dark hair? She waited for a second.

The guy in the band?

That was it. That's where he was from. Yeah.

Billy Harris. He's there??

Looks like it.

He's hot.

Want me to ask him out for you? Kayla typed back.

Sorry I'm taken. But YOU aren't.

Kayla smiled. She wished Lisa were taking this class with her. And I'm not going to be for a long, LONG time.

And as the film continued on, and Kayla glanced back at the head of the dark-haired guy her roommate found to be "hot," she knew one thing: That was the last thing her life needed now. Not just another guy in it, but a guy like that.

As if on cue, Billy turned around and gave her a thumbs-up, as if to say *We're stuck in this together.*

And they were.

Over the next few hours, Billy somehow kept coming across her path. She would be roaming through an exhibit by herself, in silence, when he would suddenly appear out of nowhere and say something to her.

In front of the massive U-505 submarine. While she was staring at the baby chicks that had just hatched. During the lunch break, as she sat with the giggling freshman girls.

He struck her as a younger, more attractive and lucid version of the *What About Bob?* character who kept showing up even when the family thought he was gone.

Each time, he popped up with a smile and a comment.

Each conversation was short, simple, nondescript . . . and annoying.

But each time, she found herself laughing at something he said or did.

His cool attitude wasn't for show—it was genuine. But so was his gentle approachability. It was easy to think he might be full of himself until he talked, and then he sounded self-deprecating, silly, and almost . . .

Don't go there.

. . . endearing.

It was true.

But that was a mirage. That was all. Because compared to that jackass named Justin, all guys were endearing.

Still . . .

Something about Billy was . . .

She stifled the thought.

⌒

It was three thirty, and in another half hour the museum would be closing. Dr. Hart had excused himself to try and locate the other students as Billy and Kayla walked along the main floor. They had just passed the transportation gallery and the Great Train Story with its hundreds of moving trains and had come across Yesterday's Main Street. It was a recreation of a 1910 town street, complete with an ice cream parlor.

At this point in the day it was impossible to try and escape Billy. But that was okay. Kayla had decided he was harmless.

"This looks fun," she said as they walked on the cobblestone and brick in the muted light of the gas streetlamp.

"Do you ever wish you'd lived in another era?" Billy asked.

"Yeah, I often do."

"Me too," he said. "The problem I have is trying to pick which one. Sometimes I think the seventies because of all the cool music and movies that came out of it. Then I think back to the twenties. Even something like this would be great. The simplicity of it all. Living in a world that doesn't have downloadable everything at your fingertips."

They passed a dentist's office, a clothing store, a corset shop. At the end of the street, they entered a small building with *Cinema* marked above the door. Sure enough, there was an old black-and-white silent movie playing. A few people sat in the hard wood rows, watching.

They sat there for a while, then Kayla got up and Billy followed. They walked back down the street.

"I'm tired," Kayla said as she sat next to a sign that said *The*

Berghoff (Established 1898).

"Mind if I sit too?"

"Go ahead."

Billy sat quietly at the small table. It was almost as though he were waiting for an opportunity, not wanting to intrude on Kayla's thoughts.

"So you're in that group, right?" she asked.

"Yep. Song of the Day."

"That's what it's called?"

"Don't like it?"

"No, it's fine."

"It was a game my roommate and I started playing freshman year. You know Chad Whitford?"

She shook her head.

"He's a tall guy, walks like Frankenstein. Sorta acts like him too. Every day we'd choose a song to sum up our day, or that we hoped would sum up the day."

"What's today's?"

Billy's eyes lit up. "Good question . . . and one I take very seriously."

"Really?"

"Oh, yeah. I've always felt like each day should have a new song attached to it. A soundtrack for that moment."

"I see. Hence the band name."

Billy nodded. "You're Kayla Rowe, right?"

"Yes."

"We've been in a few classes together."

"Really?"

"Well, I try not to make it a habit to attend classes regularly."

"I see. Conflicts with your whole rock-star image?"

He laughed. "Exactly. You're dating Justin McKannon, right?"

"No."

"That was a quick no."

"We *were* dating."

"I see."

"We signed up for this class together. Then he decided to take an interim class in Europe."

"That would be sweet. If I had any money to go."

"Yeah, well, I'm sure he and his little girlfriend will have lots of fun."

"Whoa—wait a minute. Don't tell me he broke up with you."

"He didn't. His actions made me break up with him. But I was hoping the day wouldn't be ruined thinking about him."

"Okay, sure," Billy said. "I never liked him anyway."

"Really? And why's that?"

"Nobody likes the big jock who's dating the prettiest girl around, you know? That was my impression. I saw you at the U2 concert."

Kayla ignored the compliment. "There were a lot of people there."

"I noticed you. And then happened to see the big guy standing next to you."

"He's sorta hard to miss."

"So are you."

As they all headed back to the cars, Billy offered her a ride.

The lights in the parking garage seemed to make his green eyes radiate.

And even though she desperately didn't want to ride back with the freshmen girls, she said thank you but no.

"You sure?"

"Yes. Thanks."

But she wasn't sure.

Everything he had said came out so naturally.

Not as a pickup line.

And she wanted to keep the conversation going.

But she knew this was just her anger and frustration at Justin speaking. Hearing some other guy's compliments made her feel better about herself. And made her forget (or almost forget) the girl that Justin followed to France. But the last thing she needed was to jump into something else.

"I'll wait if you want to think about it some more."

"Have a good night," Kayla said, forcing herself to walk away.

She thought about turning around and seeing him still standing there, grinning, the way couples always did in the movies. But she didn't have to. She knew that he was still behind her, still looking at her, still smiling.

Somehow she just knew it.

9. In My Place

Through sculpted heads and modern furniture they walked. Down long hallways and open, airy rooms they walked. Past ten-foot paintings and ten-inch paperweights they walked.

Billy followed Kayla through the Art Institute, talking, asking questions, laughing, pointing, examining, listening, letting it all soak in.

One gallery led to another, which led to another, which brought them back to where they started. Sometimes they retraced their steps, walking slowly, together, like a couple.

A couple of minutes turned into a couple of hours. But they weren't thinking about time.

At least Billy wasn't. And Kayla certainly acted like she wasn't.

"Tell me about yourself."

Kayla didn't take her eyes off the painting. Despite the beauty surrounding them as they strolled through the museum, Billy couldn't take his eyes off her.

"What do you want to know?" she asked, whipping her long blonde hair back, either nervously or flirtatiously. Or maybe both.

"The important stuff."

"I'm five-foot nine, and I weigh, let's see—"

"The important stuff," he said.

"That's not important? Oh, that's right, you're one of those kind guys. Looking only at the heart."

He laughed. This was Friday, their fifth day together. No matter how long he spent around her, it never seemed enough.

She was finally—finally—letting down her guard. The museum helped.

"The outside stuff I can see just fine. I'm curious about *you*. Who you are. Where are you from? What do you like? What do you want to be when you grow up?"

"Who says I'm not grown up?" she said.

"I certainly didn't mean that."

"I was forced to grow up at an early age."

"Really?" Billy said. "I never want to grow up."

"My father passed away when I was two years old. And my mom—she left us right after I was born. Too much pressure for a twenty-two-year-old going through postpartum depression back at a time when it wasn't a household word."

He hadn't seen this coming. Kayla's demeanor didn't change, but she did sneak a glance to see his reaction.

"I'm sorry," he said.

"Yeah, me too. I grew up with my Aunt Cynthia. She's my mother and father all in one. She never married—though I wish she had. For her sake. She's got such a big heart. It's a shame she can't share it with someone."

"She shared it with you, right?"

Kayla looked surprised for a moment, then smiled and nodded her head. She continued looking at the French paintings.

"So why'd you choose Columbia?"

"It's in Chicago—the city, the arts. Far enough away from my aunt but not too far. I don't think she'd like it if I moved halfway across the country."

"Would you like it?"

Kayla shrugged. "No. Probably not."

"I keep toying with going to New York."

"What's in New York?"

"That's where a lot of new groups go. The music scene there is ridiculous. Chicago is awesome, but it's nothing like New York."

"What's stopping you?"

"Oh, I don't know. The guys, for one thing. They're not overly . . . how can I put it . . . ambitious? Motivated? Well, maybe Chad is, but he's quite eccentric to say the least. Plus, well, my family lives here, in Hinsdale. South suburbs."

"So here we are, two suburbanites meeting in Chicago."

"I was afraid there wasn't going to be anybody in this interim. I waited until the day before to sign up—most of the classes were full. Except for knitting or homemaking."

"I don't recall those classes."

"So what do you want to do after college?" Billy asked.

"I don't know. Before college I thought—I had crazy dreams."

"No such thing as a crazy dream. What about?"

"Doing something with film, maybe photography. But I changed my mind."

"Why?"

"Because there are so many things I want to do. So many things I *should* do."

"I get that."

"Do you?" she asked, again looking genuinely surprised.

"Oh, yeah. Like I love writing. I'm not particularly good at it, but I love it. And the visual arts. Even painting. I mean—look at this. How cool would that be, to create something like this? To have it last so long for others to appreciate? But for me, I guess it always comes down to music in the end."

"So do you have a CD of your songs?"

"We're working on an album now. I have some songs—they're rough."

"I'd love to hear them."

"They're really rough."

"I can deal with rough," Kayla said.

"If you're really that curious, you can come to a concert we're playing this weekend. Nowhere big, just some pub downtown—but you can hear some songs."

"How many songs do you play?" she asked, her blue eyes locking on his.

"About four or five of our own, then a bunch of covers."

"You take requests?"

"Sure. What do you like? Alanis Morissette? I can dedicate one of her songs for your boy Justin."

"Funny. I love Coldplay."

Billy smiled. It was good to find a common connection.

"How's this—if you come to the show, I promise we'll play a Coldplay song. Or maybe even two."

"What if I think you guys are really bad?"

"Well, we'll always have the Art Institute, won't we?"

Kayla smiled and brushed her hair back, her eyes quickly shying away from his glance.

⟋⟍

Earlier they had strolled down a Paris street on a rainy day in

1877, thanks to Gustave Caillebotte.

They passed a bullfight, courtesy of Édouard Manet.

They spent a morning on the Seine, saw the Houses of Parliament in London, and sifted through stacks of wheat all thanks to Claude Monet, whom Billy particularly liked.

It was a strange thing to see these classic works of art up close and to think that a hundred or more years ago, some person sat at a blank canvas carefully crafting and creating what now hung in this museum. They weren't gods or immortals—some were completely unknown. But they were incredibly talented and gifted and were trying their best. And their work had stood the passage of time.

And now, Billy and others could walk through these walls and appreciate them, be moved by them, take in their beauty and their aura, even marvel at them.

"What are you thinking?" Kayla asked him late in the afternoon.

"Just taking everything in."

But the words felt insufficient. Taking everything in.

It was more than that.

He felt alive, at home in this world. It wasn't that he necessarily fully appreciated or even *got* art—it was something he hadn't studied much. But he could appreciate it. He saw the value in it. And he understood something about what those artists might have gone through.

Every artist is the same was what he was thinking.

But of course, how could he compare himself to these greats?

In the silence and security of his mind, he could.

Looking at Kayla, he wondered what it would be like to share this with her, to be completely open and honest about his dreams and notions and not be ridiculed. Something deep down told him that she would get it.

"I like being here," Kayla told him.

"Yeah? The art is amazing, isn't it?"

"I like watching your expressions."

"What do you mean?"

"The way you look when you're checking out a picture. It's funny."

"I didn't realize you were looking."

"I know."

Billy waited for Kayla in front of the Art Institute. He wanted to see if she would take the L with him back to campus. For a second he thought she might have left without saying good-bye, then he saw her coming with a bag in hand.

"Here you go, Mr. Artist," she said.

"What's this?"

"Open it."

Billy reached into the bag and pulled out a notebook. On its cover was a Monet entitled *Sandvika, Norway*. It featured a snowy white scene with a bridge in it.

"What's this for?" he asked, in both delight and disbelief.

"It's a blank canvas for you. And since songs are your thing, there's a hundred pages for you to start filling up."

He couldn't say anything. It was perhaps one of the best gifts he had ever received from anybody. And the crazy thing was this: Kayla barely knew him.

"Did you get one for yourself?" he asked.

She shook her head.

"Why not?"

"I don't have anything to say. I think it'd just sit in a corner making me feel guilty."

"An empty notebook is full of endless opportunities."

"That's why I bought it for you and not me. Good night, Billy."

"Maybe I'll see you at the show," he finally managed to say before she was out of earshot.

She turned back and smiled. "Maybe."

He looked again at the notebook and knew he'd fill those pages, especially if someone like Kayla stayed around in his life.

10. A Rush of Blood to the Head

The place was crowded, claustrophobic, and cloudy with cigarette smoke. Kayla followed Lisa into the warmth of the narrow pub as they weaved through the people.

"Good thing we didn't miss them," Lisa shouted at her.

She'd only been twenty-one for half a year, but already Kayla found bars and clubs obnoxious. Overpriced drinks, overbearing people, overindulgence everywhere she looked—she wondered why so many of them were packed. Sure, it was a Saturday night in downtown Chicago, and it was the middle of January. But she could think of a dozen other places she'd rather be. Lisa had been the one to persuade her to go tonight.

That along with a mild curiosity about Billy and his band.

"Hi," some guy said to her, a guy who looked as though he'd spent longer getting ready than she had.

She nodded, but kept following Lisa. Some other guys stopped Lisa, but she brushed them off. Her roommate was good-looking but tough, and had little patience for guys with lines, especially now that she was off the market.

"Let's stay here," Lisa said, wiggling into a spot at the bar that was close to a small stage near the back of the pub. "I don't see any of the band."

"Think they already played?"

"It's only nine. What do you want to drink?"

"Surprise me," Kayla said. This wasn't the sort of place to order a cosmopolitan or a glass of white zinf.

Lisa brought her a pint glass of beer.

They saw a few people from campus, but nobody that either of them knew well. A group of frat boys came over and started joking with them, but Lisa wasn't interested. She'd come with an agenda.

It was an hour before Song of the Day came on.

There wasn't a momentous lead-up, like the crowd silencing and the lights going dim as the band started. It was surprisingly subdued. The four band members came on, Billy waving to the uninterested crowd as he got behind a keyboard in the middle of the small stage. They quickly starting playing a song that Kayla had never heard—the song was loud, upbeat, and average. Nothing that was going to get them on the cover of *Rolling Stone*.

"Pretty good, huh?" Lisa said.

"Life changing," Kayla joked.

"He's a good singer."

"You don't have to try so hard."

"I'm not trying anything."

"Oh, no? Not even just a little?"

"Okay, maybe just a little." She smiled.

And as Kayla watched the band on stage perform, she found it easy to forget Justin and the mess that had happened a couple weeks ago.

In ten songs, something happened.

Something magical, almost miraculous.

Kayla was no longer just watching Billy, fellow junior from Columbia. She was watching an artist open up his heart and soul for a small moment in a small venue. And even though the music wasn't particularly groundbreaking, she was touched by his earnest delivery.

He acted as though he was performing in front of a crowd of 50,000. And he sang in a singular way. He had a low voice, strong and bold and melodic. A bit grainy, if she were to try and describe it, but grainy in a good way.

With each song, the crowd got more into the music.

The seventh song they played was a cover of U2's "Running to Stand Still." Kayla hadn't heard it for some time, but the crowd all announced their approval by their raucous applause at the start. The song was mellow, with Billy playing the keyboard and singing in the microphone as if he were the only one there.

As he sang the words *singing ah la la la de day*, something happened. The song grew, the melody expanding, and Billy's earnestness bled over his keyboard and microphone.

And the crowd, at first loud but mostly indifferent, suddenly found themselves quietly transfixed.

Just as she was.

The band was fine—they were fine. But Billy was more than fine. *He's beautiful.*

It was a distant thought, whispered gently, but she couldn't help it. She wasn't thinking of what he looked like or even sounded like but of what he was doing, what he was trying for, what he was summing up in front of all of them.

Something deep inside of her moved.

And it terrified her.

On the last song of the night, Billy talked to the crowd.

"I want to dedicate this song to a lovely lady I just met who shares my love of this group. It's called 'Amsterdam' and it's by Coldplay."

Lisa nudged her as Billy started playing the piano and singing.

He smiled as he sang.

She could tell that he loved this—singing, playing in front of the crowd, sharing a little of himself with everybody else.

The wave came suddenly. A wave of melancholia. It flooded her, even as the piano chords continued, as Billy's voice grew louder, as the band continued playing.

Distant memories. And a million might-have-beens.

She watched the figure in front of her and could only think of one thing.

And it broke her heart.

As the song grew to a climax, Kayla felt like she couldn't breathe, couldn't see, and couldn't keep standing.

She pulled away from the bar and through the crowd toward the doors.

She needed to get away from this—from the earthquake that had unleashed in her soul.

The cold, dark Chicago street greeted her, and she sucked in air and tried to keep from collapsing.

Tears streamed down her cheeks.

"Kayla?"

The voice sounded as if it hovered over her.

"Kayla—what's going on?"

She looked up and saw Billy standing there. Wearing only a T-shirt and jeans, standing in the cold, his forehead still sweaty.

"Are you okay?"

She nodded and looked away, embarrassed. "It's nothing, really, please—"

"Why are you crying? What happened?"

"Nothing."

"I know it's none of my business, but I just—"

"Were you done playing?"

"Are you okay?" he asked again.

"It's stupid, really. I just got reminded of my father. When you were playing—you reminded me of him. He was a musician, and I just got this thought—he did what you were doing tonight—getting up and playing in front of small crowds. That's what he always wanted to do and—I don't know. For the first time in—maybe the first time ever—I think I suddenly got what he was doing. What he wanted to do, at least. And you reminded me of him. Of what I pictured he might have been. Crazy, I know."

"I'm sorry—I didn't mean to stir up anything."

"It's just me—it's just tonight—my mood or something, I don't know."

"I'm glad you came. And—for you to even say anything like that—I'm honored, Kayla. I can't imagine what it would be like not to have my parents, you know? So it's okay. Tears don't bother me."

She looked down on the ground, feeling stupid. When she looked back at Billy, he looked blue and was shivering.

"You were really good up there."

"Thanks for coming."

"You need to get inside before you freeze to death."

"Only if you come with me."

Kayla smiled. "Deal."

11. God Put a Smile upon Your Face

They walked underneath Saturn toward the orange glow of the sun. The rest of the class, including Dr. Hart, roamed the Adler Planetarium somewhere else. Billy had completely forgotten about the others, along with forgetting that the planets hanging above them were made of plaster. He'd forgotten everything except for the stunning blonde who strode with him through this imaginary universe.

He'd stay here for the rest of his life if he could.

"Why do you keep looking at me like that?" Kayla asked.

"Because you keep looking like that."

"Like what?"

"Like—like that."

"There has to be a definition of *that*."

"If I were stuck between Jupiter and Mars, looking out at all the stars and galaxies, nothing would look as beautiful as you. That's *that*."

Kayla laughed and put a hand on her face. "That may be the corniest line I've ever heard."

"I don't do lines."

"Yeah, I know. Or at least I believe that. Which makes it . . ."

"What's it make it?" Billy asked her.

"Nothing."

"Just say what you're thinking."

She let out an exasperated sigh. "Why do you have to say things like that?"

"Because they're true."

"Well, first off, they're ridiculously *not* true, and second, they're just—why?"

"What?"

"You drive me crazy."

"Ditto," Billy said.

"Nobody's ever said those things to me—not in that way. Not like that."

"Good," Billy said.

"No, it's not good, and I want you to stop."

"Why?"

"Just because."

"Because why?"

"This is getting old," she said.

"We're floating toward the sun." He gestured toward the bright giant orb on the floor in front of them.

"So I see."

"Your last chance."

"For what?" Kayla said with a smile.

"To tell me something meaningful and poignant."

"You need a haircut," she said.

"Ah, such poetic words on our last day downtown."

Billy watched Kayla reading the information in the exhibits. She would occasionally read aloud something that interested her, and he would nod. He was only interested in her. And he couldn't keep his eyes off her. Off every part of her.

She's breathtakingly, utterly beautiful.

After a few more minutes of walking around the exhibit, Kayla sat down on a bench that looked out toward the frozen, snow-capped waters of Lake Michigan.

"May I sit next to you?"

"You don't have to ask."

"Just being polite," Billy said. "Sometimes you get this look about you that says you want some space."

She tapped her hand at the spot next to her. "Come on."

Billy sat next to her, squinted his eyes from the brightness of the day. It was cold with a bitter wind outside, but at least they could see the skies.

"So have you found any memento to bring to the final class?"

"I'm thinking about your bangs," she joked. "You?"

"Yeah, I'm going to see if I can borrow Venus. I think it'll fit in my apartment."

For a few minutes they just sat, looking out toward the lake, toward the brilliant white outside.

Eventually Kayla turned toward him with blue eyes that looped and locked themselves around his. "You're something, you know that?"

"I try to be," he said, attempting to be funny.

"No, I mean it. I don't think I've ever felt so—comfortable, I guess, is the word I'm looking for. I don't think it's ever been so easy to be around a guy and just feel comfortable."

"Just call me your lazy chair."

"Then again, I actually tell you meaningful things that I wonder if you get."

"I get it. You don't need to explain."

Kayla looked around and stretched. "It's nice. Just being here. No pressure, not having to be 'on.'"

"You never have to be *on* with anybody, Kayla. Especially not me."

She laughed. "I'm on all the time. Always trying or doing or thinking or acting."

"Well, you don't have to try with me. Or do with me. Or think. Or act."

She gave him a look that made him think she might not object if he were to move over and kiss her lips.

But that was going against everything she had just told him. He could be pushy, but he wasn't pushing her now. He was giving her space to breathe and think.

If she decided to kiss him at some point down the road, well— she would need to make the move herself.

Billy would be there. And he wouldn't say no.

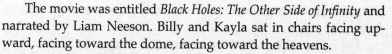

The movie was entitled *Black Holes: The Other Side of Infinity* and narrated by Liam Neeson. Billy and Kayla sat in chairs facing upward, facing toward the dome, facing toward the heavens.

As the narration started, Billy whispered, "Well, he should know. He's a Jedi Master."

"Who?" she whispered.

"Liam Neeson."

"Shush."

The solemn voice spoke about black holes while the screen gave a realistic depiction of what they might look like: *There's a place from which nothing escapes, not even light, where time and space literally come to an end.*

"I know that place," Billy said. "That's the bathroom in my apartment."

"Stop it," Kayla whispered. But she couldn't help laughing.

They showed the death of a star that created wormholes. Kayla kept her eyes on the scene above and around them, but as Billy watched her, he knew she wasn't paying attention.

"I know you're thinking about me," he whispered.

"No, I'm not."

"Yes, you are."

"Stop."

"You can't help it."

"Quiet."

"You're being pulled. It's impossible to resist."

She laughed, but didn't look his way.

Billy knew she was afraid to.

A thousand moments build up to something. An amazed first greeting—a comfortable train ride downtown—smiles and laughter and easy conversation—strolling around this museum talking about other planets and galaxies and solar systems—eventually finding themselves in a room looking up at a dome covered with stars.

It was natural and it was new.

And it was almost as though the heavens were favoring Billy today.

Because in the darkness, with hundreds of stars dotting this imagined night above them, Billy suddenly felt something touch his hand.

For half an hour, sitting in the darkness, they held hands.

Simple and easy and natural.

He didn't say anything. And for the first few minutes, he didn't even look at her. He was too afraid.

Eventually he looked over and could see the dark outline of her face.

She smiled at him, and her eyes pierced his soul.

I want this to be the start, Kayla. I want you to stay here just you and me right here under these stars in this world.

And it was as if she could read his mind, because she squeezed his hand to let him know she got it.

She was here with him. Not going anywhere.

⌒

The smile couldn't leave his face.

The class had gathered near the entrance to the planetarium. Billy was looking for someone with a camera to take a picture of Kayla and him. Some of the students had already gone outside, including Kayla, so he opened the door and saw the afternoon sun on the lake.

It's Friday afternoon and we're in Chicago and I don't have plans and maybe she doesn't either and Kayla just held my hand and....

He stopped as he saw her going down the steps near the circular drive.

He also saw the black BMW.

He recognized the car.

And then he saw the car door open and Mr. Smiley climb out and greet her.

What is Justin doing hugging and kissing Kayla?

The thought was ridiculous. His jealousy and surprise were ridiculous.

The way his legs almost buckled underneath him was ridiculous.

For a brief moment, he saw Kayla look back at him. Way too brief.

He breathed in and watched the two of them talking, Kayla acting happy and surprised and Mr. Smiley acting smug and proud.

Why don't you pee all around the steps while you're at it?

He had wanted things to just—well, evolve. Happen.

They're sure happening now, aren't they, Billy Boy?

He went back inside to the lobby to try and gather up his shattered everything.

Then he heard that voice, the sweet voice that had been filling him all day, talking to Dr. Hart.

"—showed up and he's taking me out—"

That was all he heard. Or all he could bear to hear.

And as he started to head toward the nearest exit to try and jump into Lake Michigan, he felt a tug on his shoulder.

"Billy—"

He turned. He wasn't sure what the look on his face resembled, but he knew it couldn't be good.

Kayla looked pale and—confused, maybe? Sad?

"I'm sorry, Billy—I'm so—I didn't know. Justin took an early flight from Europe—he surprised me—he's been e-mailing me, and it's just—I didn't know he'd show up like this."

"Yeah."

"I didn't know—there's lots we need to talk about."

"Of course," he said.

"Billy, don't. Please."

"It's fine."

"No, it's not, and I . . ."

She shut her eyes, then opened them. She looked like she was trying to control her emotions and herself.

"This is all my fault. I'm really, really sorry. I should never have—I'm sorry."

He wanted to say *You should be*, or *Frankly, my dear, I don't give a damn*, or something really snappy, but all he could manage was "Yeah."

And then the princess who had traveled to the other side of infinity with him walked away, out of his life and out of his universe.

⌒

Riding on the L and looking out at the fading light of the winter day, Billy heard a song in his head. It was one of his own making. He hummed it and couldn't wait to get home, to play into his keyboard, to shake some of the emptiness away.

One lyric stood out in his mind and played over and over.

He wrote it in the notebook Kayla had given him.

The last train to infinity.

12. Green Eyes

She would have recognized the disheveled hair anywhere.

Kayla had just walked into the warmth of the coffee shop and shut the door when she saw the back of his head. He was sitting there, laptop in front of him, coffee on one side.

For a second she thought about turning around, but Billy turned first.

"Hey!"

"Hi, Billy."

It wasn't like this was a Starbucks or some big shop. It was more of a hole in the wall that catered to students because of its location and prices. There were a handful of tables, but no cozy fireplace or comfy couch.

"What brings you in here?" he asked her, standing.

"Uh, coffee?"

Billy nodded, then raised his eyebrows as if to say *stupid question*.

She knew her tone had a bite to it. A part of her wasn't sure why. *Something about this guy terrifies me.*

It was the first time they had seen each other since the planetarium.

"You didn't come to the last day of class. Everything okay?"

"Sure, yeah. I just couldn't make it."

Billy nodded, looked as if he was going to say something, stopped. "You, uh—can you stick around?"

"Just a few minutes."

"Okay. Can I get you anything?"

"No, it's fine, I'll get it."

Billy stood there for a moment, an awkward moment, that finally dissipated when Kayla came back with her drink. Suddenly she didn't want it. Suddenly she just wanted to leave.

"Haven't seen you at all the last couple of weeks. I was thinking maybe we'd have a class together."

"I'm a business major, remember?" Kayla said.

"Yeah, but one can hope."

"How was the last day of class for the interim?"

"Good. And I—well, I got you something."

"What?"

"Just a little something."

Billy took a small, flattened gift bag out of his backpack and gave it to her as she sipped her latte. "It's a little crumpled."

Kayla held the bag, not sure whether to open it or not.

"Don't open it," Billy said. "Not now. If that's okay. I had this big speech planned for the last day. But it sorta—it seems sort of silly now."

"I can deal with silly."

"Obviously. You dealt with me for a couple of weeks."

"Billy—I wanted to talk to you about that day."

"No, it's fine. Really."

"No, it wasn't fine. I apologize. I apologize for letting myself get to that point. It was a great day. I just—I shouldn't have been like that."

"It's no big deal."

"And then leaving you. Look, you need to know that I'm not with Justin. We didn't get back together. We just had some unfinished business. But I was stupid—I shouldn't have left you like that. That was awful, and I'm sorry."

"You don't need to explain. It's okay."

Why does this guy have to be so accommodating? Why can't he give me some attitude? It would make this all so much easier.

Kayla continued to look at the scrunched bag. "Sure I can't open it?"

"Wait till I'm not around."

"Okay."

"I was going to call or mail, but I didn't know if I should, you know."

"Sorry. I just—I've been a little wary of things."

"What things?"

She glanced at him. "Of you."

"Me? Why me?"

Why, Kayla? Do you even know why?

"Because—I don't need more drama in my life, Billy."

"Hey, I'm drama-free."

"A musician in a band? A singer-songwriter? Drama-free? I don't think so."

"A little drama won't kill you," Billy said. His green eyes bore into her.

She thought for a moment. "Do you come here much?"

"Well, I do lately, if you want to know the truth. Someone said you liked to come in here. I was beginning to doubt them."

"So wait—you've been—"

"I'm not some stalker," he said. "I just wanted a chance to give you that."

"What is it? Let me open it."

"Not in front of me. I'll feel more stupid then I already do. You know, I don't make it a habit to hide out in coffee shops waiting on a girl I met. I might be desperate, but I'm not *that* desperate."

"Says who?"

"Hey," he said, smiling.

Kayla ignored his request and opened the bag. She produced a round object that seemed to be full of dots with markings around them. "What is this?" she asked.

"I thought I told you to wait. It's a planisphere."

"Okay," she said, moving it to reveal one disc on top of the other. "What's it do?"

"It's supposed to display the visible stars for any time and date."

She continued to play around with it. "Does it come with in-structions?"

He nodded, looking sheepish. "There's a note inside the bag."

She pulled out a small white handwritten card.

> *Kayla:*
> *This is helpful for finding your way. But remember—*
> *sometimes you have to make sure you look up.*
> *Billy*

"What's that mean?" Kayla asked.

"Just what it says."

"Look up for what? Look up to the stars?"

He smiled. "I think it's easy when you know where you're going in life to lose track of the places you *could* go."

"And where should I go, Mr. Billy Harris?"

"I can't answer that. I'm just encouraging you to look up. See all that's out there."

"Including guys who give me gifts?"

"No. I'm talking about possibilities. For a girl who loves film and photography and art, yet is a business major."

"Okay," she said. Skeptical, dismissive.

He blushed a little and shook his head. "See, I told you to open it on your own. Now I really feel like a moron."

"Why?"

"Because—I don't know. I get these ideas and picture them in certain ways and then—and then they happen and they go in an entirely different direction. Things make sense in my head, but don't always come out right in the real world."

Just go your way and end this chapter right now.

She tightened her lips. "Thank you," she said.

"Sure."

That's enough, now go. Go. Now.

But she couldn't.

"No, I mean it, Billy. Thank you. Not only for this, but for interim. For being so willing to get me to look up. I guess sometimes I'm focused. It's hard *not* to be when you don't have the luxury of having others in your life to do it for you."

"What was your favorite part of interim?" he asked her.

"All of it," she blurted out unexpectedly, then added, "I just wish—I wish that we didn't need to go back to reality. But we always do."

"Reality doesn't have to be a bad thing."

"No. But I'm used to expecting little and handling the rest myself."

"What if I said you deserved to expect more and handle less?"

"I'd tell you to stop looking into the stars so much," she said.

"Never."

Those green eyes didn't blink and didn't waver and didn't stop looking deep inside of her.

13. Crests of Waves

Sometimes church brought more pressure than peace.

Kayla found herself lost in the middle of the sermon, riding in a sea of confusion.

She thought of two people she didn't want to think about. One who wasn't there anymore and one she couldn't get off her mind. That helpless, anxious feeling wrapped around her ankles and tried to pull her down to the deep black undercurrents.

The only thing that helped when she got like this, which seemed to be more and more often the older she got, was concentrating on the here and now. Doing the responsible thing. Doing the logical thing. Doing the right thing.

What would Dad say? What would he think about this?

But of course her father wasn't around to ask.

In moments like this Kayla wondered if she would ever move on.

Why do I think about him so much?

And as the pastor spoke words she didn't listen to, Kayla figured it out.

She knew why she was thinking so much about Billy, and why she was avoiding him. Nothing about Billy screamed responsible or logical. But everything about him screamed something else.

He reminds me of my father.

As the music began and the pastor asked everybody to close their eyes for a prayer, Kayla prayed one herself. *Give me peace to know what to do and where to go. Give me peace to let him go. Give me a way to do this.*

Moments later, when she got to her car and checked the messages on her phone, she saw the text from Billy.

Hope you're having a good weekend.

Kayla stared at the words for a long time in the silence of her car, sitting in the parking lot of the church.

She turned on the ignition and headed back to Aunt Cynthia's.

▶ 14. Clocks

"I don't want to rush things," she says on the phone one January night.

"Then we won't rush things," he says back.

"Because I'm not ready. For anything."

"I can wait."

"I shouldn't get involved with you, Billy."

"Too late."

What's the song of the day? she texts him during class one February afternoon.

Be Mine he texts back from his apartment.

That's not a song.

Track 10 On David Gray's new one.

You never give up.

What's yours? he asks.

It takes Kayla a while to think of one. Don't Stand So Close To Me by The Police.

Good one, he texts. You have a thing for Sting, don't you?

I'd marry Sting if he asked.

I thought you said you'd never date a musician.

I can always make an exception, she texts.

That's what I'm hoping.

Sometimes at night, Kayla finds herself dreaming about him, waking up and feeling sad to leave him behind, then knowing she'll see him later in the day.

Sometimes in the morning, Billy finds himself awaking with a song in his heart, rushing to write down random lyrics in his Claude

Monet notebook or hoping his roommates will leave so he can play his keyboard and compose a song.

One night, while studying at her apartment, with the roommates already asleep, Kayla drifts asleep while leaning against Billy's lap. And he stays still until she finally wakes up an hour later.

"Sorry," she says.

"No, it's fine."

"What time is it?"

"Not really sure."

"It's almost two."

"You didn't have to wake up. I'd stay still all night. I wouldn't disturb you."

"What were you doing?"

"Just watching you dream."

"I don't even know where I am," he tells her from a pay phone somewhere in Florida during spring break.

"Are you okay?" she asks quietly, from her bedroom at her aunt's house.

"No. I haven't been okay since I met you."

"You sound like you've been drinking."

"Yeah, I have. So?"

"Did you guys play tonight?"

"To like five people. I don't even know why I bother."

"Because you love music and you love what you do."

"I'm not talking about that."

"Then what are you talking about?"

"I'm talking about you, Kayla. I'm talking about you. I don't know why I keep trying. Why I call you in the middle of the night. Why we can't ever be together."

"Billy, come on . . ."

"But then I realize something. I realize that I love you and that I want to be with you and that I can't stop thinking about you and that every single song I sing is a song for you and about you. Do you get that?"

"You're drunk."

"Maybe, but I'm not lying. Maybe I'm just drunk enough to have the courage to say the things I've wanted to say."

"Call me when you're sober."

"Why should I bother?"

"Because if that's true—if what you just said is true—then you should follow me to the ends of the earth."

"Do you want me to?" he asks. "Do you really want me following you?"

"I don't know."

"Yeah, exactly."

"What do you want?"

"The song of the day is 'All I Want Is You.' Do you know that I sang that earlier tonight? To five people. I think it was probably the best performance of my life. And you weren't even there to hear it."

"I'll hear it when you come back."

"You'll be there?"

"Of course I'll be here," Kayla says. "I'm always here."

"Yeah, you are now. But what about after college? What about when you move on to life and adulthood?"

"You'll move on too, Billy."

"I'm never moving on, Kayla. It's you I want. I want you, and that's that. And I'm not going anywhere and I'll continue to follow you wherever and don't you ever ever forget that, okay?"

"Get some sleep, Billy."

"I'll be dreaming about you," he says. "Like I always do."

⁓

A hundred e-mails stack on top of each other. A hundred texts pile over each other. And the warm spring sun warms them.

And April passes in a blink, the school year fades, draws to a close.

And May arrives, and they're still friends, and Billy is still patient (though losing his patience and increasingly losing his mind) and Kayla is still intrigued (though knowing that her interest is more than just a little bit of intrigue).

And then Billy gives her the ticket that will change everything. . . .

15. The Scientist

The moment that Billy will always remember, for however long he can store memories and draw in his own breaths, will be the moment before the Coldplay concert began that June night at the UIC Pavilion.

In the center of the seats, a sea of excited strangers surrounding them, Kayla looked at him and smiled.

God, was she beautiful. She turned so many heads. But that wasn't why he loved being with her.

He loved being with her because she noticed him. Not the masses surrounding them or the faces looking at her, but *him*. When she looked at him she really saw him.

And at this moment, still "friends" (whatever that meant), Kayla couldn't contain the joy filling her face.

"You're so excited," she said to him. "Like a little boy."

"I love concerts," he said. "Especially the big ones."

"I know you do."

"Every time—it's just—these guys weren't that big a few years ago, you know? And look now. It's crazy. And awesome."

She took his hand and squeezed it tight. "Don't ever stop."

"What?"

"Believing. In this—in all of it."

"I won't."

"Just don't forget all of us little people when you make it big. And you will, Billy. I know it."

He felt a wave of something fill him, fill the holes that weren't even seen or known.

And soon the lights went off and the show started.

⌒

The lights blasted the audience as the four-man group lived up to the cheers greeting them. The lead singer, Chris Martin, was the most animated and charismatic, whether he was behind the piano banging away or rushing around the stage trying to incite the crowd.

During most of the songs Billy had his arm around Kayla, cheering and clapping and watching with delight.

And he kept hearing her words.

When you make it big . . . and you will. . . .

Nobody—well, except for his family, who couldn't help themselves because they were related—had ever uttered something like that to him. Especially with such confidence.

One by one, the songs soared off into the sky.

Billy felt light. He felt joy in his heart.

And as he cheered after one of the songs, Kayla looked up at him.

And he knew. He really, truly knew she was crazy about him.

The crowd roared when Chris Martin got them standing and singing along to "Yellow." He bounced and jumped around the stage as the lights pulsed and the audience rocked in unison.

And they sang the refrain back to him: " 'You know I love you so.' "

And it was just a lyric. A lyric written by a British band before they got big. A song sung by a singer before he became a sensation. But Billy sang the lyrics as if they were his own, and he sang them looking down at Kayla.

Those beautiful blue eyes stared back at him, and they didn't go away. They were strong and sweet and they held his gaze. Billy might have thought that was the highlight of the evening, but the show wasn't over. Their song still needed to be played.

It was a simple song. A simple little melody. Simple chords played on a piano.

It always starts so simply.

As the song began to play, Billy found Kayla tucked in front of him, his arms around her. They swayed gently together.

He was lost in the moment. Against her, smelling her, feeling her, touching her, all while the song gently played and began to build.

He couldn't imagine a better moment.

A stirring song, the lights and the performance and the energy around them, the girl of his dreams snuggled against him, the realization of a hundred dreams finally coming true.

The crowd sang along as the singer belted *I'm going back to the start* from "The Scientist."

The drums played louder and the guitars kicked in and the piano still guided away and the bass stomped along.

The crowd moved and swelled and sang out.

And then Kayla turned around, jostling in the short area in the aisle.

She smiled.

And there were tears on her face. Good tears, if such a thing existed. The blue eyes didn't hold back. Not now. This wasn't a place to hold back.

And forgetting the song that was still playing and the people still cheering and swaying along, Kayla moved to put her arms around Billy. Then she moved her head toward his. She gave him a gentle, lasting kiss on his lips.

His head catapulted around the arena even as his eyes closed.

The song neared to a close with the soothing vocals singing *Ah ooh.*

And when it finished, the crowd cheering, Kayla looked up at Billy and nudged him close. Her lips pressed gently against his ear. "Thank you," she said.

"For what?"

"For waiting. For letting me take my time."

The crowd still cheered, and he made sure that she heard his response. "I'd wait my whole life for you if I had to, Kayla."

And then, as if somehow Chris Martin knew what was happening in the audience, he broke into a piano version of the classic Louis Armstrong song, "What A Wonderful World." The audience applauded and sang along: " 'And I think to myself, what a wonderful world.' "

Kayla stayed snuggled up next to Billy as he held her.

He might live to be one hundred, but he doubted that he'd ever have another concert experience like this. But that didn't matter.

He had Kayla.

And it was, indeed, a wonderful world.

16. A Whisper

Thomas listens to James wrapping up Kayla and Billy's story and pauses for a moment.

"Why didn't I see any of this happen?" he asks.

"You weren't allowed to until now," James says.

"So he's a musician, and she loves his music. Is that why they're supposed to be together?"

James shakes his head at Thomas. "Not exactly."

"He sounds like a nice enough guy. But that was what—five years ago?"

"It's a start. Just a way for you to understand."

"But why did they break up? And how in the world am I supposed to get them back together?"

James reaches in his coat pocket and produces something.

"What's that?"

"It's an iPod. Are you wondering why we met on this plane bound for Chicago?"

"It's only one of a hundred questions I have," Thomas says.

"You still have a little more time. Listen to these songs. Some are by Billy's band. Others are songs that mean something to Billy and Kayla. And others are—well, you'll recognize them instantly."

"And this will help how?"

"Everyone has songs in their soul, not just musicians. And Billy and Kayla, they share the same playlist, the same melodies."

Thomas doesn't get it. "What's that supposed to mean? If they're so perfect for each other, then why aren't they together?"

James smiles. "I can't tell you everything, Thomas. I'm simply giving you some tools."

"To play matchmaker?"

"Yes."

Thomas shakes his head and lets out a sigh as James stands in the aisle of the plane. "Where are you going?"

"To let you be alone. To let you find the rest of the story in the music. To let you remember."

"But what if I—what happens if I can't get them together?"

James thinks for a moment, then smiles, raising his eyebrows and leaving Thomas.

For a few minutes, Thomas tries to figure out how to use the iPod. Whether it was planned or not, the first track that plays is a song he remembers too well. One of his favorite songs performed by one of his favorite groups.

He can picture James smiling as the song plays.

part three

ghost in the
machine

From the very beginning, I knew you were strong.

The nurses even told us this after your mother had the emergency C-section and they led you and me out of the operating room so they could tend to her. You fought this new place. Your lungs and your fists lashed out. All the nurses around me told me I had a fighter, a spirited and determined little girl. They said you were very "strong-willed."

I soon realized they didn't say that to everyone.

But that strong spirit wasn't all bad.

I've watched that spirit grow and be used for so much good.

I've seen you take your passions to help others in need, to voice out opinions that need to be heard, to share your thoughts and beliefs openly.

Passion can be a good thing, and you embody it.

And all along, even while watching from the sidelines in this unique way, I wondered what sort of soul would be the one to slow you down, to make you sigh with a full heart, to make you smile and think of nothing else.

I never knew that it could be someone like Billy.

It's an awesome and scary thought.

17. Secret Journey (May 2008)

The Chicago skyline brings tears to Thomas's eyes.

Perhaps it's because of the music he's listening to.

Or perhaps the memories in his heart.

He swallows and feels nervous.

What will I say? What will I do?

There's so much in his heart that he wants her to know. But how can he hold back? How will he be able to see her and not say anything, not break down and tell her the truth?

A few minutes before the plane will be landing, Thomas finds the notebook and pen that James left for him. He starts writing.

The words come naturally.

There's so much he needs to tell her.

And he starts with the following sentence: *You don't remember when we used to dance together, but I do. . . .*

18. One World (Not Three)

Billy rounded the city sidewalk and collided with some suit-wearing, Starbucks-carrying businessman.

Normally, he might apologize and keep going without thinking. Unfortunately, this was one of the rare days when he cared about getting coffee spilled on him.

Somehow, business-suit man didn't get a drop of his venti-cappuccino-sweet-and-sour-whatchamacallit on himself. Instead, the entire cup (and it was filled to the rim) gushed over onto Billy's button-down shirt and khakis.

"Son-of-a-bitch!" the stranger said.

Billy looked at the man in disbelief. "Sorry."

"Yeah, why don't you slow down a bit."

The coffee was dripping over Billy's shoes.

It looked like he'd been shot and was bleeding to death.

The businessman kept cursing and glaring at him until he walked away.

Billy still stood in amazement.

He was already fifteen minutes late to this nonsense. All because he'd gotten stopped driving drunk (which he could understand) and he got some tyrant as a probation officer (which was unfair). He was doing this because his probation officer was forcing him to. Billy wasn't even sure he could do this legally, but then again, he didn't want to argue with the guy. Several things stood out on his PO's desk: a Marine insignia, a bullet from God knows what, and a photo of the man in full camouflage gear.

Billy looked at the address the probation officer had scribbled down for him.

It took him another five minutes to realize that he was heading down the wrong street.

Wasn't that what got him into this mess in the first place? That and a combo of Brewtown beer and shots?

The stain on his light blue shirt and pants was just that—a stain.

He wasn't sure if it would even come out. Then again, he didn't really care.

I just need to get this over with.

When he finally opened the door and entered the four-story building, Billy was irritated and out of breath. It took him five minutes to locate the offices of Angel Hands. When he got off the rickety elevator, he examined the mess covering him.

And that's what he was doing when the Angel Hands director walked by him with a cup of coffee.

"I'd ask if you'd like one, but looks like you've already had your share," the man said with a smile that instantly put him at ease.

Billy couldn't help but nod and laugh. He already liked the guy.

"So what brings you here?"

The director's name was Dale Thomas. He looked to be in his midforties, maybe older. He had given several paper towels to Billy that only seemed to shred over his wet pants and shirt, adding paper debris to the wet.

"Helton didn't tell you?" Billy asked, abandoning any hope of cleaning up.

"Not exactly."

"My probation officer sorta forced me to come. To do some extra community work. 'To give back' were his words. He said it sounded like I'd been taking a little too much lately, that I needed to give back. So here I am."

"And how did you end up with a probation officer?"

"DUI," Billy said.

"Your first?"

He nodded.

"So do you have a drinking problem?"

"Wow," Billy said, surprised at the question.

"Just a question."

"No. I was just being stupid. Drank too much, made a bad decision."

They were in a small, bare office that looked as though the man had just moved into it today. Billy couldn't see or hear anybody else around. Even Mr. Thomas's desk looked strangely neat.

"So you decided to help out with elderly people."

"Mr. Helton thought I should. I guess he's involved in Angel Hands."

"You ever done anything like this before?"

Billy shook his head, still looking around, wondering why it was so empty.

"We're moving offices," Mr. Thomas said to him.

"They leave you behind?"

"Something like that. Do you know what we do here?"

"Like, uh, babysit old people or something like that?"

This comment didn't seem to amuse Mr. Thomas. The man looked at him with eyes that seemed to see right into him. They also looked strangely familiar, though Billy couldn't say why.

"Billy—you go by Billy, right?"

"Yeah."

"So imagine this. All your life you've been able to do what you want, when you want to. You have a family, friends, a social life, a home, a car. Imagine one day you wake up and you find those things gone. Your health—gone. You can't drive. Your spouse passed away from cancer. Most of your friends have as well. And the only people you have left in this life—your kids and grandkids—well, they live too far away, or they're too busy. So what do you do? How do you pass the time away?"

Billy didn't say anything. Helton hadn't put it this way.

"Want to know the worst thing about getting older? It's not the ailments or the shriveled skin. It's loneliness. And that's what we combat at Angel Hands."

Billy nodded, feeling guilty for being so cavalier about being here.

"Most people don't think much about the elderly. We're too busy in our own little worlds. But—for one summer, Billy, I want to encourage you to do something."

"Okay."

"I want you to spend this summer using your imagination. Don't just breeze through the motions. Be there with the people you meet. Embrace them. See yourself in them."

For a second, Billy just sat there, staring at Mr. Thomas.

Where had he heard that before?

See yourself in them.

"What's wrong?" Mr. Thomas asked.

"I—nothing. Just had a bit of déjà vu. How exactly does this work?"

"First we need to do some tests. A blood test, a urine sample. When was the last time you drank any alcohol? That's a big one. Also, are you a virgin?"

"Wha—are you—are you kidding?"

Mr. Thomas let out a laugh, his eyes gleaming, those eyes so familiar. "Of course I am. Sorry, I couldn't help it."

Billy sighed as Mr. Thomas handed him a folder.

"There are some papers in there explaining what we do, our history, all that good stuff. Also, there's information on a few events we're hoping to do this summer. If you make it through the summer."

"What do you mean?" Billy asked.

"Well, let's say you go and get another DUI."

"I won't."

"You got the first one, right?"

"And I'm paying for it."

"Hey, Billy, one thing, okay? This, this experience you're about to embark on. Don't go into this thinking that it's punishment. Your DUI allowed you to get to this point, but who knows. It could be one of the best things to ever happen to you."

"Okay."

"I know you're thinking 'Whatever.' And that's okay. Just don't consider this as something negative. That's something that we tend to do down here—view so many experiences through pessimistic eyes."

"What do you mean 'down here'?"

"Did I say that? Sorry—I just got back from a trip up north. Guess that's what I meant. Just—have fun with this, Billy. The main thing you'll be doing is befriending an elderly man."

"Do I get to pick him?"

"Nope. We do that for you."

"What if he turns out to be creepy or something like that?"

"Then you'll have some good stories to tell your friends one day."

"Great," Billy said.

For a second Mr. Thomas just stared at him, thinking something, seeming to be far off. Then he gave Billy a strange smile.

"What is it?"

"Nothing. Just—it's a pleasure to meet you, Billy."

"Yeah, same here."

"Don't lie."

"Okay, fine, I'd rather be wearing dry clothes and watching ESPN."

Mr. Thomas laughed. Billy was a bit relieved that this guy actually seemed halfway decent. But he still wasn't sure what this whole Angel Hands thing was going to be about.

19. Rehumanize Yourself

"What do you mean the date is August 30? Of 2008?"

"You have plans for that day?"

Shannen laughed. "That's in three months."

"So?"

"So? Are you planning on going through a wedding drive-up or something? When Liz started planning for her wedding, it was insane how far off she needed to book to get a church, not to mention a reception hall."

"We thought that through."

"And?" Shannen waited for a response as Kayla took a bite of her sandwich.

They had spent the last few hours in stores downtown looking at bridesmaids' dresses and hadn't found anything they liked. They were all too slutty or too frumpy or they clashed with Shannen's red hair. After an unproductive but nevertheless amusing parade of dress-shopping, the two friends sat in a restaurant having some light dinner and avoiding the rush hour traffic heading toward the suburbs.

"We're going to have the wedding and reception at Aunt Cynthia's."

"Really?"

"Think about it. The backyard is beautiful. I always thought it would be a perfect setting for a wedding."

"Still, what about invitations and getting a pastor and the ten million other details?"

"Ryan is okay with a simple wedding. So we're going to have ten people, max."

"What?" Shannen shouted.

"I'm kidding. But it's going to be small and intimate. As weddings should be. Weather might be a factor, of course, but otherwise, it'll be just like the wedding in *Father of the Bride*, minus the father part."

"Please. That movie is so ridiculous."

"You just hate it because you can't stand your father."

Shannen shook her head and held her tongue, surely out of respect for Kayla's love of that movie and for the fact that Kayla didn't have a father to not stand.

"Aunt Cynthia loves the idea of showing off her place. Of course, I get to rein her in since we'll only have three months."

"That's not leaving you much time. Especially since you have to look for a job too."

When Kayla didn't respond, Shannen pushed back. "You *are* going to look for a job?"

"I'm going to work on my bucket list."

"Do you even have a bucket list?"

Kayla laughed. "No. I'll start by making one."

There was some half-truth inside the remark. Ever since turning twenty-six, Kayla kept reminding herself that her father passed away when he was her age.

You never know when you're going to kick the bucket. You just never know.

"So you're just going to have a three-month vacation, then marry the rich guy and start pumping out babies?"

"Exactly," Kayla said. "Hoping for quadruplets right off the bat."

"Don't look for a babysitter here."

"I'm smart enough for that," Kayla teased.

"Ouch. Okay, I deserved that."

"I've thought about looking, but every time it's like I get to this big brick wall. I just don't know if I can see going back to some corporate grind."

"What are you going to do? Work at Starbucks?"

"That wouldn't be bad. When your options are open, think of all the things you can do. I just—I keep having crazy thoughts."

"Like what?" Shannen asked.

"Like—I don't know—lots of thoughts."

"When it's all said and done, you're going to be working for a big fat corporation making a nice paycheck and living a nice life."

"Hey!"

"What?" Shannen asked, tapping Kayla's hand. "It's true. That's not an insult. That's who you are."

"Maybe it's not."

"No?"

"I want to do something meaningful."

"You're getting married. That's meaningful."

"I mean *me*. I want to try and . . ."

Kayla didn't finish the thought because she wasn't sure where it led. For some crazy reason, she thought of strolling through the Art Institute with Billy so many years ago. She thought of the inspiration that entire interim had given her.

A voice reminded her softly, gently, *It's easy when you know where you're going in life to lose track of the places you* could *go.*

"You want to try and what?" Shannen asked.

"I want to just keep my options open. Keep my eyes open."

"K—you sound anxious."

"No, I don't."

"Are you?"

Kayla sipped her iced tea. "I could tell you no, but you know me too well. It's not like I feel I'm making the wrong choice."

"Really?"

"Well, okay, there's a part of me that's worried. It's just . . ."

Should she tell her friend about the songs she kept hearing on the radio? Or the mementos she kept finding in her apartment? Or the dreams she kept having at night?

"Is this about Billy?"

"No," Kayla said a little too loudly and forcefully.

"Okay, then."

"Maybe just a little."

"So you happened to see him a few days ago. What are the chances?"

"I know."

"He's going places, isn't he?"

"Shannen."

"I'm sorry."

"This isn't about Billy. It's just—I didn't know part of the change I was about to undergo would include getting married."

"Wish I was getting married."

"You need to let a guy take you out first."

"Not everybody finds a Ryan in her life. Or even a Billy. I'd settle for a Billy any day."

"I'm sure he'd love to hear you say that."

"I'm sure that Billy would like to never see my face again. He probably still blames me for what happened."

"I'm sure he's over it."

"Did he look 'over it' when you saw him?"

Kayla shook her head. She could close her eyes and see his face. Sad, hurt, boyish, fragile. "He's over me," she said, leaving it at that.

"So where are you going to start with your summer of freedom—er, I mean reflection? What's going first on your bucket list?"

"I don't know. I'll let things come to me. I'm sure a few of those things are going to include you."

"Just no skydiving," Shannen said. "You know how I hate heights."

"You just gave me number one," Kayla teased.

As they talked, out of the corner of her eye Kayla noticed a younger girl, maybe college age, sitting with an older gentleman. It was a cute scene, the way they talked. It made her long for grandparents. The only one alive was her aunt's and mother's mother, a crabby old lady who grew more incoherent with each passing day.

As they were walking out of the restaurant, they passed the girl sitting by herself, a half-eaten monstrosity of a sundae in front of her.

Kayla couldn't help herself. "Excuse me. I don't mean to be nosy, but is that your grandfather?"

"No," the girl said with a smile. "No, that's Simon. No relation. I take him to lunch every other Tuesday."

"Really?" Kayla's curiosity must have shown on her face.

"Yeah. It's pretty cool. I got involved with a program called Angel Hands downtown. They coordinate friendships between seniors and young people."

Kayla saw the elderly man sauntering back to the table. She thanked the girl and greeted the man as she passed him by.

"What was that about?" Shannen asked.

"Oh, nothing. Just curious. Just keeping my eyes open."

20. Spirits in the Material World

It was a busy and bright day in Millennium Park, downtown Chicago. It was the first event Thomas was running, the first coordinated effort with the elderly folks and their designated friends. It was also the first function that Billy Harris attended, looking slightly lost when he showed up early this morning.

And, if all went as planned, it would be the first time Thomas would see Kayla.

The event was simple on paper: bring a set of the Angel Hands "friends" to the park with their "guests." Calling them *friends* sounded better than *old folks*, and *guests* better than *babysitters*.

Part of the fun was simply getting the friends to the park.

Thomas, along with ten guests, had shown up at his offices, where they received coffee and doughnuts and instructions. Billy was late, of course, and looked tired and a bit pale. They loaded onto two small buses and drove to the retirement home where the friends awaited.

Inside the home, there had been an amusing mix of both tender and awkward moments, like Janis kissing Billy's cheek and causing the guy to blush, and Richard trying to fend his guest off with a cane. It had taken twice as long as Thomas expected to lead the wandering group out of the home and outside on the clear and beautiful June day.

Billy had met his friend: a wild-haired, tall, lanky gentleman who looked like Abraham Lincoln's lost brother. His name was Flint, or at least that's what he said his name was. Thomas found Billy listening to one of Flint's stories on the bus ride over to the park. Billy gave him a look that said *Please get me outta here* and only made Thomas's pleasure in the day even greater.

At the park, the friends and their guests simply enjoyed the beauty and the sights. Thomas tried to make sure everybody was doing okay, helping out with wheelchairs or disoriented friends, getting water for a woman who seemed flushed, putting sun block on a few people, talking with everybody.

He was standing next to the Crown Fountain when it happened. The fountain was a black granite reflecting pool positioned between a pair of fifty-foot glass brick towers. The two towers displayed random faces projected from within, with water spouting through a nozzle positioned in the location of the mouth.

As he stared at one of the walls, he suddenly saw the beaming face of James.

And then he turned and saw a figure bathed in sunlight. He could only see her outline, tall and slender, with long hair bound up and bouncing from shoulder to shoulder.

Right then, Thomas knew.

It was Kayla.

She was talking to a figure that was shorter and hunched over.

For a moment, hidden behind his sunglasses, surrounded by the moving masses, Thomas felt something in his heart break.

No, it didn't break. It filled. And the sensation was shattering.

The tears came as quickly as he'd seen her. And he breathed in and nonchalantly brushed them away and faced her.

Imagine, for a moment, twenty-four years gone.

A blink, and she is grown.

A breath, and she is gentle, graceful.

The hair that never seemed to want to grow now reaches below her shoulders. The chunky little arms and legs are gone, replaced by a long and slender physique. The bouncing baby has turned into a beautiful woman.

Even though he had stood on the sidelines and seen her mature in his own unique way, this was still more than he thought it would be. Almost more than he could handle.

Thomas walked toward her and finally saw her up close. And it was like nothing he had ever experienced on this earth. Except, perhaps, holding her in his arms for the very first time and seeing her crying and knowing that somehow in some way he'd helped create this little life.

Kayla glowed.

That's all he could think for the moment. She glowed. Her smile was immense, infectious, the kind you'd see and you'd just *have* to try and get to know.

She looked like her mother in so many ways, but she had some of him too.

Including his smile.

That's what it was.

The way the eyes crinkled in amusement and delight.

God, she is so beautiful. Thank you. Thank you for this life and for this gift of seeing her again.

As he approached, she looked up at him, laughing from something the little old lady next to her was saying.

"Hi," she said, as if slightly bashful. "I hope I'm not interfering with anything. I'm Kayla."

And all he could think was *Of course you are.*

His eyes glistened up and he found himself thankful for the sunglasses. Everything in him wanted to abandon it all and simply hug her. He forgot to breathe. And the two seconds after hearing "I'm Kayla" felt like two years.

Time is so relative, he thought, *so relative and so futile and so incalculable.*

"Hi, Kayla," he finally managed, shaking her hand. "I'm Dale Thomas."

"Nice to meet you. I just met Leona here."

He smiled and continued to try to get hold of his emotions. "Leona. Where did Patti go?"

"I'm not with Patti. She already has two others to babysit. I'm with Kayla."

"Oh, really?" Thomas laughed. "Kayla, I think you've made a new friend."

"I ran into a girl in a restaurant who told me about Angel Hands. And I looked it up and thought—I don't know. I was looking for something like this. So I thought I'd just come down here and check things out."

"Let's go over by the art show," Leona told Kayla, grabbing her hand.

"Looks like you got caught."

"I know," Kayla said with an animated face. "Guess some things are meant to be."

And just like that, Leona led Kayla away.

That was easy.

But as Thomas walked back by the fountain, he looked up and once again saw James's face staring at him. It gave him a wink, reminding him. This was all the help he was going to get. James got Billy and Kayla in the same arena, in the same world again.

The rest was going to be up to him.

21. Hungry for You

This was going to be tough. Especially for a whole summer.

But at least the old guy's nice, Billy thought as he sat listening to a story about sailing out on Lake Michigan.

Billy thought again and decided against calling Flint nice. He simply wasn't cranky. That was it. He could've been stuck with a crotchety old guy who had that old-person smell and seemed annoyed with everything in life. Flint, on the other hand, was Mr. Tangent Man. Every story and every step and every breath reminded him of something else.

It seemed like Flint hadn't had the opportunity to share his stories with anybody for a long time.

"Did you know that when I was your age, I was working in the factory. I started when I was only fourteen."

"I'm twenty-six."

Flint laughed, but didn't seem to understand. Either that or he didn't hear Billy. He was almost seventy-three and still seemed to be in remarkable health. He was tall with a slight slouch in his walk and mostly thin except for his neat and round little gut. He had long hands, the kind a piano player might have. His hair was wild and dark, and combined with his wide eyes made him look a bit hysterical without even trying. Those long hands flailed and those expressive eyes grew big as Flint told his stories.

"How's everything going?"

Billy turned to see Mr. Thomas. He nodded, but he couldn't say anything. He didn't want to interrupt Flint.

"Did you guys get a chance to see Cloud Gate?"

"You mean the Bean?" Billy asked, referring to the mirrorlike sculpture that was one of the centerpieces of the park.

"I once rode my bike over the Golden Gate Bridge," Flint said.

"Maybe you guys can take a walk over there," Mr. Thomas said.

Billy raised his eyebrows as Flint continued to talk.

"Or maybe not."

Billy considered himself to be an okay listener, and he was genuinely trying to pay attention. The problem was that there was no back and forth. Flint talked and Billy listened. And even when Flint asked him a question, he would continue on as though Billy hadn't even answered.

A whole summer of this was going to get tiresome.

But it's your own fault.

"Do you know that my first wife used to make the worst meatloaf known to mankind. I'm tellin' you, it was wretched. And she didn't believe us. She started making it to spite me. I think she started making it worse on purpose. Her memory started to go—she ended up with Alzheimer's, God rest her little soul—so she'd forget things. But she kept making it."

As Flint talked about meatloaf and other meals—apparently moving to the topic of food because Billy had uttered the word *bean*—Billy gazed off toward the crowd and pictured Kayla.

It was like he was in a desert picturing a mirage of a fountain.

There she was, in black shorts and a white top. Her hair tied up, those long legs walking toward him, next to some little old lady whose hand she held. With a bright smile and a laugh and a charm that could make the wind in this city hold its breath.

The vision kept coming closer.

And she suddenly saw him, and stopped.

This was no mirage.

Right down the sidewalk from him stood Kayla Rowe.

"Billy?"

Suddenly Flint's voice faded out. As did the rest of the strangers surrounding them.

Suddenly it was just he and Kayla in this park, in this city, in this world.

"What are you doing here?" she continued.

Billy stared at Flint, then back at her.

Flint stared at Kayla too, and for once he was actually quiet.

"Uh, Flint, this is Kayla. Kayla, Flint."

Kayla laughed, looking incredulous. Then the elderly woman tugged at her, ignoring all of them and apparently interested in something in the opposite direction.

"This is Leona," Kayla called out to him.

"Are you—with these . . . ?" Billy began to ask.

"Are you?" Kayla asked him, the crowd suddenly crossing between them, Leona taking her down the sidewalk and Flint starting to talk again.

And as Billy tried to say something, he lost sight of her.

But then he saw her again. She was listening to the woman next to her, then turning her head in his direction.

And there was the smile he remembered. The smile he adored. The smile he would always love.

⁓

Half an hour later—thirty minutes of confusion and delight and bewilderment for him—Billy saw Kayla walking toward him. He was waiting for Flint by the restrooms. Kayla stormed toward him in a way that didn't look promising. He knew that look and that walk.

"What are you doing here?"

He let out a disbelieving chuckle. "Nice greeting."

"Well?"

"Well, what? Wow—nice to see you too."

"Billy, come on."

"What? Want me to grab you an appetizer?"

"How did you know?"

"How did I know what? What are you talking about?"

"How could you? Did Shannen tell you?"

Billy almost choked on his own laugh. "Yeah, totally. Because, as you know, we're total BFFs."

"Then how did you know about this—about me being here? I didn't tell anybody else."

"Wait a minute," Billy said, the past resurging as quickly as the mirage had turned into a real person. "You think I'm here because of—wow."

"Don't give me that look."

"What look?"

"That look. That wounded, sad-sack look of yours."

"Oh, I'm sorry. I haven't seen you—well, except for that nice little outing at the brewery where I actually *served* you—I haven't seen you for a year and a half, right? And now you're accusing me of something ridiculous."

"Just answer my question."

"Maybe I don't want to."

"Maybe you need to grow up."

"I've planted surveillance cameras in your apartment and car and all your pairs of shoes."

"Then answer my question," Kayla said.

This could be happening several years ago. The same tone and same fire and same irritation.

"What are *you* doing here?" Billy said.

"I just came down here today to check out the Angel Hands program. It sounded interesting. But I didn't know—"

"No, you didn't know, did you? Didn't think you'd see Billy Boy, did you? The scene at Brewtown was a little too much for you, huh?"

"So how long have you been volunteering then? You didn't know anything about me coming down here?"

"Does the world *always* have to revolve around you? Do you think that I wake up and go to sleep thinking about precious little Kayla Rowe?"

"Yeah, that's *exactly* what I think."

"I'm such a selfish prick, I'd only do such a thing like this in order to get closer to the one and only Kayla Rowe. Right?"

"You never change."

"Neither do you."

Kayla turned to storm off.

And that was when Billy saw Mr. Thomas standing there, his face grim and white and his lips tight.

Billy just shook his head and sighed.

Fights with Kayla always took his breath away.

22. Invisible Sun

"I'm sorry, but I don't think this is going to work out."

For a moment, it almost appeared as if Mr. Thomas was amused. But he cleared his throat and gave her a serious look as he asked, "And why do you think that?"

"I wasn't even sure about this—I just wanted to take a look."

"Seems like you made a friend."

"I know—and I—I'd feel awful if I just disappeared. But I—I don't think I can help out here because of Billy."

"You know him?"

"Yeah. And, well—there's a history. Actually, we were engaged once."

The man's eyes widened. They were blue and kind and genuinely interested.

"It's just awkward now, you know? I'm not sure about it."

"This program isn't about matchmaking. I see you have a pretty diamond on your finger. A good-sized one too."

"Yes," she said, suddenly feeling stupid.

"What's his name?"

"Ryan. We're getting married August 30."

"End of summer. That's coming fast. Congratulations."

"Thanks."

"So, Kayla, why did you decide to come down to Angel Hands?"

Kayla shrugged. "I happened to meet a girl who's in it. I looked it up, thought it might be something good to get involved with. Something different from the stuff I'm involved in at church."

"Then maybe you should give it a try for a while."

"I don't know. I just quit my job—I should be in the process of looking for another one."

"This doesn't have to interfere with that."

Kayla smiled. "I'm probably just making excuses because of Billy."

"I can tell that Leona really likes you. She's a special lady."

"I just—I can't have any drama. And being around him—I don't know what that will be like."

"Kayla?"

She glanced at Mr. Thomas and suddenly felt strange, like a little girl. "Yes?"

"Is Billy a decent guy?"

She looked away as she nodded.

"Then just talk to him. Explain to him what you're thinking. He can respect that."

"I know, it's just . . complicated," she said.

"Love always is."

She was going to answer him back, tell him he was off base, but she couldn't. She nodded and smiled.

Mr. Thomas sat in his chair and waited for her to reply.

"Thanks. I'll think about things. Maybe talk with Billy."

Mr. Thomas handed her a card. "That's got my cell number on it. Call me if you have any other questions or want to talk. I'd really love having you in our program this summer, Kayla."

"Thanks."

"I'm surprised you still remembered my cell number."

"Billy . . ."

There were so many things she could say, that she wanted to say, that she couldn't say. But the look she gave him probably said it all.

"Well, I'm here," he said. "Even though I would've preferred something a little later."

"It's ten a.m."

"I worked until one last night."

She held a cup of coffee and watched Billy yawn. He still looked the same, with his boyish face and a faint shadow of facial hair that could never fully become a beard. His green eyes looked tired with dark bags underneath them.

"How are you doing?" she asked, unable to resist the urge.

"Oh, I'm fabulous. And you?"

"Stop."

Billy picked at the blueberry muffin he'd ordered. He wasn't a morning person, and neither was she, but this wasn't even morning.

It was halfway to midday.

"I want to talk to you about Angel Hands."

"About me breaking into your apartment and discovering you were going to be in the program?"

"Funny," she said.

"Yeah, I know. But that's basically what you accused me of when you saw me at the park."

"I freaked out a bit."

"I miss those days of you freaking out."

"I'm sorry, okay."

"And I miss those days of you apologizing like everything's okay afterwards."

"See, this is why. This is why."

She stood up to walk away, but Billy grabbed her arm and held it firm.

"Okay, sorry, okay? Please—don't—Kayla, don't go."

"Then lay off me."

"Okay, fine."

"I'm afraid of—of this. Of going through a summer of this."

"What's 'this'?"

"You know what 'this' is. Fighting. The mean, sarcastic comments. I can't put up with it."

"I told you, I can't help being in the program. I can't get out of it."

"I know. And that's why—why I'm seriously considering not doing it."

"What do you want?" Billy asked. "Want me to try to persuade you to stay?"

"Of course not. But an attitude like that might persuade me to go."

"I'm not sure what sort of attitude I'm supposed to have. Considering everything."

"You can be nice."

"I am being nice. I was nice when you showed up at one of my tables. And thanks to you, I ended up getting a DUI that night."

"That was not my fault!"

"I know. I blame him."

"His name is Ryan."

"What's he think of the whole Angel Hands thing?"

"He doesn't think anything of it. He thinks it's great that I want to get involved with something like this."

"Of course he does. You should win a prize."

"Billy—"

He sighed and sipped his coffee. "I'm sorry, okay. I'm grumpy. It's just, yesterday I got attacked while I was helping Abe Lincoln around the park, then I had a crap night of work. Just like every night. I woke up this morning wondering how I got in this mess in the first place."

"With your DUI?"

"No, with my life."

She knew where he was going with this and didn't want to go along. "Billy, I need you to promise me something."

"I've already promised you enough in my life."

"Well, I need one more promise."

"What's that?"

"That this—that this attitude—that the past—that you control it when you're around me. I don't want to *not* do this just because you're in this program."

"You don't like anybody telling you that you can't do something."

"Maybe it's something like that," Kayla said. "But I also feel that I need to do this. For some strange reason. It's just—I'm getting married at the end of the summer."

"So I heard."

"See?"

"What? What'd I do?" Billy asked, his eyes looking innocent.

"It's that attitude. You should hear yourself."

"What do you want me to do? Show up and sing you a song at the wedding? I'm sorry if I'm not exactly elated for the two of you."

"I know you're still angry at me."

"I don't know exactly how I feel toward you, Kayla. I know I'm tired. And I know that I didn't purposely show up in your life again. It's not my fault."

"I know that."

"So then give me a break."

"Only if you give me the same," she answered.

"What do you want? I'll leave you alone. I've done a pretty damn good job of it the last two years, wouldn't you say? I still remember your cell number but haven't used it. Not once."

"I don't want drama."

"Then lay off me a bit with the attitude, okay? This wasn't a part of some big plan. This was random. Not everybody is like you with the way life should and shouldn't be, you know?"

"So what are you like, Billy? Huh?"

"Me?" Billy laughed. "I'm a train wreck. That's what I am. But I won't give you drama, okay? You might not even see me much. It's not like you have to babysit me."

For a few moments there was silence. Kayla saw a couple in the corner, another couple waiting on coffee and holding hands.

Never in a million years would she have imagined that things would be like this. It was painful simply looking in his eyes. There were too many memories, too much history, too much life left to live.

"Billy, I'm sorry."

"For what?"

"For—for everything. For how things turned out."

"It's life. It's okay. It was a while ago."

"It doesn't seem like it was so long ago," she said. "Not to me."

"It feels like another universe to me. Another life. Ten thousand years ago."

For a moment a thought came to her, and instead of holding back she uttered it. "Did you buy the new Coldplay CD? I thought of you when it came out."

"No," Billy said.

"Are you serious?"

Billy glared at her, angry now. "Are *you* serious?"

"What?"

"How can you ask something like that?"

"It's just a question."

"That's not *just* a question."

"I'm sorry—I didn't mean anything. I just—I just thought of it. I'm sorry."

"I have a hard enough time when they play those damn songs at work. It's like a soundtrack for a loser. A soundtrack for my failures."

Kayla looked at him and suddenly wanted to reach out and hold his hand. She wanted to hug him and tell him things were okay. But they weren't. And she had tried that before, and it hadn't worked.

Billy looked at her, then his angry face cracked away and turned into amusement. "I mean, did you hear that song at Brewtown?"

She nodded.

"It's like God is cursing me or something. What was that? I was like, seriously?"

"That was . . ."

"Yeah, there's no word to describe what that was," Billy said.

Kayla laughed, letting off tension. "I'm sorry."

"No more apologies. Between the two of us—man, there have been a lot of them."

"That's why I'm afraid of this summer."

This time it was Billy who reacted, reaching across the table and grabbing her hand. "I'm not going to do anything to you, Kayla. I'm not going to hurt you, okay? I'm not a bad guy."

"I'm not afraid of that."

"Then what are you afraid of?"

"I'm afraid of you. I always was. And always will be."

For a moment they shared a glance, the kind that only the two of them understood. It was familiar, comfortable, terrifying.

Billy let go of her hand, swallowed as he appeared to search for the right thing to say. "You don't have to be afraid of anything, Kayla. Especially not me. It's just a summer. No big deal. Just one summer, and then you'll have the rest of your life to live. I promise—I won't do anything to mess that up. I already gave it my best shot."

23. Every Little Thing She Does Is Magic

Kayla smelled like summer.

She wore a halter dress, a vibrant blue that matched her eyes. She looked more like a page from a magazine than a volunteer helping out with the elderly.

For a couple weeks now, Billy had been downtown helping out with Angel Hands. But he hadn't seen Kayla once during that time. He wondered if she was still involved, yet knew he couldn't simply give her a casual call to ask. It was only when Mr. Thomas enlisted him in a unique project that he learned Kayla was still involved with the program.

And now that the project had arrived on this clear and perfect Saturday morning, Billy stood sipping a cup of a coffee at a Starbucks and watching Kayla pacing as she talked on the phone. When she finally hung up, a look of concern filled her face.

"What is it?"

"Mr. Thomas said he changed his mind at the last minute."

"On what?"

"On the group today. It was supposed to be five of us. Turns out it's just you and I."

Billy thought of a hundred quips in his mind.

Uh-oh, watch out!

The babysitters are gone!

How dare you even think of spending a day with me!

But he kept them all to himself and just nodded.

"He said that two of us should be enough to scout out the city."

He didn't say anything, just sipped his coffee and waited for her to talk more.

"This probably isn't a good idea," Kayla said.

He nodded.

"I mean, I suggested that perhaps you and I could do our own separate scouting, but he wanted the camaraderie of the experience. He said that it was important to bounce ideas off each other."

"Hmm."

"I told him it might not be the best idea. Mr. Thomas asked if I was uncomfortable being with you, and I said that I wasn't. Because I'm not, you know. It's just—with everything. I just feel a little—"

"Uncomfortable?"

"No. It's not that. It's just—well, I had a hard time explaining it. You know what I mean."

"Uh huh."

Kayla looked at him.

"Are you going to say anything?"

"What should I say?"

"What do you think?"

"Not really sure, to be honest."

"What's that supposed to mean?" Kayla asked.

This was normally the place where Billy would tell her exactly how he was feeling. How he was thrilled to hear that he would be spending the day with Kayla in Chicago. How he was bewildered as to how it had even happened. And how he was ticked off at how Kayla was acting.

Normally he would tell her all these things and more. And normally the "more" part got things out of him that he hadn't even known. But that was from another era, another time.

"What?" Kayla asked.

"Look—if you don't want to do this, it's fine with me."

"I already told Mr. Thomas I would."

"Okay then," he said.

"Maybe you want to call him."

"What for?"

"Tell him you're sick."

"Geez."

"What?"

"I get the whole 'no drama 'cause I'm getting married' thing. But this is really—it's just—"

"It's just what?" Kayla asked.

"It's sad. You can't even fathom the thought of spending a day with me. Heaven forbid."

"It's not that."

"It's not? Then tell me what it is."

"I already explained it to you."

"Yeah, maybe. Kind of."

"What more do you want me to say?"

How about you explain to me why you broke things off in the first place? Because I still don't know and I wonder if I ever will.

"Nothing," Billy said. "You don't have to say anything."

Kayla glanced at the city street outside the coffee shop. It was around nine o'clock. "Okay, let's go then," she said.

"What? Now?"

"Sure."

"You're okay with it?"

"I'm fine. No big deal. We've got a job to do, right? Find half a dozen possible places where we could have outings. That's simple and easy, right?"

Sometimes she could change her mind that quickly.

Billy knew.

He knew too well.

He was careful not to walk too close to Kayla.

But simply being in her vicinity made his mind swirl and his body weak.

It was hard to know that he had come so close, that they had come so close. So close to being at a point where they could be walking down this sidewalk in Chicago together, a couple shopping or maybe getting away for the weekend. So close to being able to hold her hand and see her glance and know that they belonged to each other.

But she belonged to someone else.

"You're walking slow," she said to him with a smile.

It was a friendly smile. Innocent. Sweet. Caring.

He couldn't hate her. He had tried.

Oh, how he had tried.

And even at that last concert, when he finally said enough was enough and said no and put an exclamation point at the end, he still knew he didn't hate her.

He hated being away from her. He hated not being with her. He hated wondering if she loved him. He hated knowing he still loved her.

"Sorry," he said, quickening his pace.

Kayla gave him a glance, and he quickly tried to snap out of it. She could read his mind, always could and always would be able to.

"You know where you're going?" he asked her.

"Of course."

Billy had a list of possible places to check out. But every time he suggested one, Kayla would say, "We don't need to go there." It became the phrase of the day.

They went to Michigan Avenue and to the Watertower Place. Both of them had been before, but they went trying to imagine a sea of elderly people walking around with their helpers. Kayla quickly decided that it wasn't an ideal place.

Billy suggested Wrigley Field.

"We know what that's like," Kayla said. "We don't need to go there. Plus it probably would be pretty expensive."

"The Cubs are going to win it all this year," he told her.

"That's faith."

"It's gonna happen," he said.

"They're going to break your heart."

"Just because you don't support them doesn't mean you have to rain on my parade."

"I support them. I'm just not fooled that easily. I'm jaded. I've had my heart broken too many times before."

Kayla didn't seem to realize what she had said until it came out of her mouth. Billy didn't respond, just handed her a map of Chicago and let her make up her mind on where to go next.

"How about the Art Institute?"

"We don't need to go there," Kayla said.

"It's only a couple blocks away."

"So?"

"You don't think it's a good place to go?"

"I don't know. I have other ideas."

At Navy Pier, Kayla didn't want to eat anything. Billy went

ahead and got a couple of hot dogs and sat watching strangers pass.

"So we can go to Navy Pier, which is Grand Central Station for tourists, and yet not go to Wrigley Field or the Art Institute or the Shedd Aquarium."

Kayla tried to ignore him as he talked with his mouth half full.

"You don't want to go to any of the museums, any of the interesting places. I mean—what about the planetarium?"

Her head shot up, and she glared at him. Billy stopped chewing and looked at her. "What?"

"You're an idiot."

"What?" he asked. "What'd I say?"

She stood up, shaking her head, putting her sunglasses on. "Do you even have to ask? Are you *that* dense?"

"I love how special you make me feel."

"Think for a second. About what you just said. Those places. The Art Institute. The museums. *The Planetarium.*"

Billy shrugged and tried to think. For a few moments there was nothing.

And *then* he got it. Boy, did he ever get it.

Yes, he was *that* dense.

"I recall going to all of those not long ago," Kayla said. "Seems like you forgot about them."

"Of course I didn't forget about them."

"You didn't?"

"That's where I fell in love with you."

"Stop."

"What? I can't say the L-word around you?"

Kayla stood, so tall and so vibrant and so fiery. "You actually thought—" She laughed.

"What?"

"You thought we could just stroll through the planetarium and not remember? Not mention it? I know you couldn't do that."

"I'm sorry. You're right, okay?"

"Right about what?"

"That was pretty stupid."

"Yeah."

"Last thing I want is to have billboards of my failures surrounding me."

"Oh, it was *your* failure?"

"You broke up with me, right? Last I recall you did."

"So it was a *victory* for me, then? Is that what you mean?"

"Let's just drop it."

"No. It's not just about you and your failure, you know? You don't understand what I went through."

"And I don't think I ever will."

"No, you won't," she stated firmly.

He wished he could see her eyes behind those shades. Billy crumpled the other hot dog in a napkin and stood to throw it away. He had envisioned sharing it with her, both of them sitting on the stone wall eating dogs and laughing and passing time away looking at strangers.

The old days were gone.

"I want to know something, Billy. Did you really mean that at the last concert?"

For a second, he didn't say anything. He already knew the answer. But he didn't want to give it to her.

"Did you? Did you really mean all of that? I just—I went there in hopes of—in hopes of something. I was confused. There was a lot of stuff going on, and I just—I didn't know. And then, right in front of everybody—"

"I know. I'm sorry."

"Did you mean it?"

"You know the answer to that."

"I want to hear it from you," she said.

"I was hurt and angry. I was confused. Hell, I'm *still* confused. I get confused every time I spend more than five seconds with you."

"It was mean."

"I know. I'm sorry."

"But was it true? Were the words—all those songs—did you really mean them?"

"No," he admitted. "You should've stuck around when I trashed the stage." It was still easy to be honest with her. Far too easy.

"Then why?" she asked.

"I told you—I was angry. And I was tired. Tired of waiting."

"But you told me—"

"I know. You don't have to remind me."

"I just thought—after that, I really didn't know what to believe."

"I never lied to you, not once."

"But you told me you'd wait. And then you did that."

Billy looked at her and felt his world swaying. He had wanted to have this conversation two years ago. "What do you think I'm still doing here?" he asked. "Have you ever thought of that?"

He walked away, trying to regain control, trying to find some ounce of dignity he had left.

He had already told her enough.

Too much, in fact.

He didn't want to hear what she had to say in response.

He'd gotten enough rejection for the day.

24. Darkness

This is ludicrous.

Thomas looked at the clock on the wall and stared out the window of his office. This room felt like a prison. It was drab, lifeless, so desperately quiet.

He wanted Billy to get there simply to get rid of the silence.

It was an hour and twenty minutes after they were supposed to meet.

After the three of them were supposed to meet.

Thomas had arrived at the office this morning—a gray morning reminiscent of this office—and had gotten the voice mail from Kayla.

"Hi, Mr. Thomas. This is Kayla. I want to thank you for your patience with me these last few weeks. I've enjoyed getting to know Leona and the other people in Angel Hands. I've just decided that I need more time to devote to my upcoming wedding—there're a lot of things going on that I need to either plan or be a part of—so that's why I've decided to quit Angel Hands. But I did enjoy my time with Leona and plan on letting her know this in person. I don't know what I'll say—but I'll let her know. I just—there's lots that I could— well, anyway, thank you. It was good to get to know you. Take care."

Take care.

He had almost cried, listening to that voice mail.

It was just a message from a confused young lady, but it devastated him.

If only she could know. If only I could tell her. If only . . .

Immediately he began trying to think of ways to get Kayla back into the program.

And now this. Now Billy was gone too.

Who knew if that was a decision that Billy had made or if he was in jail or hung over sleeping it off or God knows what?

Thomas rubbed his temples. "I thought this was going to be easy. Or easier than this."

He wasn't sure where to go or what to do, but he knew he needed to get outside of this confined space.

Even though the day was cloudy with a hint of rain to come, he felt better breathing in fresh air and seeing life around him. He walked a few blocks and kept walking, the energy helping him think.

"Help me to know what to do," he prayed.

And as he was lost in thought, ignoring the strangers around him and the city bustle, he almost knocked over the figure on the sidewalk.

"Excuse me, I'm so—James?"

James stood there smiling, unbothered. "Hello, Thomas."

"I was wondering—hoping, I guess—that I'd see you again."

"This is the last time I can do this."

"Do you know?"

"Of course."

"Don't you have some special love potion I can just slip them?" Thomas asked.

"They don't need that. That's not their problem."

"It seems like all they are is one big problem. Or at least Billy is."

"Can we talk? There's a nice little Indian restaurant down the street. Sound good?"

"Anything to stay out of that office. That is my definition of hell."

"For some people, that's their life, five or six days a week."

"Sad, isn't it?"

"It's a job. And some people don't have that."

"Just kidding," Thomas said. "Can't you take a joke?"

"I'm watching you play matchmaker. That's funny enough."

⁓

Before they got their food, not that Thomas was even hungry, he couldn't help but state the obvious. "I don't get why they should be together."

"You don't?"

"No. They had this bond in college and afterward. And they got close. But that happens to a lot of couples. So?"

"There's more to the story. That's why I'm here."

"To explain what happened?"

"To at least share a little more of their story. Then maybe you'll understand why things are the way they are."

"I just thought—I thought it was going to be easier than this."

"Did you?"

"Sure. Maybe that was overconfidence."

James studied a packet of sugar before putting it in his tea. "So, you thought you could send them on an outing that would get them to relive the past?"

"Yeah, something like that."

"Didn't work out, did it?"

"Nope. It actually backfired."

"Reminding them of the past doesn't mean they'd simply jump right back into it. It's still too fresh for both of them."

"But I just don't get—what is Kayla afraid of? I mean—I know she still has feelings for Billy. I can see it in her. I know my daughter. There are many things I don't know—I haven't been there—but I still *know*."

"And you're right, Thomas. There are still feelings. There always will be. Think about Kayla's mother. There is still a love for her deep down inside you, isn't there?"

"Well, sure—in some ways. But that was a universe ago."

"But for Billy and Kayla, it wasn't that long ago. These are two complicated people, Thomas. But for different reasons."

"So where did things go wrong?"

"There's not one simple explanation."

"There never is."

"Let me tell you what happened after college. But that's it. After that, you're on your own."

"It would sure help if I could just explain to Kayla that I'm her father."

"That would only make things worse. Not to mention the fact that she won't believe you."

Thomas nodded and sighed. "Okay, go ahead. Tell me the bloody details of how the love ended."

"The love didn't end, Thomas. It would be easy if it had."

part four
x & y

I always wanted to bottle up time with you, Kayla. I wanted to stop it or at least try to slow it down. But day after day, week after week, I'd notice something new or different about you. Your hair growing longer, your eyes growing more attentive, your mouth finally figuring out words to say.

Sometimes the love I held inside scared me. I didn't know what to do with it. That's because it was an imperfect love held by an imperfect person. But I still feel this way now—it was the best part of me, this love inside. It was real and it was awe-inspiring. I knew that it would only grow.

And it has grown.

Little did I know that my tiny baby girl would be so strong. That she would be so smart. That she would be so feisty. That she would turn into you. But then again, nothing about it surprised me, because even when you were a year and a half old, I saw it in you. That spirit and that mind and that wit.

I hope that strength you have even to this day comes from the first couple years of your life when your father took care of you. I don't know how things like that work, but I know that we remember those impressionable first few months and years. And I hope that who you are today—the bright and bold

young woman you've turned into—is maybe in part
because of me.

25. Square One (December 2005)

Every flake seemed to have a mind of its own. They swirled around the jogger, filling in the solitary tracks, resting on the blue warm-up suit. The white limbs of trees arched out over the forest path, the silence of the late morning haunting. The year was nearly done, yet the figure ran deliberately, as though her whole life waited somewhere just beyond the next turn.

Kayla's heart beat fast, but it wasn't because of the exercise. She was used to that, even if the snow made running a bit more difficult. It was the news she carried that weighed her down, the anticipation of revealing it to her father.

The trail in the woods, meant for bikers and joggers, ran along the Fox River. It edged up a small hill, then curved toward a clearing. As Kayla approached the open field she slowed down, catching her breath and trying to capture the right words.

A small cemetery stood in the clearing, surrounded by a low fence. The sight was familiar enough, in the heart of summer or the pit of winter. The headstones looked cushioned between newly laid snow. Kayla opened a small gate near the front and walked several rows to the square block of granite.

For a moment she stood, still breathing in, one gloved hand covering the other, jaw clenched. Wavy blonde hair, shoulder-length, spilled out of her white cap. She tightened her lips, then smiled, staring at the name on the stone.

"Hi, Dad," she said out loud, her words quickly lost in the swirling winds.

On the stone it read *Thomas Rowe, loving father with a song in his heart. 1957-1984.*

Kayla wiped snow off her nose and cheek.

"It's been awhile. I know that. And I'm sorry. I needed to come here—I need to tell you something."

She slipped off her gloves and clutched them tightly. She had been here so many times, and those times had been easier. As a small girl, she could recall coming here and recounting what had just happened in third grade or what she received from Aunt Cynthia for her birthday or what movie she had seen. Never once did she doubt that her father watched her from Heaven, looking down or around or from wherever. She knew he heard her words. This had always been her hope, her belief.

But today was different.

For some reason—she wasn't sure why—Kayla felt like her father couldn't see her now, that he didn't know what was happening.

"I should be celebrating," Kayla said. "I should've come earlier. The day it happened or the day after. I just—I miss having you here with me. Knowing what you would say. It's one thing to just talk—and you know I can talk well enough, don't you—but it's another thing to get advice. Wisdom. Simple encouragement. And I . . . I need that now."

She sighed and wiped away a tear with her left hand, the ring on it inescapable. Kayla smiled as if someone had spotted it, as if she had finally given away a secret.

"There it is. What do you think? Or more like, am I making a big mistake?"

Her hand was raised high, the ring facing the headstone. She could see her hand shaking.

"Billy asked me to marry him Christmas morning. And of course I said yes. And I'm excited and I love him and I can't wait to get married."

Her eyes looked upward at the falling snow, the thick, gray clouds. "So what's wrong with me? Can you answer that?" She shook her head, frustrated at herself and her feelings. "I just wish you were here to tell me—to let me know if this is right. I feel it's right, but I just don't know for sure."

She sighed, digging at the snow with her tennis shoe. "I just wish . . ."

She couldn't finish the thought.

Kayla didn't like self-pity, didn't like wallowing in sadness. She wiped away the tears and breathed in.

"All my life I've felt that you've watched over me, that you've protected me, that you love me. I just wish you were here, just this once. I wish I could really talk with you and get your opinion, hear what you think. Get your blessing . . ."

Wind whipped across her and made her shiver.

"Dad—I want to know I'm doing the right thing. I've prayed, and I just want to know—because I *don't* know. There's something in me. Something I haven't felt very often." She laughed. "Yes, believe it or not, I can be afraid. Crazy, huh? Kayla Rowe afraid. Miss Independent. That's what Cynthia says you called me. And I was only a couple years old. Who would think, huh? But I'm afraid. And for once I just want—I just wish—I just—"

She looked at the headstone, the words, the name.

"I wish I could have known you. And I wish that you could know the man I'm marrying."

She shut her eyes and prayed and then opened them again, her eyes teary. "Don't tell anybody I cried. Although they probably wouldn't believe it if you did."

She started to walk away, then turned around. "Happy coming new year, Dad. I love you and always will."

It took her a few minutes to resume the jog, back toward her aunt's house, the house she was raised in. She should have felt better, her feet lighter, the day brighter.

But nothing had changed.

Her father was still gone, and she was still left with something she hadn't experienced much in her life.

Doubt.

26. What If

The call should have been a cause to celebrate.

But instead, in the silence of his apartment, Billy stared at the smudged wall and sighed.

He had the job.

The job he wanted, the job he needed, the job that would help pay the monthly bills along with paying for the sizable ring he'd bought with money he didn't really have.

He was going to be a part of the corporate world, part of the establishment, part of the matrix he'd been denouncing for some time now. He didn't have to wear a tie, but he might as well.

For a second, Billy thought of calling them back and saying thanks but no thanks.

But then he thought of Kayla. And he knew he couldn't do it.

She had been patient long enough. And he understood. The dreams of—of whatever it was that he wanted to be—were simply dreams. It was time to get with the program, get with the real world, get a job and settle down.

New York was a mirage, just like the music, just like the bright lights and the cover of *Spin*. Just like Song of the Day. All a mirage.

He knew he should call Kayla and tell her the good news. But he was afraid to. He still couldn't shake the look she had given him when he proposed. The look should have been one of excitement and elation, but it was one of apprehension.

If he didn't know her as well as he did, Billy wouldn't have had a second thought. But he knew Kayla. He knew everything about her.

What if she changed her mind? What if all of this was a mirage, something to fill the gap until the next thing or the right thing comes into her life?

Billy shoved the thought away, but it still clawed at him, undeterred.

He found his cell phone and called her.

But instead of Kayla, he got her voice mail. Kayla was with the rest of the working world, stuck in some meeting or working on some project or doing something important that helped the bottom line.

The bottom line for him was that he was finally entering that universe. Even if he really, truly didn't want to.

He hung up without leaving a message, then looked at the heaping pile of garbage in the kitchen. His roommate sure wasn't going to take it out. Reuben had two part-time jobs that seemed to take up his entire life. He was never around. And Billy was always around, working on songs that never got sung, chords that never got played, ideas that never got uttered. And Chad was—well, who knew where Chad was these days. Billy never heard much from him, especially as he'd gotten closer with Kayla.

All of this—the sitting around and the playing songs and the dreaming—he was living a lie, a fantasy, a fiction that he needed to close the book on.

A mound of bills sat on the kitchen counter.

This place gave him a headache. This small hole-in-the-wall apartment. The smell. The drabness of the paint color (or lack of color). The crazy neighbors.

Billy could list a hundred things that gave him a headache. But mostly, it was the fear.

It seemed like he had never had fears until meeting Kayla. And then, one fear after another popped into his life.

The fear of rejection.

The fear of her discovering he was really somebody else.

The fear of losing her.

And he dragged this last fear around with him on one foot, and on the other the fear of never seeing the door to his dreams open. Or, he should say, open again.

Billy went into his room and played some loud music. He found the e-mail that he'd printed and opened it up again.

> Hey, Billy. I got a place for you up here. We need
> a good singer and songwriter. You'd love New York.
> Give me a ring. Sam

The e-mail was six months old. He'd met Sam and had basically gotten an offer to play in his up-and-coming band in the New York indie rock scene.

It hadn't been blind luck. Sam had heard Song of the Day playing downtown and had shared some drinks with the guys afterward. But it wasn't the band he wanted. It was Billy.

And when the e-mail came, Billy hadn't told anybody. Not even Kayla.

Because he was afraid she might tell him to go.

To leave her.

To follow his dreams.

He folded the letter back up. It was done. The small crack had been opened and now it was shut. Just like many things in life.

But Kayla was still there.

And he'd just gotten a decent job working at a business in their customer service department. Nowadays, with the economy failing like a dying horse, having a job that paid biweekly checks and gave him benefits was indeed something.

He stared at the letter from Sam. Then he decided to head out and go shopping for some clothes. He needed to find some business casual attire, whatever the hell that meant.

Kayla sat in her car, the rain/snow/hail skittering over her wind-shield. The engine was off and she sat in the diminishing warmth, the blurred windshield resembling her thoughts.

I don't want to go in there.

It wasn't that her mother scared her. It was just that every single time she spoke with her, Kayla would spend the next week in a funk. For many years, she didn't recognize it, couldn't understand it. Only after a year in therapy did she figure out this nasty habit.

The icy chunks tapped all around her, not helping her think, not encouraging her to get out.

Only an hour ago, the phone had rung. It was seven on a Satur-day morning, and she found the cordless, assuming it was Billy. He would be checking up on her just to make sure—well, just to check up.

"It's early," was the first thing she said.

But instead of Billy, it was her mother. "Kayla?"

A mother should recognize the voice of her daughter, even if it was hoarse and faded from going to bed late the night before.

"Yeah?"

"It's your mother."

It had taken Nicole Swanson many years—sixteen, to be exact—before she could actually call herself that. But then, for some reason, she had decided she wanted to be part of her daughter's life. That lasted one whole month, during Kayla's junior year in high school.

"Hi." Kayla instantly spoke from a guarded position.

"Can we meet for breakfast?"

"Are you okay?"

"Yes, I'm fine. I just—I'm coming out to the area and wanted—well, I spoke with Cynthia last night and she told me."

Kayla waited for a *Congratulations* or an *I'm so happy for you,* but then she remembered who she was talking to. She'd felt as much love from one of those automated voices that guided you through a bunch of menu options on the phone.

"I'm assuming you're talking about my engagement."

"Yes. I'd like to talk to you about it."

For a brief moment, Kayla almost said no. But she couldn't. Despite not being in her life until Kayla was almost a grownup, her mother still had control over her. She would always be her mom. And deep down, Kayla wanted as much time and attention from her as she could get.

So why was she sitting here in the cold car, the rain turning to ice scattering around her?

Once again, she felt like she was leaking.

Why does she still have so much control over me even though she's not in my life? Even though she didn't want to have any part of my life and my father's life when she went through her postpartum depression?

Kayla rubbed the engagement ring, a habit she had picked up out of fear of losing it—and reassurance that it had actually happened.

For a moment, she thought about calling Billy. He would pick up, even if he was sleeping (and he was still surely sleeping). But then she decided not to.

She needed to face her mother.

Kayla could take whatever her mother was going to say.

Once again she wondered if her father was up in Heaven, watching her. Or possibly watching over her.

The restaurant was a family-owned establishment that served great food for great prices. It was busy, but thankfully her mother had gotten there early enough to get them a booth. Kayla took off her damp hat and coat as she approached the table.

Nicole sat there, sipping a cup of coffee. She smiled at Kayla as she sat, but she didn't give her a hug or a kiss or even a warm greeting.

"Is it still raining?" her mother asked.

"It's turning into ice and snow."

Her mother was pretty. She was tall and slender, a little too chiseled for Kayla's liking, with short blonde hair and wide eyes. Kayla did resemble her in many ways, but her mother had a harsh edge to her. From her jawline to her rough hands to her cold green eyes—there was nothing warm or soft about her.

"Thanks for meeting me."

Kayla poured herself some coffee from the carafe on the table. She opened the menu in front of her and started looking.

Silence like this wasn't unusual. Her mother had a hard time communicating. Not because of some guilt or anxiety about not being there. No—Nicole clearly didn't regret her decision. She sometimes gave Kayla a look that seemed to say *You probably deserve more,* but she would never actually say it.

After a few minutes of conversation about the weather, a waiter came up and took their order. Kayla wanted the guy to stay simply so she wouldn't have to talk anymore to her mother.

"I would have called sooner, but I just got back from Jamaica."

"Christmas in Jamaica. How festive."

"Like my tan?" Nicole asked.

"You're always tanned."

"Guess you're right. When I got back this week, things at the office were crazy."

"Aren't they always?"

Her mother was a secretary at a law firm downtown. She worked five days a week, doing the commute, dressing the part, talking the talk.

"So what happened?" her mother asked.

"What do you mean?"

"You're engaged. When did you guys decide to go and do that?"

"You act like we just adopted five children from Africa."

"Marriage is a big step."

"And you know this how?"

Nicole sighed, looked annoyed. This conversation felt more like one Kayla might have with a friend, or an older sibling.

"Just because I never got married doesn't mean I don't understand its pitfalls."

"Thanks for the vote of confidence."

"I'm just looking out for you," Nicole said.

"Good that you're starting after a couple of decades."

"Kayla—"

"What? You haven't even said congratulations. Or at least wished me luck."

"Kayla, you're still very young."

Kayla could feel her anger beginning to quake inside her. "Don't you think you're the last person in the world to talk about being too young?"

"No," her mother said. "Not with you. If there's one thing I'm qualified to talk about, it's that. I was too young. Your father and I were too young. And too stupid, too."

"Thanks. That makes me feel so swell when you talk like that."

"We were foolish by not taking precautions, Kayla. That's what I mean."

"Maybe it's the way you say it. As if I'm not really here. As if I was just an afterthought."

Nicole closed her eyes for a second, trying to think, her tight skin showing lines under the makeup and the tan. "I was too young to have a child, Kayla. And I was too young to even understand the concept of love. Even now I sometimes wonder if I truly understand."

"I'm not you."

"No, you're not," Nicole said almost too quickly. "You are your father in so many ways."

"I know what I'm doing. I don't need you to tell me that I don't."

"But, Kayla—have you thought about life ten years from now? Even ten months from now?"

"Of course."

"Your rocker friend isn't going to be able to support you, much less if you guys start a family—"

"Whoa. Just stop right there."

Her mother had always called Billy her "rocker friend." And she always said it with disdain in her mouth.

"I'm just trying to talk some sense into you."

"Did you know that Billy just got a job? With a good company? No, of course you didn't."

"So he's giving up his dreams?"

"No. I told him he didn't have to get the job. But he's doing it for both of us. He still is going to make it. I know it."

"I believed your father was going to make it too."

"My father died trying to make it."

Perhaps it was her tone, or the way she emphasized *my father*. Whatever it was seemed to quiet her mother.

EVERY BREATH YOU TAKE

It almost seemed to scare her a bit.

"Don't you dare say anything about Dad's dreams," Kayla continued. "At least he had some. And he couldn't help it. It wasn't his fault that he died. Blame the trucker that ran into him."

"I'm just trying to warn you about things."

"About what? What 'things'?"

"Kayla, I've walked your shoes. I've been there."

"No, you haven't."

"Yes, I have."

"You left Dad and me."

Nicole shut her eyes and remained silent for a minute. She didn't look sad, but she acted as if she couldn't say anything against Kayla's accusation.

"You left Dad and me, so don't you *dare* talk to me about my choices. Because I'm the only one who can make them. Not you. And not Dad."

"Kayla—listen to me. I was . . . your father and I believed that we loved each other. But my mistake wasn't in leaving him. It was in believing that we were ever truly meant to be together in the first place. There's no such thing as a soul mate, Kayla. Your father talked that way, but he was a helpless romantic."

"So call me one, too."

"Romance and dreams didn't help pay the bills."

"Neither did bailing out. And that's *exactly* what you did: you bailed on Dad."

"Yes, I did. And I've told you. I wasn't ready to be a mother. I'm still not. I just—I can't blame myself for your father's death. It was a tragic accident."

"But I wasn't."

Her mother looked at her, and for the first time that Kayla could ever remember—*ever*—her mother's hardened eyes covered up in tears.

"You weren't planned, Kayla. But out of mistakes come miracles."

Kayla put her head down and suddenly, unexpectedly started to cry. She buried her face in her hands and breathed in and breathed out and tried to regain control.

Not here, not now, not in front of her.

She tightened her fists and then wiped her eyes.

"I didn't come here to upset you," her mother said.

"Then what do you want?"

"I just don't want you to make a mistake. You still have your life ahead of you. Don't get stuck in some romantic dream and then wake up and realize that you made a big mistake."

"I think the only mistake I've made is coming to talk with you," Kayla said.

"I don't want you to simply settle because of what you believe might happen."

"With what?"

"With anything. With your career or with Billy's musical dreams or with love or life. Nothing in this world comes easily. You don't want to be fortysomething looking back wishing—knowing that things could have been different."

Their breakfast arrived, but Kayla was too sick and angry and hurt to eat.

She looked her mother in the eyes and spoke deliberately. "The only thing that I wish could be different is that Dad was still alive to tell you how wrong you are."

And with that, she stood and walked out of the restaurant.

As usual, her mother had wreaked havoc in Kayla's heart and soul.

And Kayla was the only one around to clean up the mess.

28. Fix You

It would always be like this, as long as he performed, as long as he even played. Being behind the keys of the piano and the stare of the microphone, Billy poured out his heart and sang with his soul.

The January gig had been planned several months ago. It was on a Wednesday night, which was fine for the other guys but meant he would be going into work bleary-eyed tomorrow. They got a little money, but it wasn't about that. It was about continuing to pursue the dream, the dream that was getting dimmer and dimmer with each passing day.

Billy had told Kayla that she didn't have to come, that she had been to enough of their concerts with few interested audience members and late hours and the same songs. She had a new job of her own, and the last thing he wanted to do was add to the pressure of that.

It already seemed like she had been under a lot of pressure lately. Ever since—well, really, ever since he had proposed.

Up here on this small stage, he could put aside his worries and doubts and fears. The music squelched them. It was only for the length of the song, but that was the beauty behind the chords and the choruses. For a brief time, he could forget his problems.

With every show they did, Billy would put in a few extra songs to pad their set list. And tonight, he had a song he was dying to sing. They had practiced it several times. They would end with it, and maybe a few of the twenty-something people in the bar would be impressed or moved or at least stop talking and drinking and listen to them.

They'd found an old vintage drum machine from the eighties that Reuben tinkered around with. It was perfect for this song: "Duchess" by Genesis, a tune that he had discovered thanks to the magic of iTunes. It told the story about the rise and fall of a musical diva, but the story could apply to anybody who made it big in this industry.

The song made sense to him, and the lyrics moved him. So as they closed the small joint in Chicago on this cold, wintry Wednesday night, Billy performed as if he was in the United Center in front of twenty thousand people.

He felt comfortable behind the keys of the keyboard as he belted out the lyrics.

And then, near the end, as the guys surrounding him jammed away, Billy saw her.

Sitting on a barstool near the back of the room.

And he kept singing, smiling, singing now to her, a rush washing over him, the sweat dripping onto his moving hands.

And when he uttered the final lyric, he looked over and saw her turn and walk away.

Billy didn't understand. They finished the song and heard the mild applause and he thanked everybody and then tried to find her.

For a brief moment, he remembered the first time he'd performed in front of her.

That felt like another lifetime ago.

But it was the same Kayla. And some things never changed.

She smiled at the rest of the band and made small talk. But Billy knew better.

She bought them a round and congratulated them on the music. But Billy wasn't fooled.

She didn't seem worried about the time or the place or the cold night air. And neither of them had time to share a solitary conversation. Billy couldn't ask her why she had left at the end of the song, as if she was upset. Now, she smiled and laughed and acted normal.

But he knew something was wrong.

And soon Kayla said she needed to go, and Billy told the guys he would walk her out to her car.

"K, what's the deal?"

Snow coated them as they walked, the kind of thick, wet snow that was great for making snowmen. The city streets were mostly silent.

"Nothing."

"Come on."

"Are you upset that I came?"

"Of course not," Billy said. "Why would I be upset?"

She kept walking until she reached her car.

"I can't," she said.

"You can't what?"

She stood there in her long, black overcoat, snowflakes on her long blonde hair, looking like some long-lost model who should be in New York rather than Chicago. Who should be with someone else besides Billy.

"If only you could have seen yourself."

"What? Was I *that* bad?"

She shook her head in disbelief. "When are you ever going to get it?"

"Get what?"

"Get how good you are?"

Billy laughed. "I don't know about that."

"Of course you don't. You don't get it. You never have. Even though you can carry off that cocky attitude at times, you *so* don't know how good you are. Sometimes I think you never will."

"What's going on?" Billy asked her again.

"This. This—all of this."

"What? The weather? The night?"

"You're a fool."

"Thank you," Billy said.

"No, you really are. *This* is what you should be doing, Billy. Not getting up at six and going to some dead-end job that is as inspiring as filing your income taxes."

"The job is fine—we've talked about this."

"No—*you* talked. And you told me what you were going to do and what we were going to do."

"Kayla, what's wrong?"

She shook her head, still standing in front of her car, the snow coating her, her breath slightly visible in the muted light on the corner of the street. "The only time I've seen you look like that—ever—is when you're with me, in my arms, when we're holding one another."

"That's a great place to be."

"But you can't be there all the time. You have a life to live, Billy."

"*We* have a life to live."

"I'm holding you back."

"That's crazy."

"I'm serious," Kayla said. "I just—I can't—not anymore." She unlocked her car and climbed inside.

Billy slipped around to the other side and got in the seat next to her. The windows were draped in white, but by the dome light he could see that she was crying. He grabbed one of her gloved hands and held it tight. "Kayla, talk to me. Ever since—ever since I proposed, something's been wrong."

"No."

"We don't have to rush things. I can wait. You know I can."

"It's not that."

"Then . . . what?" Billy put his face close to hers and forced her to look at him. "Look at me, please. What is going on?"

The tears were coming on strong now. For a few minutes, he just held her in the silence and seclusion of the car. The snow continued to fall and the tears continued to stream and Billy waited.

"I'm sorry," she said. "I just—Billy, I can't." Her eyes were swollen and red and she looked desperate and young and lost. "I don't want to hold you back. I don't want to be a burden."

He laughed in disbelief. "Hold me back from what?"

"From tonight. From more nights like this. You should have seen yourself. You should have heard yourself. And that last song. Don't you get it?"

"Get what?"

"Did you listen to the lyrics? You didn't just randomly pick that song, Billy. That's one of *those* songs. One of those you have tattooed on your soul. I get it. I always have. And it terrifies me."

"Why does it terrify you?"

"Because I understand. And that—that path—that road—I just don't know if I can go down it with you."

"What are you saying?"

She took off her gloves as he shook his head.

"Listen, K, just—look, it's late. And I don't—"

The ring he had given her was now grasped between Kayla's fingers. "This is yours," she said.

"No, it's not."

"Take it, please," she said.

"Kayla, please. I don't care what path I'm on as long as it's with you."

"That's what you say now. But I don't want you looking back ten or twenty years from now and wishing things were different."

"The only way I'd do that is if you're not by my side," Billy said.

"Damn it, Billy, take it."

He took the ring, but continued shaking his head. "We can wait, okay?"

"No, no waiting. I already prevented one person from being able to follow his dreams. I couldn't help it then. Now I can."

"What? Who?"

"I really need to go."

"Kayla, this isn't about your father, okay? This is about you and me."

"I know. And I've made my decision."

"Your decision? What decision is that exactly?"

"I need some time."

"Some time to think about marriage? To think things through?"

"I need some time," she repeated.

"Kayla, please."

"I need to go. The guys are back at the bar waiting for you."

"Let me come home with you."

"That wouldn't be a good idea."

"Yes it would," he said.

She gave him a glance that he recognized, that he knew was dangerous. "Billy."

"This ring belongs to you, Kayla. And we can wait. We can wait five years if we have to. But this is yours and always will be."

"I just—I really think I should go, okay?"

"Yeah, okay."

He went to kiss her, but she moved her face away. Billy kissed her on the forehead.

"It's going to be okay," he told her.

But as he climbed out of the car and watched the snow-covered taillights of her car drive away, he wasn't sure he believed his own words.

He held the ring firmly in his hand, shaking from the cold.

Can you see inside my heart, inside my head?

The darkness enveloped her, the silence suffocating. The covers seemed to want to strangle her.

Sometimes this apartment felt so lonely.

She wanted to talk to him, but she couldn't.

She wanted to see Aunt Cynthia, but she shouldn't.

But what she really, truly wanted was to know.

To know what her father was like.

Why am I the way I am? How much "like" him am I?

She couldn't get the image out of her head. The snapshot of him holding her, both of them laughing.

What a waste. What a waste that my father couldn't live longer. That I couldn't grow up with him by my side. That he couldn't see me become who I am and that I couldn't see him be who he was.

And the same thoughts nagged at her. Did he watch her? Did he know her? Did he protect her? Did he still live, somewhere in Heaven? Could the dead watch you like a never-ending reality show? *Kayla Rowe Unleashed—Stay Tuned on Channel 27.*

Kayla could feel the sweat on her forehead.

Can you read my thoughts, Father?

Only three weeks after her mother had gone and thrown a grenade in her lap, and a week after having seen Billy perform and giving his ring back, Kayla found herself wishing she could talk with her father.

Just this once.

God, I would give anything to be able to hear from him again. To see him. To spend one day with him.

She had always accepted the fact that he was gone. Life was tough, and life was like that. But she wanted some simple advice. Not the advice of a selfish woman who still couldn't really truly call herself Kayla's mother. Not even the advice of a caring and well-intentioned aunt who sometimes couldn't help herself.

She wanted her father's perspective.

A thousand thoughts cut at her.

Where am I going in life? Is this the life I want?

Should I be with Billy?

Am I weighing him down?

Is he weighing me down?

She felt sad, and scared, and silly feeling this way.

She was twenty-three years old. She was an adult. With a good job. And good friends. And a good life ahead of her.

But that could all change.

Every day was a breath. A blink. And one day, it could all be over.

Please help me, Dad. Please help me know what to do and where to go.

But nobody answered.

Maybe he was in Heaven, watching and waiting. But she was alone.

And it was up to her to move on.

30. X & Y

"What are you doing here?"

Billy looked up and saw his father walking toward him wearing his ancient black bathrobe and slippers the size of groundhogs. Daniel Harris looked like a relic from the sixties or seventies, his hair still long even though it was thinning, gray stubble on his rough face, his eyes bright like a lighter at a Grateful Dead concert.

Billy had arrived at the house in Hinsdale after his folks were in bed. He'd come down to the finished basement, which had sound-proof walls that allowed him to crank up the stereo if he wanted. Which was exactly what he was doing.

"Just wanted a little space."

"From your roommate?"

"From life."

His father nodded, sat down and looked at the records strewn about on the carpeted floor. "Looking for some inspiration?"

Billy laughed. "Nah, I got enough of that. Looking for some-where it can go."

His father picked up a record. "You know the beauty of this?"

"Don't," Billy said.

"What?"

"Don't get into the whole 'I remember the days of vinyl.' I know. I've heard you say it a thousand times."

"I wasn't going to say anything about that, Mr. Know-It-All." His father looked amused.

"No?"

"No. I remember where I was the day I bought this album." He held a battered and faded copy of *Revolver* by the Beatles.

"Prison," Billy said.

Dad laughed.

Billy loved his parents' sense of humor. They were the two most laid-back parents he had ever met. He sometimes wondered why the genes hadn't got passed down. The musical/artist genes sure did, but not the even-keel attitude toward life.

"Put this on."

Billy slipped the record into the player. His father, a musician himself who idolized John Lennon, had every type of sound system in place down here—a record player, two in fact; an 8-track player; a cassette deck; and of course a high-quality CD system. All of these were attached to an amazing sound system, so complicated Einstein couldn't figure it out. His dad couldn't figure out the television remote, yet he could fine-tune this complicated stereo system.

They listened to the album for a while. That was another thing Billy liked about his dad—he could just sit and listen to music with him.

"I was sixteen years old. 1966. Your grandparents didn't like rock, to put it lightly. So I had to go over to my friend's house to play the album. And he didn't like the Beatles. I remember he wasn't home, so I snuck into his house to play it. His mother came home and called the cops on me before realizing who was there."

"Are you serious?"

"Of course," Dad said.

"That's dedication."

"It was worth it. I love this album."

It felt like Paul and John were there, jamming in the other room, the sound was that good. Billy sat back in the plush sofa, just listening.

"So what's up?" his father finally asked as Lennon sang away on "I'm Only Sleeping."

"Oh, just drama. Nothing really."

"Lady problems?"

"The only lady problem I have is that I don't have a lady."

"What do you mean? What happened?"

Billy reached in his pants pocket and produced the box that he'd opened for Kayla on Christmas morning.

"What's the ring doing back in there?" Dad asked him.

"Exactly. She gave it back. And not because it didn't fit. Well, I guess it didn't fit—none of it—the marriage and the happily ever after."

The Beatles "Love You Too" song came on with its Eastern influence. Daniel turned it off and gave Billy a serious look. "Want to talk about it?"

"It's been a couple weeks now. I didn't want to say anything to you guys—I thought it was temporary. Kayla's moody, she can go to extremes, even when she desperately tries not to. But she hasn't wanted to talk—it's been impossible to see her. I don't know what's going on."

"What did she tell you?"

"She's hasn't exactly said it, but I think she's afraid of the whole musician thing. She knows how much I love performing. And it all goes back to her father—to losing him, to feeling like she was the reason he never made it as a musician. She blames herself for some reason. So, with me, it's like this big reminder."

His father waited for a while, not feeling the need to say anything or share some bit of advice or wisdom. Another thing Billy liked about him. He didn't need advice or wisdom.

He needed Kayla.

"I took this job for her—for us. It's not like I'm giving up my dreams. I'm always going to be playing. But it's just—the music thing pales in comparison to her. To being with Kayla. To living a life with her."

"Does she know this?"

"Yes. A hundred times. But she thinks I'm selling myself short. I don't know. I just keep hoping that she's going to snap out of it. She's done things like this before—breaking up because we were too serious, you know. Then coming back and calling herself an idiot. That's what I love about her. Her passion and intensity. And the fact that you never know what she might do."

His father nodded. He took out another Beatles record, but Billy put a hand on his dad's arm.

"It's a little too perky for me."

"Ah, let me think. Let's find something truly despondent. Then we can wallow in our sadness."

Billy sighed and sat back on the couch as his dad continued glancing through the hundreds of albums arranged in some way only he knew.

"Did you know the first time I proposed to your mother, she said no?"

Billy stared at his father, puzzled. He didn't remember that story. And he prided himself in knowing all of his father's stories. "You ever told us this?"

"No, come to think of it. It's not one of the happier stories to tell."

"Yeah, but she married you, and you had five of us."

"I know, but the first time she really, truly believed she was in love. With someone else."

"What?"

"Yeah. A guy named Alistair."

"Alice-who?"

"Alistair. Yeah, I mean, come on. On the name alone she couldn't marry him. His last name was even worse. Krotchen."

Billy laughed. "You're making that up."

"One hundred percent true. And your mother, well, she thought she knew. She had all the vibes and all the signs and all that nonsense. Well, it was nonsense with Alistair Crotchety, as I called him. But then when the signs came with me, then they were okay."

"What happened?"

"To Alistair? Oh, I shot him. Buried him in the woods."

Billy chuckled.

"No, I waited. Of course, I was lovesick and love-struck and all those kinds of things. I dated a few other girls, but I knew. I just knew."

"What are the chances that could happen twice?"

His father put another record on. He found the track he wanted and delicately set the needle down. The drumbeats sounded, and the melodic sounds of Simon and Garfunkel started to play. *Cecilia, you're breaking my heart,* the upbeat song said.

"They always break your heart. Maybe there was someone once named Cecilia. These guys created something great out of it."

"Yeah, but they probably didn't end up with Cecilia."

"True. That's how great art works sometimes."

"I'd settle for Kayla and mediocre art. Or no art at all."

"But isn't that the problem, according to Kayla?" his father asked. "She doesn't want you to settle."

"Not sure how I can have both."

His father sat down on the couch beside him and nodded. "I waited for over a year for your mother."

Billy nodded. "But I already waited before she even decided to officially date me."

"So then keep waiting."

"And do what? Everything I try seems to somehow backfire."

"Don't 'try' anything. Just let things be. Women are fickle and funny creatures. Sometimes they need to make their minds up themselves."

"Heaven forbid someone tells Kayla what to do."

"She's headstrong. But that's why you love her, right?"

"Yeah. One of a thousand reasons why."

They sat on the couch and listened to records far into the night. It was one of those scenes that would be worthy of recalling twenty or thirty years down the road, perhaps.

If Billy was talking to his son or daughter.

Hopefully telling them about their mother.

Hopefully.

31. Speed of Sound

You there? the text reads.

And for a long time it's unanswered.

No the response finally comes.

I am. And I'm still waiting.

But the text to Billy comes back quickly this time: **Don't. It's not worth it. I'm not worth it.**

And one hour turns into one afternoon. One sunset turns into a week's worth. One month turns into spring.

Time passes, as it always does.

The memories remain, as do the songs.

Kayla immerses herself in work, trying her best to run around but getting nowhere.

Billy immerses himself in music, playing as often as he can and debating about a fulltime job that's going nowhere.

And then he recalls a song, and sees the lyrics and the notes for it from another time not too long ago, in a notebook with Monet's *Sandvika, Norway* painting on the cover.

He builds on it.

And with that, he gets another idea. Another idea for another show.

But this time, he'll be singing to just one person.

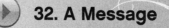

32. A Message

Billy recalled his father's words: *She doesn't want you to settle.*

And after a few months of letting that sink in, he decided that he didn't want to settle.

In the course of one week in mid-April, several things happened.

First, he quit his job. Not in a dramatic fashion. There was no drama in the job in the first place. No drama, no passion, no career, no anything. He simply told them he was quitting and needed to leave as soon as possible. He said his heart wasn't in it and that there was more he needed to do. They didn't get it, but they didn't need to get it. All they needed to know was that he was done.

The concert was scheduled on his birthday, April 21. He hadn't even thought about the date when they first booked it. Then it dawned on him, and gave him an idea.

He had only had brief conversations with Kayla in the last few months. The more he pushed, the more she pushed him away. He'd initially thought time was going to be the key. But unfortunately, it worked against him. He found Kayla drifting further away until he asked her point blank if they were a couple or they were anything at all, even friends. She had told him no. That was a month and a half ago.

So a week before he played the concert on his birthday at the popular pub on the north side, Billy got Shannen to have lunch with him. He hadn't seen Kayla's friend in several months. When he found her waiting at the table at a restaurant downtown, he could feel the tension filling her.

"Wow, look at you."

"Hi, Billy."

"You look like you're having lunch with the devil."

"Stop. This is not easy."

"It's lunch. That's all."

"I don't know what's going on with her," Shannen said.

"I didn't ask."

"I know, but I figure you're going to. Why else did you ask to see me?"

"How are you?"

"Me? I'm fine. I mean, my best friend is not doing well, so I've been holding her hand and being patient with her."

"That's good. She's lucky to have someone like you."

Shannen looked sad. And unafraid to show it. Every glance she gave Billy seemed to be full of pity and regret.

"You know, I'm not dying," Billy said.

"I know. It's just—I'm so sorry."

"Is she okay?"

"What's your definition of okay?"

"I mean—with her work and her life."

"She's busy. She's trying to run away even though she's not going anywhere."

"Look—I have an idea. But I need your help."

"To do what?"

"We're playing a gig at the Stony Pub. On April 21. Kayla will know that it's my birthday."

"And you want us to come?"

Billy nodded. "I don't know how you get her there, just figure out a way."

"And then what?"

"I always think that, well—in the end, music will prevail."

⁓

But in the days leading up to his birthday, and the hours leading up to playing at the Stony Pub, Billy had his doubts that Kayla would hear any music at all. Even when they started playing, he couldn't see her in the crowded pub. It was a large rectangular room, and since it was Friday, the masses were mingling. There seemed to be three times the number of girls in the room as guys. The guys in the band were happy about that, but the only thing that mattered to Billy was spotting one particular blonde.

They opened with "Shout About," their second most popular song. It had been almost a year since they released their self-produced, self-published album, *Song of the Day*. They'd already managed to sell through the thousand copies they'd ordered. Billy kept telling the rest of the guys that this was basically their demo—that it would be the way they'd find a label and build a fan base. And while the fan base seemed to be working—unless there was some free beer special going on tonight—they still hadn't found a label.

Not yet, Billy often told the rest of the guys.

          ◡◝

They were five songs into their set when he saw her.

An angel in the packed crowd standing in front of him. The pub was definitely at full capacity, maybe two hundred or so. But suddenly, all those people disappeared.

All Billy could see was Kayla.

And something surged inside of him.

God, is she beautiful, he thought as he sang.

He noticed her smile, her wavy hair glowing, those bright blue eyes, her sun-drenched soul so out of place, yet so right, in a room like this.

Billy smiled as he finished the song.

So far, they had played five of their own songs. Billy liked to think of all the bands before them that went on with unheard songs and slowly built a following. It took time—night after night and song after song. And since Kayla was there, and he didn't know how long she might be standing there in front of him, Billy knew that the plan needed to spring into action.

As they prepared to start playing another song, Billy looked at the rest of the band. He nodded his head to let them know.

"I want to thank everybody for coming out tonight," he said into the mike. "I thought this would be a great time to play a new song that I recently finished writing. Hope you'll like it. It's called 'Last Train to Infinity.' "

And he started playing the chords on the keyboard, the sound of the piano soothing the crowd.

And for the first time, Billy sang the opening words in front of the crowd, in front of her: " 'It still counts, if you want to know. All the distant sounds, and all the places you go.' "

As Billy sang he forgot about everybody and everything else. He didn't look at her at first, with his eyes closed and his fingers playing and his mind focused on the music. The guitar and the bass landed in the song, along with the drums. And they played it well.

It wasn't the next coming of The Beatles, but then again, who was? There were probably a thousand rock groups trying to land a new deal. Every day, someone somewhere was playing a new song and composing a new riff and structuring a new chord and making up a new lyric. And none of them knew if it would take off.

But if it mattered to them—if it moved them deep inside their souls—then that's what made it worthwhile.

The rest—the magic—that was like all of life. Sometimes things happened, and sometimes they didn't.

But for Billy—twenty-four years old today, only months removed from being engaged and having a corporate job and having another life—he realized that the magic had already happened.

And it stood in front of him as he sang this new song.

He could see Kayla smiling.

Were those tears in her eyes?

Did he have tears in his?

I wrote this for you all for you all of it for you Kayla.

" 'And we can take the last train to infinity. God knows we'll get there eventually. With you at my side, there's nothing else that matters to me, riding this last train to infinity.' "

At the end of the song, the applause was not simply standard. The crowd erupted in joyous noise.

But when Billy looked at Kayla, he knew.

She understood.

She remembered.

And as she smiled, he believed that music would prevail.

Before doing the last song of the night, Billy looked squarely at Kayla as she glowed in the crowd.

"Thank you all for being here tonight. This last song is dedicated to a lovely lady whom I still love."

The rest of the band stepped off the stage. Billy grabbed an acoustic guitar and then started to play one of his favorite songs.

One of *their* favorite songs.

And if you've ever fallen in love and ever had a song move you and make you think of your beloved, remember that song now.

Whatever it is.

And imagine that your beloved is there in front of you, in front of a crowd, and you're on the cusp of a dream come true, performing this song with every ounce of passion you can muster.

And if you can imagine this, then you can picture the scene with a boy singing to a girl and the girl wiping her eyes in response.

" 'You don't have to be on your own,' " Billy sang.

Music has a power and that is why people listen, why people keep coming back for more. To be moved. To be inspired. To be amazed.

And for this clustered crowd in the middle of a pub in Chicago, Kayla and Billy weren't the only two hearts moved.

But that was all secondary—the song and the music and the emotion.

What Billy wanted was to love Kayla.

Now and tomorrow and the next day and for the rest of eternity.

" 'And I'm not going to stand and wait,' " he sang triumphantly, emphatically, roaring with life behind the strumming guitar. "I'm nothing on my own. . . ."

And he didn't care that as the song came to a close, his guitar the only instrument playing, that tears streamed down his cheeks.

They were tears of sadness and of joy. Of relief and of disbelief.

And he sang the final words.

" 'My song is love, is love unknown, and I've got to get that message home.' "

"This would be one of those things I'd ask Dad about—if he was still around."

Aunt Cynthia stopped what she was doing in the kitchen and then walked over and gave Kayla a hug. Her aunt was always giving her a hug. It was almost as if her aunt tried to compensate for Kayla's missing parents through hugs and touches and kisses, not to mention a hundred other ways.

"Or if your mother wasn't such a flake," Cynthia said about her younger sister.

"Tell me about it."

Kayla had been back at the sprawling house in St. Charles for over an hour, talking to her aunt about everything that had happened. Aunt Cynthia knew some of the details, but not all of them. Especially not the bit about the breakfast with her mother that had, in fact, messed things up with Kayla. She told her aunt about the concert a few nights ago and how Billy had written a song for her (even about her) and how he had basically put his heart and soul out there for everybody including her to see.

"So what happened after the show?"

"I couldn't help myself," Kayla said. "Billy took me home. And it was—it was a magical night."

They had talked deep into the night, not about "Billy and Kayla" but more about catching up with each other's lives these past few months. And they fell asleep on the couch in one another's arms.

But the morning came, as morning always does, and Kayla needed to get to work, leaving unemployed Billy behind.

Now, a few days later, Kayla still didn't know what to do.

"Did you even talk about it?"

"No," she said. "And he didn't pressure me. Billy has never pressured me. He knows that I often do the opposite when I am."

"What do you want to do?"

Kayla shook her head, looking at the massive kitchen around her.

Aunt Cynthia and Kayla had moved into the Victorian house when she was a young child. Insurance money from her father's passing had paid for it outright. The selling point for her aunt had been the large and unkempt backyard. Over the years, she had worked extensively on both the inside and the outside of the house, doing everything from remodeling to carving out a large formal garden in the back and adding on a wing that attached to the garage. The house was over 3,000 square feet, ample enough space for the two of them, and now just her aunt.

"I'm not sure what I want to do. Or what I *should* do. That's why I'm here."

Aunt Cynthia smiled, sipping her coffee. "I've been waiting for forty-nine years to be in a wedding. And since I'm not going to be the one getting married, it might as well be you. You know how much I want to have a wedding here, K."

"I know."

"But that's irrelevant. I want you to be happy. You deserve to be happy."

"Billy makes me happy."

"Then what's holding you back?"

Kayla stood up and grabbed a picture from the baker's rack against the wall. It was picture of her in her father's arms, her eyes beaming and her smile radiant as she gazed at him. Kayla could only see the outline of his face, his cheeks stretched in a big grin.

"What was Dad like?"

Aunt Cynthia looked surprised at the question.

"I mean—I know what you've told me. But what was he *really* like?"

For a few moments, her aunt sat silent, seemingly lost in memories.

"I wish I'd known him better, simply for the sake of being able to share that with you. But I know this one thing, as I've told you before. He was a kind man. A good man. And I know that he loved you more than anything else in his life. Even more than his music, which was his life up until you came."

"I always feel like I came and ruined everything."

"No. I know without a doubt that you gave him something that had been missing in his life."

"What?"

"You gave him love. And you brought this . . . fullness . . . into his life."

"But don't you think there were times when he wished I wasn't there?"

Aunt Cynthia shook her head. "No. He was hurt and didn't understand why your mother left both of you. He was a new father dealing with raising you by himself. I knew he was scared. He never told me he was—Tom was so strong, of course. But he was scared. You scared him. Not only because he suddenly was responsible, but also because you took so much after him."

"But how do you know? I'm not some musician or anything. I mean—I'm pretty boring."

Aunt Cynthia laughed. "Boring? Child, you might be a lot of things, but 'boring' is not one of them. I'd call you responsible, but definitely not boring."

"Yeah, but how does everybody know I took after him? I was only two when he died."

"I see him in you every time I look at you, or hear you, or hear your laugh, or see that intensity about you. He approached life the way you approach it—full on. He didn't want a partial chunk of life like most people. He wanted it all."

"I don't have a clue what I want," Kayla said with a sigh.

"Don't you see it? Look who you've fallen in love with."

"I know, I know. I get it. But that's what scares me."

"Why?"

"Because," Kayla started, putting the photo back on the shelf and glancing out the window toward the garden. "Sometimes I don't know if I'm in love with Billy because he reminds me of the father I never had. Or if I'm in love with him because he's the man I want to be with—who I *need* to be with."

"Both reasons are good ones."

"Not necessarily."

"What do you want, Kayla?"

Perhaps it was because she was tired or because of PMS or because of everything going on the last week and the last few months, but Kayla glanced at Aunt Cynthia and felt tears crawl out of her eyes. "I just want to be content. I'm not even asking for happy. I'm not asking for perfect. I'm just asking for peace and contentment. Is that too much to ask for?"

34. The Hardest Part

"Dude, what's this?"

"CDs."

Chad stood at the edge of the couch, his expressionless face waiting for something more from Billy than the obvious.

"I threw 'em away. Take them. They're yours."

"What? All your Coldplay CDs? Did Chris Martin send you a hate e-mail or something?"

"There are others too."

"Why not get rid of the posters in your room?" Chad asked.

"I will. Just didn't get around to it yet." Billy kept his eyes focused on the television screen.

Chad walked around in front of Billy and sat in the chair facing him. His roommate was stocky from working out and drinking beer, probably not in that order. He carried a face that rarely changed in expression. Dark eyes stared at Billy. "Is this about Kayla?"

"Of course not," Billy said.

"Didn't she buy you the Keane CD?"

"Yep."

Chad nodded, getting it. "So, you delete the songs from your iPod too?"

"Of course."

"So they're gone?"

"Forever," Billy said, still pretending he was watching television.

For a few moments, there was silence. Chad didn't pressure.

Finally Billy cursed. "I just don't get it."

"Yeah," Chad said.

"I'm tired of waiting. Tired of sitting around and waiting for her to figure out what she wants. Waiting for her to wait. It's stupid. And I'm done."

"Done with what?"

"I'm done. Period. End of the story. End of the CD. Finished."

Chad nodded.

"I'm serious," Billy said.

"Sure."

"Stop smiling."

"Okay."

"This isn't funny."

"You can't just unplug Kayla out of your life."

"I sure as hell can try."

"Why now? Why today? I thought things were better since the show."

"Oh, they were. Until it got her thinking and feeling and talking and all that crap. She just—she just sent me an e-mail. Kind of a thanks but no thanks. I mean—if someone loves you, then why shouldn't they be with you? You know?"

Chad shook his head. "No, I don't know. The last girl I hooked up with told me the only person I'd ever love in my life was myself. Well, that and Lindsey Buckingham. I was impressed she even knew who that was, then realized I'd told her about my obsession with Fleetwood Mac."

"You are a bit obsessed."

"You're one to talk."

"No more obsessions for me," Billy said. "Ever. From here on out."

"Sure about that?"

"You promise me. Promise me that if I ever get sucked into the morass, then shake me out of it or let me sink to death."

"Morass, huh?"

"This muck. This smelly pile of horse dung."

"I know what morass means," Chad said.

"Just promise me."

"I promise to buy you a beer in a few minutes, okay? Let's go."

"Where?"

"Doesn't matter. Somewhere out and away from here."

Billy nodded. "Sounds good to me. Anywhere away from here is good for me."

It had been two weeks since she had heard anything from Billy. E-mail, text, anything—there hadn't been a peep in a month.

She knew it had been a bad idea to be with him the night after the concert, but she couldn't help herself. And neither could she help herself when she distanced herself and didn't answer his voice mails or e-mails or texts.

The worst was when he came to her office.

There was nothing she could tell him, especially not then and there.

And all she could do is watch a pale, angry figure stand in front of her desk and demand an explanation. The scene had been embarrassing and had broken her heart.

Since then, nothing.

Because she'd still needed time. She'd still needed space.

But tonight was different.

Kayla wore her best (and not coincidentally her tightest) jeans along with a hot red top that was very flattering. Billy had always like red on her. Then again, he liked blue and pink and black as well. Her boots had thick heels that made her stand above a lot of the crowd. She drew a lot of glances as she waded through it, following Shannen.

"Don't get too close to the stage," Kayla called out.

This time, it had been her idea to go to Houdini's to watch Song of the Day perform. It was a stifling June night and the city was ready to party. The crowd already sounded loud, and the band hadn't even started.

She sipped the fruity drink with the risqué name that the bartender had made for both of them, no charge. Kayla wondered if that was his pick-up bit, making drinks like "Sex on the Beach" or "Dirty Banana" and then handing it to the girl for free with a complimentary wink as well. Well, it had worked, she guessed. At least it had made them chuckle and helped lighten her mood.

"You need to relax," Shannen told her.

"I'm relaxed."

"You keep looking up at the stage as if you're expecting a ghost."

Kayla put an arm around Shannen. "Thanks for being so patient with me."

"It's fine."

"I just hope that he's as patient."

"He's probably going to get on one knee and propose when he sees you in the crowd. Remember last time?"

"I just—I don't know."

"Trust me, K."

She nodded, sipping her drink, waiting.

She had finally decided, and that was why she was here.

She was going to try.

Despite her fears and her questions and all the whispering voices in her head, Kayla was going to try.

She only hoped she hadn't waited too long.

⌒

The four guys came onto the stage, but something seemed different.

Normally Billy would greet the crowd with a wave and a smile and a "thanks for coming tonight." But instead, he just walked up to microphone and then waited, looking out in the crowd, looking above everyone's heads to the back of the room. He looked especially scruffy, with disheveled hair and several weeks' worth of beard.

Shannen glanced at her with a bewildered look on her face.

Then the drums started. Reuben pounded while Gus, usually playing bass, played the keyboard.

And after the first stanza, Kayla knew what this night was going to bring. But she wasn't moving. Whether or not he knew she was here, Kayla was staying.

Shannen looked at her after he finished the chorus.

"What the f—?"she mouthed.

And Billy stood, his eyes closed, singing a song that Kayla hadn't heard before.

Over and over, he sang the words *I don't care anymore.*

And with each verse, her heart broke a little more.

And with each verse, Billy belted out the words stronger, harder, louder.

" ' 'Cuz I remember all the times I tried so hard, and you laughed in my face 'cuz you held the cards. I don't care anymore.' "

Shannen looked at her, asked if she wanted to leave. But she wasn't afraid of Billy's intensity.

She wanted to see where this was going.

Perhaps there was more he had to say.

She was going to listen. One way or the other.

It was a set list for a broken heart and troubled soul.

Some of the songs she recognized, and others she didn't.

There didn't seem to be any original songs that the guys played— they all sounded like covers. Billy didn't talk between songs; he seemed to be in his own little world on the stage. He didn't seem interested in applause or accolades. Even the other guys seemed indifferent about the whole thing.

Shannen said they should leave.

"No. I'm staying."

"I don't think it's a good idea," Shannen said loudly in her ear as the music wailed away.

"I want to know if he knows I'm here."

"I don't think he knows anybody's here."

On stage, Billy sang, "This is our last good-bye."

It was ridiculous.

They were supposed to be playing for this crowd and getting everybody psyched about summer and about the end of the week. They were the entertainment. Instead they were dragging everybody down with lyrics about failed relationships and good-byes and anger.

But still, the applause kept growing with each song.

And maybe it was because the crowd saw what Kayla already knew.

It was Billy putting himself out there, for better or worse.

It was Billy saying, *Like it or not, this is who I am and this is what I'm about and this is where I am right now, and if you don't like it you can just piss off.*

And the songs were all over the board.

There was a Nine Inch Nails song that got the crowd moving even though it was one hundred percent anger. There was "Live and Let Die," where Billy pummeled the piano. There was a slow, bluesy version of the Bee Gees "How Can You Mend a Broken Heart," where Billy conjured up a voice that Kayla had never heard before. There was a guy's take on a recent Gwen Stefani tune.

It was amazing, in one way. The thought process going in this set list.

And the fact that somehow Billy had persuaded the guys to play the songs. Especially something as fluffy as Gwen Stefani.

But the beauty was that they followed it up with something darker, like a song by a group like Interpol or Editors.

But there was no Coldplay.

And no Song of the Day.

⁓

The favorite song of the night seemed to be "Wonderwall" by Oasis.

This was perhaps one of the only glimpses of hope that Kayla saw that night.

It was also the first time that Billy saw her. And she realized that he hadn't known she was there. The look on his face gave it away, gave away his feelings, gave away his thoughts.

He almost stopped.

But he kept going, playing the song and singing and looking directly at her.

Shannen stared at Kayla to see her reaction.

Kayla wasn't sure how to feel.

⁓

After that, Billy stood up and said a few things to the other guys, then came up to the mike.

"We've got one final song tonight. Glad you guys could come and celebrate with us the absolute bullshit notion of this thing called love. But, hey—thank God for music. And for tequila."

The crowd cheered, even though they really didn't know what

EVERY BREATH YOU TAKE

they were cheering for.

Billy picked up a guitar, then stood beside Chad.

The beats began.

And both Billy and Chad sang.

Kayla didn't recognize the song.

But she could hear the lyrics clearly.

" 'And if you don't love me now, you will never love me again,' " Billy sang. " 'I can still hear you saying you would never break the chain.' "

And the more he sang, the more he glared at her.

He seemed to spit out the words.

He wasn't just heartbroken.

He was angry.

" 'Damn the dark, damn your lies,' " he sang.

And he kept belting out the words, daring her to leave, daring her to look away.

Kayla had stood there for the last hour listening to this nonsense.

He was lost in his own world, a sea of insecure melancholy.

And as they played their guitars and jumped around on stage, Kayla just shook her head.

He was just a boy. A kid who needed to grow up.

She had come to see if there was a chance. But now she knew.

Billy had made up his mind.

"I'm done," she said as the music continued to play and she walked out.

▶ 36. Twisted Logic

It all begins—and ends—here.

Billy stood in the center of the airport terminal, the rush of strangers surrounding him. Faces passed, smiles drifted, conversations echoed. He noticed a Hasidic Jew and his young son, a businesswoman in a suit, a family speaking what he thought was Italian, a couple of jocks filling up the passageway with their muscles. He noticed all these people, but they didn't notice him, an average-sized average-looking twenty-four-year-old ready to bolt from his average life.

Four-thirty on a Thursday afternoon, the thunderstorms finally relenting to let flights go, Billy knew this was it.

He carried a backpack—that was all he needed. He'd put the rest of his belongings in his car and left it parked at home. Eventually his parents would find out when he called them from New York. Eventually his buddies would find out too.

And yes, eventually she would find out. Whether or not she cared was another matter.

He began striding down the walkway, a wall of advertisements on either side, signs and sounds and hanging globes all assaulting him. He reached for a pocket on the backpack and pulled out his new iPod, a Christmas present from his parents. He'd spent the last six days filling it with as many songs as he had on his computer—somewhere around 30,000. Billy slid in the earpieces and then shuffled to find something.

Just any song wouldn't do. No, he needed something poignant, something fitting, something perfect for this big moment in his life.

He had already gotten rid of any songs that he labeled Kayla-esque. And there were quite a few.

He tried out a U2 song, but it was too clichéd. The Killers didn't fit the mood. Explosions in the Sky—yeah, that worked, but it wasn't "big" enough. He needed something huge. This was the climax in a rather mundane movie. He wanted it to be momentous.

As he shuffled through the iPod and walked at the same time, he bumped into someone rushing the other way, toward the baggage claim. Billy looked up, then heard the song that started to play accidentally.

Oh, come on.

The ghost of Christmas past was playing with his iPod now.

This wasn't the triumphant swan song he was looking for.

It was a sucker punch that slowed his walk, that made the masses blur, that made his heart ache just a tad bit more.

This was their group, their love, their shared delight.

He couldn't believe it. Hadn't he gotten rid of this song?

He could remember driving along with her to this song, kissing her to this song, hearing her declare her love to him to this song . . . hearing her say good-bye.

He should've just turned it off at once. She would have. She wouldn't be listening to the iPod, bathing in melancholy, pining away.

But that's what he did. That's why he wrote songs and performed them, why the moods impacted the melodies.

Yet today was different. It was different because there was nothing left back there, in that suburb, in that apartment, in that *life*.

The voice slid through his skin and plunged toward his heart, the blade cutting up and down.

And Billy closed his eyes and saw Kayla and her blue eyes and her blonde hair and her beautiful soul. Her voice lingered in his ears.

I'm sorry Billy. I don't want to hurt you, but it's the right thing.

But what was right about love? Since when did love have to be right?

That was the last time he spoke with her, back in June, a few weeks ago.

Even after giving up on her, he had tried to win her back. And all the e-mails and voice mails and texts were making him seem like a desperate, sick man.

Billy had tried. He had really tried moving on. Yet here he was, still crushed, still hurt.

Still pining, like a poor little sad soul.

The faces around him blended together, their grins gutting him, their happiness haunting. He hated this and hated them and hated the fact that he was running away and mostly, he hated himself for ever falling in love with Kayla Rowe.

For falling in love and never falling out.

He reached the gate. In his back pocket was the boarding pass he'd printed out. The plane would be boarding in just a few minutes. And in less than an hour, he would be flying away from Chicago to New York, toward dreams of playing in bars and joints and getting far, far, *far* away from this place, away from the stench of failure, away from Kayla's utterly perfect life.

Away from her life and her love and whatever "happily ever" she was after.

He stared at the strangers around him.

Could a new city create a new life?

Could it patch an old heart and soul?

He replayed the song, and even as he did, he cursed himself.

The tune played and he felt Kayla in his head, felt her hand in his, felt her smile on his.

When in the world will I let her go?

He had waited, and tried, and waited, and composed a hundred lovesick songs over her and for her, and waited, and put his heart on his sleeve and on everything else.

All for nothing.

All for this.

And that was why he was leaving.

Billy replayed the song. Again. And again.

He barely heard the announcement for boarding over the song.

But he could see the line forming and he took his place in it, ready for his new life, ready to start over again, ready to get far away from this place.

"But he didn't go, did he?" Thomas asks.

Before James can answer, a server clears their empty plates, leaving only glasses of water on the table. Thomas waits to hear how the story ends.

James shakes his head. "No."

"I don't get it."

"You don't? I thought you would."

"I mean, I do, but after all that—I don't get why he would stay."

"Do you understand a little more why you're here?"

"I still don't really believe that they're meant to be together."

"Billy once told her he'd wait for her until kingdom come. And he lived out that promise. That's dedication. That's love."

"So he stayed behind? And she ended up falling in love with someone else?"

"Yes."

Thomas chuckles and sighs at the same time. "Poor kid."

"That doesn't mean that he doesn't still love her. Or that she doesn't love him."

"But why, then? Why can't they be together?"

"Love isn't always that simple. It's not always that easy."

"It should be," Thomas says.

"And you know this?"

"No. Of course not. I didn't know the meaning of love—not really. Not until Kayla came along."

"Billy and Kayla do. It's more than just passion. It's more than just shared common interests."

"But if they're so good for each other, then why—"

"I think you know why."

"Because—because of me? Because I wasn't there?"

"One reason. Because this world is broken and hurting. And there are many people like Kayla that are scared. They have a hole inside of them that will never be filled, not as long as they're alive

TRAVIS THRASHER

on this earth."

"But will Billy fill that hole?"

"Of course not," James says. "But he will understand it better. And, even though Kayla doesn't think this now, he will be more gentle with it. He will be able to add a little something to it. More than anybody else can."

Thomas rubs his temples. "Can't I get a little help down here?"

"What do you think this has been?"

"I'm talking about the parting of the Red Sea type of thing."

"Even though she doesn't know that you're her father, Kayla will listen to you. You can do this, Thomas. You can help fill that hole."

"I forgot how complicated love could be."

"It is, in a fallen world."

"If only Kayla could know—you know?"

"She will. But not for a long time."

part five
synchronicity

If I could have switched places with anybody when I was in my early twenties, before you came, it would have been Sting. He was the charismatic, brilliant singer of my favorite band, The Police.

They were your favorite band too.

Perhaps it was wrong for a father to be singing "Roxanne" to his newborn.

Or to mimic playing the guitar to "Message in a Bottle" with his little one-year-old baby girl.

Or to sing "De Do Do Do, De Da Da Da" to his sweet child and have her sing the words back to him.

I used to play them so much that you would say "Police" in a way that made it sound like you were saying "Please." I couldn't resist. I would turn them on and you would jump around like they did in their videos (and like Daddy did too). Sometimes you'd get stuck on one song, so much so that you'd wail and scream until Daddy turned on "Please" and we'd sing and dance away.

Your favorite song was their biggest hit, "Every Breath You Take." Back in 1983, that's all you heard on the radio. And you would dance with Daddy, and the song took on a whole new meaning.

That's the beauty of music, the beauty of art, the beauty of life. To interpret something in a different way.

For so many years, that song has echoed in my mind.

Because your father has been watching every step you make.

And yes, you belong to me.

And yes, my poor heart aches as you've gone from a toddler to a teenager to a young woman.

The music is in your soul, Kayla. It always has been and it always will be.

That doesn't mean you need to turn into a singer or a songwriter.

You can have a musical spirit and not do anything with it.

And that's why when you meet a fellow kindred spirit, well—you just feel like you belong.

38. Synchronicity 1

"Wake up."

Somewhere under the covers and the pillow lay Billy, perhaps comatose as far as Thomas was concerned. He called his name a few more times, then nudged him.

Like a bear coming out of hibernation, a scruffy face peered just over the blanket. Billy opened his eyes, then closed them again, then blinked as if he was seeing a vision.

"I'm really here," Thomas said.

Billy seemed out of it for a moment, as if he were still debating whether or not he was wading through a dream. Then he jerked out of the covers and sat up.

"What happened?" Billy asked.

"I was going to ask you the same question."

"What's wrong?"

"Nothing. Don't freak out—your roommate, the one that slightly resembles Frodo Baggins, let me in. We shared a cup of coffee."

"Reuben?"

"That's the one."

Billy rubbed his eyes. "I, uh—did my probation officer send you?"

"Oh, no. No, not at all. And I'm not about to tell him that you've missed a couple of weeks at the program. I wouldn't do that."

Billy groaned.

"Long night?" Thomas asked.

"Yeah."

"Did you work?"

"Yeah. And then—just—I need another . . ."

"Another what?"

"Job. Life. Brain."

"Well, I'm here to help."

Billy looked at Thomas and appeared puzzled. "I don't get it— what's going on?"

"Oh, I'll explain later. Why don't you get up and take a shower—get some color back in that skin. You look like a vampire."

"Okay."

"Nice posters, by the way," Thomas said, looking at the wall of Billy's musical heroes, from Radiohead to Jeff Buckley.

"Yeah. A little juvenile, but whatever."

"All you gotta do is frame them and they'll be considered art. That's what I did when I was your age."

"Did you have a dead-end job serving drunken idiots who don't tip?"

"No. I wasn't good enough to get a job like that."

Billy chuckled.

"I'll have a cup of coffee waiting. I'll be catching up with Reuben."

"Have fun."

"Does he work?" Thomas asked out of curiosity.

Again, Billy just chuckled. "Not really. He's just got very generous parents who still think he's sixteen."

⌒

Twenty minutes later, Billy came out with a wet head of hair and a dab of shaving cream still on his ear.

"Thanks for the coffee," he said as he raised the cup to Thomas.

"No problem."

"It's 10:40?"

"Early day for you."

"More like late night."

"I still got up at eight," Reuben said from his chair in the messy living room of the apartment.

"Yeah, well, I worked twelve straight hours yesterday."

"Whine," Reuben said.

Billy looked at Thomas and seemed to still have the burning question on his mind.

"I know it's probably crazy seeing me here, at your place."

"Well, yeah, sorta," Billy said.

"Everything going well with you?"

"Absolutely wonderful."

"I see," Mr. Thomas said.

"I plan on coming back, you know."

"I knew you would."

"Well, I kinda have to. I don't have much of a choice."

"Yes, I know."

"I just—the other day—I needed a break. I just needed space."

"Billy, I know what you need."

For a moment, the young man looked at him as if he thought Thomas was going to say a name. As if he thought Thomas was going to say *her* name.

"Song of the Day."

Billy waited for more. He looked at Reuben, who was nodding his head in agreement, as if they had spoken about this when Billy was sleeping.

"I want to help you get Song of the Day back together."

"Back together?" Billy asked. "What do you mean back together?"

"Well, you are missing a guitarist, aren't you?"

"So?"

"I heard that you started the group with your guitarist. Chad, right?"

"Who told you that?"

"I read it online. Amazing what you can find. And what you say on your MySpace page."

"Yeah, well, Chad will be back."

"Reuben said you guys are supposed to be playing Lollapalooza."

"Uh huh."

"And when will that be?"

"The start of August."

"It's already June."

Billy nodded.

"Seems like you guys might want to rehearse a little."

"Yeah, that would be a good idea. Or maybe we can just perform without a guitarist."

"How are we going to do that?" Reuben asked.

"It was a joke," Billy said.

"I want to help you find Chad. And help you guys."

"Okay—so, look. Don't take this the wrong way. But why would you possibly want to help out our band? Have you even heard us?"

"Sure. And that's why I'm interested."

"And why's that?"

"Just trust him, Billy."

Billy looked at his roommate with an incredulous look. "How long have you guys known each other?"

"Oh, about an hour or so," Thomas said.

Billy walked into the kitchen, opened a door and looked into a half-empty cabinet. He made a grunting sound.

"How about I take you guys out for breakfast? Or lunch?"

"Sounds good to me," Reuben said.

Billy looked confused and tired. "I still don't get this. What— what are you doing here?"

"I'll explain over a bite to eat. My treat. Sound good?"

"Okay."

"Where would you like to go?"

"Anywhere but Brewtown," Billy said. "I've been living there lately."

~

Reuben picked the place. It was a small family diner that served breakfast all day. Reuben got a Mexican omelet that would surely be hurting him later, while Billy got a Belgian waffle.

After ordering and sipping on more coffee, Thomas began his pitch.

He'd been thinking about this for a while and finally knew how to do it.

He believed that music could prevail.

With others, they might not *get* it. They might not appreciate it. But Kayla and Billy, they got it. They appreciated it. They lived it.

"I didn't tell you this, but I used to be a musician. Well, I guess once you are, you are for eternity. But I used to go on the road a lot, performing at bars and pubs."

"That's cool," Billy said.

"Tell him where you've played," Reuben said.

"The biggest was the Metro."

Billy stared at him in disbelief. "What? Shut up."

"Yeah. Back in, let's see, I think it was 1983. Showing my age."

"You played at the Metro?"

"Yeah. It wasn't as widely known back then. It was fairly new. I opened up for Echo and the Bunnyman."

"Okay, yeah, whatever," Billy said. "For a second, I almost believed you."

"No, I'm serious. Their opening act bowed out, so they got a couple of local acts to come in. There was some other local group—I forget their name. Then there was me and my guitar."

"You play guitar?"

Thomas nodded, staring ahead as though it was something he hadn't thought about in some time. "Yeah, I dreamed of being the next—well, I wanted to be Sting. Though I didn't necessarily want to be in a group."

"Have you seen The Police on their reunion tour?"

Thomas was surprised to hear about that. And surprised at how excited he was to hear it. "No, I haven't had the chance to. Life's been—it's been busy."

"So you really performed at the Metro?"

"Nobody paid me much attention. They were there to see the main act."

"I've heard Echo and the Bunnyman."

"They were great. I don't remember much except for that."

"The eighties were a great time for music. Some of those British groups like The Smiths and The Cure."

"Oh, yeah, I loved them."

"Really?" Billy asked.

Thomas laughed. "Yeah. I swam in the music scene for a while, trying to do what everybody tries to do."

"What's that?" Billy asked.

"Make it.'"

"What happened?"

"Oh, life happens. You realize one day that *Rolling Stone* isn't going to be calling. And then you fall in love and have a family. It changes things."

"Love can do that."

"But that's why I want to help you guys out."

"How?" Billy asked. "What are you going to say to Chad?"

"That I can help. I've played my share of gigs. I can help you guys get ready for the upcoming concert in Chicago."

"He doesn't need help playing. I think he's just sick of being around me."

"And why's that?" Thomas asked.

"My attitude."

"I'd agree," Reuben said. "You haven't been the best to live around either."

"Chad has other issues, too."

Thomas looked at Billy. "An opportunity to play at something like Lollapalooza doesn't come around often."

"Yeah, I know."

"So you guys play then."

"And what if Chad decides not to?"

"Then I play his part."

Both Reuben and Billy laughed.

"That I'd like to see," Billy said.

"I can play the guitar."

"Well, I can too, but not like Chad. He doesn't just play. He is really an exceptional musician."

"So we go to see him. Tell him that I'm going to help not only with your upcoming concert, but that I'll also help produce your next album."

"You're a producer, too?" Reuben asked.

"No, but I could try. That's not a lie, to say I'll help. Chad won't know who I am. And trust me—once we find him, I'll play for him."

"Can you *really* play?" Billy asked. "I mean—really?"

Thomas nodded. "Yeah. I might be a little rusty, but trust me—I can play. I used to write my own stuff too."

"This all sounds great. The only problem is this—I have no idea where Chad is."

"I can help you out there," Reuben said as the server brought them their meals. "He's staying with his brother in Michigan."

"When'd you find that out?"

"His brother called to tell me he had to bail him out of jail."

"Jail?" Thomas asked in surprise.

"Oh, yeah. Chad is a bit—well, unpredictable. Good luck trying to bring him back around here."

"I have something to tell you."

Ryan's handsome face looked at her with a self-assurance that allowed her to be able to tell him anything. They sat in a booth at the fancy French restaurant, already finished with their dinner and now waiting on dessert. Kayla knew that she couldn't keep this from him. Not any longer.

"I quit Angel Hands."

"You already told me that," Ryan said.

"I know. I just—I didn't tell you why."

"It's okay if you don't like hanging out with old people."

"But I do. I really, honestly do like that. I just—I didn't tell you this because I wasn't sure how to say it."

"Say what?"

"That Billy Harris is in the program."

"Billy Harris . . ."

"The waiter we saw at Brewtown."

"Oh, yeah. Messy hair, looked like he saw a ghost."

She nodded. "He did see one. It was me."

"What was he doing in the program?"

"He was forced to do it after getting a DUI."

Ryan raised his eyebrows. "That's pretty sad."

Kayla looked down at the table for a moment, thinking, wondering if she should tell him.

All this time, and he still didn't know.

"I was engaged to Billy once."

Ryan's expression didn't change. He didn't look shocked, didn't stand up in surprise, didn't even seem confused in the least. "When was that?"

"He proposed to me Christmas of 2005. I gave him the ring back five weeks later."

"Mind telling me why?"

"I wasn't ready."

"This isn't a theme in your life, is it?" Ryan said with a kind smile.

"No."

"So you guys were serious, huh?"

"Yeah."

Ryan nodded. "That explains the awkwardness. And just how— I don't know. He acted really strange."

"We hadn't seen each other in a while. And then that. Followed by seeing him at Angel Hands."

"And that's why you quit?"

She nodded. She was going to say more, but a server came and did an elaborate presentation with their bananas foster, cooking it right in front of them. Kayla was glad for the break in the conversation. She didn't know what else to say, or what else Ryan would ask, or what her answers might be.

When the dessert was finally put on the plate in front of them, it looked just like the rest of the food portions had looked: tiny.

"All that work for four bites," Ryan said. "Go ahead, help yourself."

"I'm sorry I kept it from you."

"It's okay. I'm sure you had your reasons."

"It's been hard to think about those times. It's like I turned off a switch and moved on."

"You're good at doing that."

"How do you know?" Kayla asked.

"Well—look at your job. All those years, and boom—the switch went off."

"I guess you're right."

"But why leave the program? You told me how much fun you were having getting to know Loretta."

"Leona."

"Yeah, Leona. What'd you say to her?"

"I haven't told her yet. I feel guilty for saying I would be around this summer and then suddenly bailing."

"Did Billy do anything or say anything—"

"No, no. It's nothing like that. He's a good guy."

"He's gotta be if you actually were engaged to him."

She shook her head. "Don't."

"Don't what?"

"Just—it was different, Ryan."

"Okay."

"It was just—*I* was different. Things were different. But we were all wrong for each other. It's just—it's been strange seeing him."

"It's not like you have to see him every time you go downtown to hang out with Leona, right?"

"No."

"And you said the guy running the thing is really cool, right?"

"Yes. He's a good guy. Very—I don't know. Very kindhearted."

For a moment Ryan waited as Kayla's mind raced. He was smart. Sometimes he could say so much simply by saying nothing.

"You think I should keep going, don't you?"

"I don't think you should quit just because of this Billy."

"It's just—I didn't know how to tell you, and I was feeling guilty for it—"

"For what?"

"Just for not saying anything. It's not like—it's not like anything happened."

Ryan smiled. There it was again, that self-assurance, that part of Ryan that was a million miles from Billy's personality.

"I just thought that—with the wedding and so much going on— that it could be a distraction," Kayla continued.

"But you told me you loved helping out."

"I do."

"It's not like it's a lifelong commitment. It's just for a summer. Then comes your lifelong commitment."

She smiled. "Wait, I thought we were only going with the five-year marriage."

"Ten-year. Then we can renegotiate."

They ate the dessert and finished their coffee and Kayla's mind still whirled, trying to make a decision.

"Why don't you just sleep on it?" Ryan asked.

"Yeah, maybe."

"Need help?"

She grinned and shook her head, reaching over to touch his strong hands. She didn't want to let them go.

One of her favorite parts of Aunt Cynthia's house was the covered walkway between the garage and the Victorian home. It was located just outside the kitchen door and not far from the garden in the back. Aunt Cynthia's love of gardening could be spotted instantly by the arrangements of flowers and potted plants surrounding the comfy chair and the narrow bench across from it that Kayla sat on.

On a table in the walkway were various floral arrangements that they were deciding on. Aunt Cynthia kept asking questions and making suggestions, but Kayla couldn't hide her lack of interest.

"K?" her aunt finally said, ignoring the flowers.

"Yes?"

"How are you?"

"I'm fine."

"No—how *are* you? With everything?"

Kayla stroked the tops of the potted flowers next to her. "I guess—I guess I don't know, really. I thought that things might be easier if I had more time to focus on the wedding. Now I sometimes think they would be easier if I had less time to think about them."

"Having doubts?"

"No, no, of course not."

"That would probably be natural."

"No—sometimes I live in one perpetual state of doubt, but no, it's not that."

"How's Ryan?"

"He's fine. He's wonderful. He's—he's Ryan."

Aunt Cynthia just nodded.

"You look like you don't believe me."

"It's not that. It's that I know you're not telling me something."

Kayla glanced out at the back garden and couldn't wait to see it on the wedding day. Her aunt had been planning this for years. "It's going to be beautiful, you know?"

"What's wrong?" Cynthia asked again.

"You know the volunteer organization I got involved with? Angel Hands?"

"Yes."

"Well, I, uh—I decided to quit."

"Why? What happened?"

Kayla sighed, then picked up a pillow that matched the chair across from her that her aunt now sat in. "Billy Harris. That's what happened."

"Have you seen him?"

"Yeah. He's part of the program." Kayla chuckled. "I went to Angel Hands and ended up with the devil."

"Billy's not the devil, that I know," Aunt Cynthia said. "How—?"

Kayla told her aunt the whole story, about seeing Billy and about his DUI and about the kind man named Mr. Thomas who encouraged her to stay on.

"I would agree with him."

"And why's that?"

"You decided to do something good, something different. I admire you, Kayla. I do worry—I can't help but worrying about you quitting your job in this sort of economic environment. But I also know that you can do many things. And the fact that you got involved in Angel Hands—it makes me proud."

Kayla smiled, enjoying the affirmation even if she felt she had been getting more out of it than Leona had.

"You shouldn't let anything—or anybody—prevent you from doing something good," Aunt Cynthia said.

"I know. It's just—to be around him on the days leading up to my wedding . . ."

For a second, it looked as though Aunt Cynthia was considering saying something. She tightened her lips and looked at Kayla and smiled. "Let me tell you a story," she said.

"Good. I like stories."

"When I was eighteen years old, I fell in love with a boy named Stewart."

Kayla looked at her aunt in disbelief. "What?"

"Yes. It's true. The same woman you always get on about being single—happily single, I might add. But I still think about Stewart. We were together for a magical summer before he went away to school and I stayed around here. I got a few letters, that's all. But I still think about him. I kept those letters. And there have been times I actually open them and read them. It's silly. That was over thirty years ago. But still. Love has a power, Kayla. Love is impossible to explain, impossible to control."

Kayla nodded, still surprised at this admission by her aunt.

"I think that if I actually saw Stewart now, I'd be unimpressed. He's probably bald and fat and hasn't written a love letter since he was eighteen. But in my mind, he's still the same Stewart as he was when he was beautiful and bronzed and liked taking me out in his convertible."

"Bronzed?" Kayla burst out in laughter.

"He's immaculate in my mind. And don't you see, Kayla. It's better for you to deal with Billy right now instead of finding yourself dealing with him ten years down the road."

Kayla finally understood what her aunt was getting at.

Billy was always going to be there, in her heart, in her mind.

But she was moving on.

She glanced out in the garden that would soon be full of people and bathed in flowers, and where she would be giving herself to Ryan.

It would be unfair of her to be holding something back from him.

It would be unfair, and probably unwise.

"I never had closure with Stewart," Aunt Cynthia said, looking in the garden too. "And some days—and some nights—he's still with me. You don't want that to haunt you, K. As good of a guy as Billy is, you need to say good-bye to him. And maybe—who knows—maybe God is giving you this chance to do that. On your own terms."

40. King of Pain

"Thanks for driving. I sorta couldn't."

Mr. Thomas looked at him and nodded. "We wouldn't have met if you still could."

"I guess you're right."

They were riding in an SUV that still had that new-car smell. Billy had been eyeing the stereo ever since being picked up several minutes ago.

"I said you were responsible for the tunes. I want to get an education."

"No, you don't."

"We have over five hours, so I'm fine listening to your music," Mr. Thomas said.

"So you can just take off time whenever you want?" Billy asked.

"You're still suspicious of this, aren't you?"

He looked at the cups of coffee and the half dozen doughnuts that Mr. Thomas had picked up for them at Dunkin. "Yeah, I kinda am."

"Don't worry. I'm not going to kill you halfway to Detroit."

"Well, I wasn't worried about *that*. Until now."

Mr. Thomas laughed. "I get the whole music thing, you know. I know that sounds like a line, but it isn't. Not a lot of people get it. Not even some of those in the industry."

Billy plugged in his iPod and began scrolling through it. For some strange reason, he felt a pressure to impress Mr. Thomas. Maybe it was just because he liked the guy, and maybe it was because he was helping Billy and his band.

But every now and then, like right now, he felt something else.

A strange compulsion to say the right words and do the right thing and, even now, play the right song. He wasn't sure why.

The first song was taking him a long time to find.

"You know, there's not one perfect song you're going to find in there."

"Yeah, I know. I'm just indecisive."

"What's the song of the day?"

Billy rolled his eyes. "Cute."

"I'm serious."

"Not quite sure."

"Here, give that to me," Mr. Thomas said.

Billy obliged. For a few seconds, Mr. Thomas scrolled the iPod without looking at it. Then he pressed on it several times.

"Do you believe in fate? In chance? In destiny?"

"Those words mean a lot of things to a lot of people," Billy said.

"You're the only one I'm asking."

"Fate and destiny. Yeah, sure. We all have a destiny waiting for us."

"I agree."

And Mr. Thomas pressed *play* and the song started.

It was one of *those* songs.

One of their songs.

Thankfully, it wasn't a Coldplay song. That would have been impossible, since there were none on his iPod.

But this was one of those songs he had missed in his purge.

"You like this?" Billy asked Mr. Thomas.

"Never heard it, actually."

"You mind?"

Billy took the iPod. He couldn't stomach listening to the whole thing. This was one of those songs that ended up at the end of one of those sappy network shows right when the characters were acting all angsty or ogling each other.

It had been a song he'd played over and over as he waited for Kayla during their last breakup. Right after getting the ring back. Right after getting the message.

"Bad song?" Mr. Thomas asked.

"Bad memories."

"I randomly chose it."

"That's how fate and destiny work. They're random. Meaningless."

"Okay," Mr. Thomas said, seeming to not believe Billy. Instead, he began eating a doughnut. "These are good. Why don't you have one? And put some music on."

Billy found a recently downloaded album that cranked out rock.

It was an antidote to the song that had just played.

"Well, this sounds more like it," Mr. Thomas said.

"Like what?"

"Like you."

Billy laughed. "I can fit in all types of songs."

"I'm beginning to see that."

The miles passed, and as they did, Billy made it a point to play Mr. Thomas all his songs. The older man seemed genuinely interested, so Billy gave him a musical history.

"Zoo Station" by U2: "First concert I ever went to. With my older brothers. The Zooropa tour. See that one? Totally amazing."

"Heart-Shaped Box" by Nirvana: "The grunge scene was going when I was ten years old," Billy said. "My older brothers loved Nirvana and Pearl Jam. That's when I decided I wanted to be a musician. A rock star."

"Paranoid Android" by Radiohead: "I wrecked my parents' car to this song. I don't think it was a coincidence either."

"Drinking?" Mr. Thomas asked.

"Nope. Just concentrating on the music and driving a little too fast."

"Nightmares by the Sea" by Jeff Buckley: "It's a shame this guy died so young. He was breathtaking to listen to."

"A Clean Pair of Eyes" by David Gray: "This is the sort of artist that I long to be on my more—well, let's just say on my more artsy-fartsy days."

"Artsy-fartsy days?"

"Well—when I'm feeling a little more melancholy. Which is, well, pretty often."

"That's why music is so wonderful. It can be so therapeutic."

"Yep."

Mr. Thomas looked at him and seemed to want to say something else, then focused back on the highway.

This continued for a while, with Billy feeling more and more comfortable talking about the music he loved and the reasons he loved it.

There was, of course, a whole universe of music that he was neglecting to mention. But that was okay.

Billy didn't need to be reminded of Kayla.

⌒

After making a stop at the apartment address that they had found online and meeting Chad's equally eccentric older brother, Billy and Mr. Thomas went to the bar where Chad was playing.

"Does Chad sing too?" Mr. Thomas asked on the way.

"No," Billy said. "And that's part of the problem."

"He wants to sing?"

"He wants to do it all. But unfortunately, he can't. He loves the notion of McCartney and Lennon not only writing together, but singing and making each other better. He knows how to come up with great riffs, but he doesn't know how to build songs around them. And he should never sing. Nor write lyrics."

"Why's that?"

Billy just laughed. The best thing would be for Mr. Thomas to see it—or hear it—for himself.

They searched for twenty minutes in the darkness for the bar, finally finding the lone road that seemed to go to the middle of nowhere. This was a small town south of Detroit, but it felt more like they were in Wisconsin. By the time they parked, they noticed only four other vehicles next to the small house that simply said *Beer* in neon lights on its side.

For some reason Billy thought of the movie *Fargo*. That was set in Minnesota, but still—he expected that type of crazed killer to be sitting at the bar. He opened the door, and the unmistakable sounds of Chad's guitar soared through the night.

Billy could remember the first time he heard Chad playing. He had gone up to the guy immediately afterwards and asked if he wanted to start a band.

It had been that easy.

Of course, things with Chad were never simply "easy."

"He's good," Mr. Thomas said.

"Yeah."

They felt like foreigners in a far-off land. Mr. Thomas led them to the bar. "What do you want?"

"Just a beer. Any beer. I'm not picky."

Mr. Thomas ordered two beers and then led them to a small table in the back. The place was dimly lit except for the makeshift stage where Chad played. So far, he hadn't seen them walk in. Normally, Chad got lost in his music, which was a good thing considering that there were only three other customers in the bar. And all seemed completely uninterested in the singer.

The instrumental ended, and Chad seemed to be debating with himself about what song to do next.

"Want to tell him we're here?"

Billy shook his head. "Not yet. Let's just see what he plays."

He started an Eagles song from their heyday in the seventies that probably should not have been played solo. And definitely shouldn't have been sung by Chad.

Mr. Thomas looked at Billy as though this was a joke.

Billy only nodded.

" 'One of these nights,' " Chad sang.

Mr. Thomas grimaced.

"Yep."

Chad sounded like someone dying. He literally sounded as though he were in pain.

"He's not just slightly bad, you know?" Billy said. "He's awful."

Somewhere in the middle of the horrific rendition of the Eagles song, Chad saw them. He seemed to sing louder, which made him sound worse.

Now the other patrons of the bar were looking up at him, wondering what was going on.

They probably felt sick to their stomachs, Billy thought in amusement. "It's like watching and listening to a car crash," he said to Thomas.

When the song ended, Chad looked squarely at them.

"Sometimes a man needs to dream, and sometimes there are those who want to destroy the dream," Chad said, speaking without expression. "I say death to those who disparage."

Mr. Thomas bent his head toward Billy. "Is he joking?"

"Oh, no. This is Chad. He's really, truly kinda crazy."

Chad's blathering continued. "And when the bough breaks and there are those who break with it, I say dream on. Dream on, I say."

Billy noticed that Mr. Thomas hadn't touched his beer. Billy was almost finished with his.

"So here's a little number that I dedicate to those who destroy. I sing for those who sigh with silliness."

Billy couldn't help but laugh. "He loves alliteration."

"I see."

Chad picked up his guitar. He looked so strange, a tall guy with a somber, expressionless face.

"This is a song I wrote that's my most personal song to date," Chad said.

"Here we go," said Billy.

"It's called 'Shave My Gorilla.' "

Mr. Thomas seemed to burst out in a laugh/cough. Billy patted him on his back.

"What'd he just say?"

"Oh, this is priceless," Billy said. "I couldn't have asked for anything more."

Chad began playing the song that Billy had heard several times. And, yet again, the song sounded off. All minor chords and strange melodies. It was the first song that Chad had ever tried writing himself. And it still remained true to what Billy said: that Chad couldn't write songs.

Then the singing came in, and that's what sent it over the top.

" 'I'm just a boy—your silent love toy—wrapped in a room of gloom so utterly out of tune.' "

Now both Billy and Mr. Thomas were laughing, and Chad was staring intently at them, as if daring them to try and be serious.

Chad's voice was off-key. When it backed up Billy, it usually didn't sound that bad. He could actually harmonize with someone else, but on his own he was a mess. And the song was a mess. And his lyrics were complete disaster.

"Here comes the chorus," Billy said.

"Help us!" Mr. Thomas said.

" 'I'm your freak, at the end of another week. Opening the window, finding myself in Manila. All I want really want now is for you to shave my gorilla.' "

For the first time since he'd met him, Billy saw Mr. Thomas in tears.

"This is why he left," Billy finally said. "He demanded that we put this on a record. Or perform it. Or do something—anything—with it. And he's dead serious. And I mean dead serious."

Mr. Thomas just wiped the tears away as Chad ended the song with a guitar solo that sounded like Slash from Guns N' Roses after a heavy night of drinking and not caring.

"Brutal," Billy said.

Chad decided to stop playing after his gorilla song. He approached the table, and Billy introduced him to Mr. Thomas. After a few minutes, Billy looked around and noticed they were the only ones in the bar. Even the bartender seemed to be gone.

"Looks like you cleared the room."

"Clearing the room implies a full room to start with."

Chad liked to talk in prose that sounded like slightly off-kilter fortune cookies.

"I didn't realize your brother lived in Michigan."

"Desperate times brought him north."

Most people might say something like this as a joke. But not Chad. His steely eyes didn't blink, his expression was serious and steady.

"And what about you?"

"I needed a breather."

"Is the air fresher up here?" Billy asked him.

"It's definitely not as stale."

Billy nodded as they sat back down. Chad went to see if the bartender was around but couldn't find him.

"Here—have mine," Mr. Thomas said. "I haven't touched it."

"Thank you."

For the next half hour they talked about very little, not really addressing the issue of why they were there. Finally Chad asked the obvious.

"So, Billy, I can imagine why you might be here right now, but I'm not sure why this gentleman sitting across from me is."

"You can call me Dale."

"Dale it is," Chad said.

"I told Mr. Thomas—Dale—about our problem."

"Our problem? What would 'our problem' be now?"

"Or maybe just my problem. The band's problem."

"And what problem is that?"

"We got invited to Lollapalooza."

Chad nodded, knowing this already. He didn't appear fazed in the least.

"That sounds like a big opportunity," Mr. Thomas said.

"Are you a manager?"

"Oh, no. It's nothing like that. I've just had the privilege to get to know Billy here, and I've heard your music. Good stuff."

"You like 'The Gorilla Song'?"

Mr. Thomas glanced at Billy. They all knew that Mr. Thomas was referring to the CD he'd heard, and not the ridiculous song that Chad had sung.

"I wouldn't quite call that a song," Billy began.

Mr. Thomas held up a hand. "No. I have to say this—that was perhaps one of the most interesting songs I ever heard in my life."

"Thank you."

"I'm not sure interesting is a good thing here," Billy said.

"But what I was talking about is your CD. You guys have a good group."

"Yes, I know," Chad said.

Mr. Thomas continued. "So why are you here?"

"I don't need the group. Not like our young Paul McCartney here."

"I never said I needed the group. I told you that you could leave anytime you wanted."

"And so I did," Chad said.

Again Mr. Thomas held up his hand. He began talking to Chad about how he used to play, about how he had some opportunities and made the most of them.

"So what changed?"

"I had a family. And that changed everything."

"In a good way?"

"In an amazing way. But I had to make sacrifices. You always do. But you guys—you're at the start of something that could be big. And getting an opportunity to play at a venue like Grant Park downtown Chicago . . . that's something I could have only dreamed of doing."

"I like to think that this world is about living and not about dreaming," Chad said.

Billy sighed. He wanted to say something, but he didn't get a chance.

"That's true. And it's also about moving ahead and not escaping."

"I would not call this jaunt an escape," Chad said.

"Then what is it?"

"A search for the soul."

"Good for you."

"And for you?" Chad asked. "What is this—this jaunt to Michigan—what is it to you?"

"It's a chance to live vicariously through Billy here. And to get to know him a little better."

"No vested interests?"

"I said I would produce your album."

"Do you have any experience?"

"None except hours of playing and some time in the studio."

"So play us something," Chad said.

Billy was interested in hearing this too.

Mr. Thomas didn't hesitate. He went to the stage and picked up the guitar that was there. "Any requests?" he asked.

"No songs about animals," Billy shouted out. "Please!"

For a second, it seemed like Mr. Thomas might not play. He held the guitar in his hands the way a stranger might hold someone's newborn baby. He seemed nervous and unsure, even mumbling something to himself as he began. "Sorry, it's been awhile," he said.

For someone with all this musical experience, the guy seemed to be having a hard time even holding the guitar. But then something clicked, and Mr. Thomas strummed a few notes that sounded good.

At first Billy didn't recognize the tune. It seemed slow and moody. But it turned out to be a song by The Police, albeit a very subdued acoustic version.

" 'But it's my destiny to be the king of pain,' " Mr. Thomas sang.

He had an amazing voice, more heartfelt and full of soul than Billy would have believed. Billy could tell he had sung and played, and the longer he played the more he got into it.

As he finished, Mr. Thomas let out a sigh. "Wow."

Both Billy and Chad clapped. "Another."

They had been joined by the bartender, who seemed to finally be enjoying something coming from the stage. "Fine with me," he said as they all looked at him.

Mr. Thomas looked younger, his face alive. "I'm taking requests. But nothing from the last—oh, twenty years or so."

For the next half hour, Mr. Thomas performed for Billy and Chad.

And slowly but surely, the two guys talked and laughed and joked around. They argued on song choices and what to sing and what not to sing.

Billy suggested a song that Mr. Thomas didn't know—a U2 song—so he and Chad went up to perform it. They had an old, out-of-tune piano on the side of the stage that Billy played while Chad played the guitar.

The two guys did a couple more songs until the bartender finally told them to call it a night.

Billy could tell Chad didn't want to stop.

"There are lots of places in Chicago and all over this country that will let you guys do exactly what you're doing," Mr. Thomas said. "Except there'll be more people watching, and you'll actually get paid."

And for some reason, Chad seemed to get this. He already trusted Mr. Thomas, and he had only known the guy for a couple of hours.

Who is this guy? Billy asked as they went out to the parking lot. *And why is he so interested in us?*

Back in the car, Mr. Thomas checked a voice mail. "Interesting," he said as he held the cell phone against his ear.

"What's up?"

"It's certainly been a night."

"And why's that?" Billy asked.

"Your friend Kayla. She left me a message saying she's decided to stay involved with the program. At least for the summer."

41. Synchronicity 2

"My second husband—no, wait, it was my third husband. He made me laugh a lot. Laughter's good. Not the phony kind, but the real kind that makes your stomach hurt. The kind where you don't need to have a punch line to laugh."

Kayla listened to Leona talk as they sat in the cafeteria finishing up lunch. It was a large room with tables for eight scattered all around. Fresh-cut flowers sat in the center of each table. The retirement center was well kept, clean, and warm.

The worst thing in the world, Kayla thought, would be spending your last days in a cold, sterile environment. Surely it would be hard enough spending your time on other people's schedules, depending on other people's efforts, passing strangers by on a daily basis. But here at Summit Hill the elderly seemed in good spirits. And since this was her third visit in a week, some of them were getting to know her on a first-name basis.

"Marriage isn't about love, you know," Leona continued.

The subject of marriage seemed to come up every time she and Kayla spoke.

"It's about spending a life with another. The passion fades. It always does. But the friendship won't. It just depends on who you're with and why you're together."

"So you were married three times?" Kayla asked the shriveled woman with the plume of white hair.

"Stan was my first husband. We married before he went off to the Great War. I was young—only in my teens. He died over in Europe. Then I married Paul, and we were married for thirty years, until he left me after the kids moved away. Not sure whatever happened to him, you know? He wasn't a good man. He stuck with things. With the children. But in his soul, he wasn't good. You know what I mean? And shortly after that, I married Frederick. He died of cancer some years ago."

"You could probably write a book."

"I could write several, but nobody really needs to hear anything I have to say," Leona said. "But every now and then I think of them. Of Stan. He had such blue eyes, sorta like yours. Piercing blue, you know. And I think of Paul. How he could fix up anything in the world. That sure came in handy. And I think of Frederick. He had a gentle heart. He was a good man. He liked to hold my hand."

Just then two figures came into Kayla's view. A tall, dark-haired man with elongated features talking and pointing and grabbing at the arm of the younger man beside him, who appeared to be totally engaged in whatever one-sided conversation they were having.

Leona was still talking.

"I'm sorry—I missed that," Kayla said.

"I said make sure you don't hold back. Life is too short. And I can say that. Right sure I can. Don't hold back your words. Ever."

Kayla glanced at the two figures, who were coming closer.

And it was then Billy saw her.

She smiled a greeting.

Billy opened his mouth to say something, but the man next to him tugged at him as though he was a little puppy.

"They say that chess can invigorate the mind. Do you play chess, Billy?"

Billy pulled him to a stop next to their table. "Hello."

"Leona, you're looking lovely today," the elderly man said.

"Flint," Leona said, shaking her head. "He's dangerous."

Kayla felt herself blushing, for some strange reason.

"Hi, Kayla," Billy said. "I heard you decided to give it another go."

She nodded, then looked at Leona, trying to regain her composure. "Leona, you remember Billy, don't you? He's dangerous too."

"Hardly," Billy said, shaking Leona's hand.

Something in the gentle way Billy shook Leona's hand made Kayla proud.

Proud, and sad.

For a few moments, Billy talked with Leona and Flint. Or more like listened to them talk and ramble on as he stood in the middle.

He still looked beautiful, with those deep eyes that could say so much with a simple glance. His amused smile stood out on a face that appeared steeped in sadness. He didn't look as disheveled as he had the last few times she'd seen him. And he actually had some color, which was a good thing.

"And how do you know Bill here?" Leona asked.

She laughed. "Well, *Bill* and I went to the same college." She knew how much he hated being called that.

Billy nodded, tightening his lips and giving her a *watch it* look.

"Bill plays in a band," she continued.

"That's right," Billy said to Leona. "And *Bill* and his band are playing a concert this summer. Have you ever heard of Lollapalooza?"

As Leona had Billy say the name five times, Kayla stared at Billy to be sure. "Are you serious?" she finally asked.

He nodded, looking proud. "Yeah."

"How—?"

But Flint began talking about the cookies that were usually put out in the afternoon and Leona started talking about her first husband and how he liked to play the banjo.

Billy gave her a look that said *maybe next time.*

And she nodded, saying *yeah.*

They would always have this shared shorthand, where a simple glance meant twenty things that only the two of them knew.

The two of them.

The very phrase scared her. It felt so utterly comfortable.

⟋

"Hey—Billy. Over here."

She sat in the muted light outside Summit Hill on a bench. The sun was disappearing, and the air felt pleasant right now. Billy looked around and then spotted her and approached.

"Hi," he said, surprised.

"What's that?"

He glanced at the item in his hand. "Oh, this? It's a gift from Flint. He said it's a genuine Virginia sword belt buckle from the Civil War."

Kayla chuckled. "That's going to look great on you."

"I know. It'll be hard to wear it since I have so many belt buckles to choose from."

"You have plans tonight?"

"Coming from anybody else that might have certain connotations, you know? But from you—"

"Yes, from me, it's just a simple question."

"Of course it is," he said. "Well, me and all my big plans. No. Thankfully, I'm not working tonight."

"How's the job?"

"Do you really need to ask?"

"Sure," she said.

"It's money. And I love the people there. Well, most of them. But it's hard work. Some nights I get home and try to go to sleep but feel like I'm still running around. But the good news is that I'm probably in the best shape of my life."

"Billy . . ."

"Yeah?"

"I wanted to tell you—that's great about Lollapalooza."

"Yeah."

"No, I mean it. That's really awesome."

"Thanks."

"You don't seem very excited."

"No, I am, really. I'm jumping in the streets deep down inside. This is just my cool exterior showing."

She thought it wasn't as much cool as it was sad. And she knew why he might be sad. "It's weird, huh? Here we are, talking at the entrance to a retirement home."

"Maybe we'll meet here again in fifty years."

"I'll have no teeth, hair falling out, wrinkled and hunched over," Kayla said.

"You'll still be beautiful."

She glanced at him, smiling, not sure what to say.

"I'm sorry," he said. "Habit."

"Thank you."

He nodded, looking uncomfortable as he stood facing her.

"You can sit down next to me."

"Can I? I don't want to say or do something that's going to make you decide that this place isn't for you. I didn't wait for you tonight, you know?"

"I know," Kayla said. "I waited for you."

"Why?"

"Because I wanted to tell you how proud I am for you. How happy."

Billy sat next to her and faced the front of the building. "You know something weird? The only way the gig at Lollapalooza is happening is because of Mr. Thomas."

"And why's that?"

"Because he helped get Chad to come back around. Chad decided to—well, you know Chad. He had another 'thing' and decided to go to Michigan. Mr. Thomas helped me get him." Billy relayed the story to her.

"So he's a pretty good musician?" Kayla asked.

"He's amazing," Billy said. "He's very talented. And it seems—I know he's older, like in his forties or so. But he seems a lot younger to me sometimes."

"He really seems to like you," Kayla said.

"Yeah. Not sure why."

"What are you talking about? Everybody likes you. Leona said that she thought you were cute, by the way."

"Great. I haven't been dating much lately, so that's good to know."

"Maybe you should."

He looked at her and appeared to be about to say something, but then stopped himself.

Kayla changed the subject. "Can I come?" she asked.

"To what?"

"To Lollapalooza?"

"I think half the city will be there. Three days in Grant Park."

"It'll be amazing."

"It's not like I'll have free tickets or anything. At least not that I know of."

"Would you care if I went?"

"I think you know the answer to that."

She nodded.

"Wedding plans going okay?"

"Billy, don't—"

"Don't what?"

"You don't have to—I mean, you don't have to feel the need—"

"Just curious. Just making conversation."

"It's a little weird to talk to you about that."

"Yeah, I know. We used to spend so much time talking about us. So I'm a little—a little lost for words."

"You don't have to be. We can talk about anything. Well ... anything but that."

So Billy told her how much the band was practicing, how Mr. Thomas was there occasionally to give input, how he thought every other day about quitting his job at Brewtown, what his family was up to. Kayla couldn't help but share some wedding details, along with her uncertainty about looking for another job.

It was easy to lose track of time.

Kayla glanced at her watch and frowned. "I'm late."

"Sorry," Billy said.

"No, it's nothing—just some more wedding stuff with my aunt. She's really going overboard. You'd think she was the one getting married."

"In a way, she is."

Kayla smiled. "It's nice to just talk, you know?"

"Talk and not argue," he added.

"Yeah, I guess so."

"Even if you don't think this—or if I don't act like it—you're always going to be my friend, K. Maybe my best friend. I can actually talk to you. It's not like that with most people."

She wanted to say that she understood, that she felt the same, that the thing they once and still had was special and unique and had started, after all, with a friendship. Then she found herself thinking about what Leona had said.

"What is it?" Billy asked.

"Nothing. Just—that reminded me of something Leona told me earlier."

"Something good?"

"Something true. I get what you're saying. I hope you know that."

"And I hope you know who I have in my life—I mean, think about it. Reuben. Chad!"

"You're right there."

They both laughed.

"Thanks for chatting. For sticking around and waiting for me."

"Sure," she said. "I am really happy for you." They stood up. "You need a ride?" she asked.

"I'm taking the L."

"I'm heading to the 'burbs."

"You know, I should be happy for you too," Billy said. "And I will be. One day."

"Thanks," Kayla said, brushing her hair to one side.

"Give me just a few decades. I'll be fine."

They laughed, and Kayla found herself nudging him.

She hadn't meant to touch him. It was just out of habit.

He looked down at her and smiled and almost said something else, but perhaps that would have been out of habit too.

They had far too many habits. And some of them seemed impossible to break.

"Here—I brought you a cup."

Mr. Thomas took the cup of coffee from Billy and thanked him. "How're you feeling?"

"Eight o'clock on a Saturday morning will always be too early for me."

"So you ready for the day?"

Billy nodded as he collapsed in the chair in Mr. Thomas's office. "All those great suggestions, and we end up going to Grant Park to watch fireworks."

"Don't forget the Taste of Chicago."

"Oh, yeah. I can't wait to see Flint snarfing down a plate of pad Thai noodles."

"The Cubs game would've cost a lot of money," Mr. Thomas said. "As would have some of those other 'great' ideas. This makes a lot more sense."

"Yeah, I guess. But did you really need Kayla and me to go scout out possible ideas?"

"It was helpful to know how much those venues cost. Who knows—maybe we'll use an idea or two from you guys down the road."

Billy sipped his coffee. "Yeah, who knows." He nodded toward a CD on Mr. Thomas's desk. "So what's that?"

"Oh, that's a mix CD Kayla made me."

"Really?"

"Yeah. She discovered I was a big Police fan."

"Watch out. She has a thing for them. And for Sting."

"She made me a mix with her favorite Sting songs."

"Pretty mellow stuff, but still good," Billy said as he examined the songs written on the case. "She knows how to make a good mix CD. Most girls don't."

Mr. Thomas nodded. He had a strange expression on his face, like a proud father.

"What?" Billy asked him.

"Oh, nothing. Just—you should hear how you talk about her."

"Who? Kayla?"

"No, the other girl we were talking about."

"We've actually seen each other a few times. And managed not to bite each other's heads off."

"That's good. You'll be seeing her today."

"It's not the first time we've seen fireworks together," Billy said. "Though we didn't have Flint and the other elderly folks in the mix."

"Hopefully it won't be the last time."

"Kayla and I?" Billy asked.

"No. I was talking about Flint and you."

Mr. Thomas let out a laugh and patted Billy on the shoulder as he headed out of his office.

It was in the middle of the sweltering day, in the middle of the horde strolling the Taste of Chicago, that Billy felt someone grabbing at his arm.

He turned as he jerked his arm away, but found Kayla, her hair pulled back and her tank top clinging nicely to her figure. Even with her face half hidden by a large pair of sunglasses, he could see she was worried.

"Leona disappeared."

Like an idiot, he blurted, "Where did she go?"

Kayla just stared blankly at him.

"Sorry, stupid question. Okay, when was the last time you saw her?"

"Over there. We just went over to porta-johns, and I went in to use one and I told her—I *told* her to stay put. And she just vanished."

Billy put his arm around her. "Listen to me. She's fine. Leona is a grown woman who can take care of herself. Okay?"

"I know, but we're supposed to be watching them, and in this heat—"

He quickly looked around. Flint was standing over by a booth, still trying to decide what to have to eat. "Now if *he* got lost, I'd be worried. But not Leona."

"Billy, where do you think—"

"Listen to me. You stay with Flint, and go back over to where you lost her, okay? I can maneuver faster through the crowds."

"And how's that? You're a lot bigger than me."

"Because I'll ram into somebody if I have to. I'll do a scan of the area. It'll be fine. Trust me. She's probably met some interesting person or who knows what."

For the next fifteen minutes he scrambled around the booths and through the crowd trying to find a little old lady. He accidentally knocked a pork chop out of someone's hands. He got half a cup of beer spilled over his leg. Each time he apologized and dashed away before he could get railed on.

As he circled around, heading back to where Kayla first lost her, a tent called The Chicago Cellar caught his attention. On a lounge chair beside it sat a small figure in a wide floral hat. Leona, sipping on a glass of wine.

For a moment, Billy took in the scene. Leona just watched people passing by, occasionally speaking to a stranger, delicately drinking her glass of vino like some sophisticated celebrity. He walked over to her. "Leona?"

"Hello. Beautiful day, isn't it?"

"Where'd you get that chair?"

"A kind lad offered it to me. I'm sorry I don't have another to offer. My feet are awful tired."

"And where did Kayla go?"

"Oh, I'm sure she's around."

Billy nodded, laughing. "Enjoying your glass of wine?"

"Do you want to know about one of the happiest days of my life?"

"I would love to," Billy said in all sincerity.

"Coming to this park and having a picnic with my first husband. Sipping iced tea and watching the strangers pass and seeing the fireworks at night. That was the only time we saw them together. That was before Stan went off to war and never came back."

"A long time ago, huh?"

"Ages. But some days those memories are the only ones that I recall very well. I don't know how this mind of mine works, but I do know how the soul goes about its business. And when you're in your final days like I am—the only memories that stick are the ones worth sticking."

Billy nodded and knelt down to be at face level with her.

"Do you have memories like that, young man?"

"Yeah, I do."

"So have a glass and share them with me."

"Well, I'd like to share them, but a certain young lady around here is worried sick about you."

"Well, I told her I'd be around. And I'm around. She doesn't have anything to be worried about."

"I know," Billy said. "I told her you could take care of yourself. But maybe we could head her way just to set her mind at rest."

Leona held onto Billy's arm as they moved through the masses. "They never go away, you know," she said softly.

"What's that?" Billy asked.

"The memories. The love. They're like books on a shelf. You can pull them off and browse through and remember."

"And what if you don't want to?"

"You always will. That's part of the deal. That's the price."

It was just a simple conversation. About nothing, really. But as he walked away from Kayla, Billy couldn't help the smile covering his face.

Apparently Mr. Thomas noticed it too. "Now *there's* an expression."

"What?" Billy asked.

"I don't think I've seen you look so light and free since I've met you."

"Yeah, maybe not."

"Something I should know?"

"No. Just laughing about the day with Kayla."

"Have you had fun?"

"Yeah, I have. I never thought that spending time around old folks would be so—I don't know. Entertaining? That sounds like I'm at the circus or something. But it really is."

"They're no different from you and me. It's just that they're a little slower. Their bodies don't cooperate as much. Or their minds."

"I think Leona's probably the sharpest mind out here."

"Oh, yes. Certainly."

Billy watched Kayla in the middle of the group, giving orders and laughing and being the center of the show. She had taken her hair down and it now floated and glowed like some radiant shampoo commercial. Everybody around her gravitated toward her. They couldn't help themselves.

"She's something else, isn't she?" Mr. Thomas said.

"Yeah."

And the bittersweet thought came to mind, the kind that he often would have when he pictured Kayla.

"What are you thinking?"

"Why?" Billy asked.

"Well—your face—your brow—everything suddenly changed. Light hazy clouds suddenly blocking the sun."

"I just—you were married once, right?"

"Oh, no. Just—just in a serious relationship. Well, I thought it was serious."

"And you have a daughter."

"Yes."

"How old?"

"Around your age."

"So you never thought about getting married?"

"I thought about it," Mr. Thomas said. "I just never happened to have the opportunity."

"Do you believe there is one person out there for us?"

"Like a soul mate?"

"Yeah, sure. That's sorta an Oprah term."

"You don't believe in soul mates?"

Billy stared at Kayla, who had taken Flint's hands and started to dance with him.

"Maybe I used to."

"I think such a thing exists."

"But what happens if you don't end up with your soul mate?"

Mr. Thomas nodded thoughtfully. "I think that happens all the time. Some people don't meet their soul mate until later in life, when they're already married. Some people never end up meeting them."

"Yeah, so if you do?"

"You do what you're doing. And you don't give up."

Billy nodded, still watching Kayla, still feeling mesmerized seeing the joy that filled her and those around her.

"If you have a dream, you don't give up on it. Right?"

Billy glanced at Mr. Thomas. "Yeah, I guess."

"No, you don't guess. You know. It's hard to wait. Life is too short. But still—that's sometimes what you have to do."

"But what if . . . ?"

"That's what life is all about," Mr. Thomas said. "What if. What if tomorrow never comes, and all we have is today? That and the billion other what-ifs are what make each person definitely unique."

"So what's your what-if?" Billy asked.

"Oh, just the old thing of responsibilities. I have fatherly duties. And I worry that I won't get them done."

"I'm sure you will."

"I'm trying, Billy. I'm certainly trying."

How do you know?

And when will you ever find out?

Billy sat in the park surrounded by throngs of people, but he could only see one. As fireworks exploded above Lake Michigan and in front of the thousands of onlookers, Billy only watched Kayla. He watched how her hair shimmered from the dazzling display, how she whispered into Leona's ear as they watched, how she pointed and seemed to take it all in, loving it all.

I still love you. And I always will.

He felt moved by being so close to her. Close enough to watch. Close enough to sweep alongside and embrace her and tell her that he wasn't letting her go. Not now, not after so much, not after they'd gotten this far and this *close.*

But how do you know, he wondered again.

How do you know if someone is really, truly meant for you, or if such a notion is complete gibberish?

The music played triumphantly and the crowd cheered and watched and all Billy felt was sadness.

She's right here in front of me and I know without a doubt that she still has feelings for me. So why, then? Why not? Why?

He wondered if he would ever find out the real, true reason she left him. Or if there even was one definitive reason. Perhaps there were a hundred, and they all added up to this. To sitting twenty yards away from her, watching her put an arm around someone who could be her grandma, watching her while she didn't watch him.

For a second, Billy closed his eyes.

He just wanted to let her go. To let this go.

He thought he had. But he knew now he never would.

He'd be writing songs about her all his life. The one that got away. The one he could never have. The one. Period.

And when he opened his eyes, the booming and crackling and swishing all high above his head, he saw Kayla looking at him.

She glowed.

And she said something that he couldn't hear.

Then she laughed and shook her head and gave him maybe the most adorable look he'd ever seen on anyone.

So heartfelt, so sincere, so unabashed, so utterly Kayla.

And he knew he wasn't alone. Not on this grass. Not in this park. Not in this city or in this world.

We'll always be something, he thought. We'll always be Kayla and Billy. That's what counts. Nobody can ever take that away. Nobody and nothing ever will.

He looked at his side and saw Flint watching him. Billy only nodded, sure that the old coot was lost in his own world and time. But then he heard something that surprised him.

"Don't give up on that," Flint said. "Don't you dare give up on her. Would be a damned shame if you did." Then the old man shifted his gaze to continue watching the fireworks.

Billy took a mental snapshot of himself, sitting in the park with this grizzled Civil War buff with the old-fashioned mustache. Sitting so near Kayla, who was engaged to someone else. Sitting here on the cusp of something new and exciting in his life. Sitting close to where he would soon be performing at a concert that could open doors and change his life.

God's got to have a sense of humor, he thought. But if there's a point to all of this, I just want to know what it is. Am I truly meant to be with her? Because every waking day seems to be pointing me toward her. But then again, I find myself alone and aloft, surrounded by eccentrics.

The fireworks boomed as if in response.

And Kayla continued to glimmer.

And Billy's heart continued to pound away.

43. Wrapped Around Your Finger

"This is a bad idea."

"It's a gift. That's all."

"I know you told him. You had to have told him."

"I didn't tell him a thing. I swear, K. He doesn't know. At least not from me."

It was a warm afternoon downtown. Kayla and Billy had come here separately, each expecting the door to the office building to be open, each assuming that Mr. Thomas would be inside waiting.

Kayla had no idea that the "surprise" that Mr. Thomas had spoken about would be this. A taped envelope on the door with both of their names on it. She glanced at Billy as she held the note in her hands.

"When did you stop trusting me?" he asked.

"It's just—this is crazy."

"It wasn't my idea."

"Let me see it again."

Billy gave her the handwritten note.

> Hi, Billy and Kayla!
>
> Both of you have been working so hard with all the folks in Angel Hands. Thank you for your time and your attitudes. It's been great to hear how everybody responds to you—not just Leona and Flint, but the others you've been helping out.
>
> I wanted to give something back to you. Consider this my way of thanking you for all you've been doing. Have fun!
>
> Mr. Thomas

"He knows about us, though," Kayla acknowledged. "I've

talked to him about us."

"I told him we've been getting along better."

"Yeah, but—I mean, what is this?" She held up the two tickets.

"Those are tickets to the Coldplay concert," Billy said.

Kayla gave him a dirty look.

"You asked."

"Is he deliberately trying to play matchmaker? Or could he really be that dense?"

Billy seemed unsure what to say.

"They're not just tickets, Billy."

"I know. You don't have to spell things out for me. *I'm* not dense."

"Sometimes you can be."

"Not this time. Not now."

Kayla swallowed and glanced at the tickets as if they contained a lethal virus.

"Are the seats good?" Billy asked.

"Does it matter?"

"Just curious."

"Here, take them."

"No," Billy said, lifting his hands.

"I'm serious. Take them."

"No."

"Go with Chad or Reuben or one of the guys."

"I didn't even buy their new album."

"Are you serious? You really didn't?"

"No," Billy said.

Kayla walked over and tried to force the tickets into his hand, but he wouldn't undo his fist. The tickets dropped to the sidewalk.

"Billy."

"*Kayla.*"

The wind flung the tickets into the street. They stared at each another, each daring the other to make a move.

A car approached.

They didn't move. The car revved its engine, and it was Billy who broke his glance and his stance. He rushed into the street and quickly collected the tickets.

Kayla stood there, proud of her triumph.

"Don't give me that smirk," Billy said. "I only did that because they're a gift."

"So have fun."

"No."

"Billy—I don't think it's appropriate for the two of us to—"

"Kayla, just hush."

"—go and see a concert by Coldplay, especially since we've ended up—"

"Kayla, shut up!"

Kayla looked shocked. "What did you say?"

"You heard me."

"That was incredibly rude."

"Just listen to me for a second. Please."

She waited.

"Look—I don't know why Mr. Thomas left these for us. I know he probably means well. Even if—even if for some reason he's playing matchmaker."

"But why would he—"

"Just—wait. Let me talk. It's a gift. You've spent a lifetime talking about letting things be the way they are. Not believing in fate or miracles or any of that stuff. Not reading into the signs. So don't. Even if he's playing matchmaker, there's no way—and I mean no way—that he could have known what these tickets would mean."

She nodded. And her anger and bewilderment turned to something else.

She felt a little light-headed.

And light on her feet.

"Nobody knows, K. Nobody ever will. And look—I might make these out to be something more than they are. Sorta like Charlie's Golden Ticket in *Willy Wonka*. So call me Charlie. But to you—it's just a concert, right? And you'll be seeing it with an old friend. Right?"

"Oh, it's that simple?"

"It can be."

She brushed her hair back and looked at the sky. "Billy, I don't know."

"If it wasn't me, would you go?"

She nodded, admitting the truth.

"So then go. Go with me. Let's make a memory that sticks."

"A memory that what?" Kayla asked.

"A memory that sticks. It's something Leona said. Something brilliant that's true."

"I already have enough memories. I'm not sure if I need one more."

Kayla glanced at Billy.

And for some time, the two of them just stared at one another. Ten thousand words were uttered, though their lips didn't open once.

But Kayla didn't look away. If she had looked away, maybe, just maybe she could have said no. But the smile that she couldn't help eventually gave way to an "okay."

Mistake or not, she had made her decision.

"We're here. You *can* talk to me if you'd like."

Billy nodded, appearing as nervous as though they were on a first date.

"What are you thinking?"

"Just—another for the books. Another in the saga of the surreal."

"The Saga of the Surreal? Is that another song title?"

"Certainly could be."

They sat near the back of the United Center, just a couple sections above the main floor, in seats #1 and #2 right next to the small entryway that led out to the concession area and the entrance to the stadium. The stage seemed both miles away and surprisingly close, depending on how Kayla looked at it.

"How are preparations coming for your big gig?"

"Good."

"Excited?"

"Sure."

"That certainly sounds like it."

"I am."

"Are you getting nervous?"

"Of course."

"You guys will do great."

"I'm more worried that there'll be five people watching us."

"That's more than none."

"Yeah."

Kayla stared at him and suddenly had one of those moments—one of those moments that she always seemed to have with Billy. One of those moments when she just had to share what was in her mind and in her heart. "Remember what I told you at that Coldplay concert years ago?"

"Of course I do," he said, finally looking at her the way he usually did. "You said not to forget all of the little people when I make it big. And you said that I would. Make it big, that is."

"That's right."

"I wouldn't call working at Brewtown, not having a driver's license, and living with Reuben, signs of making it big."

"You're playing a concert with people like Radiohead and Kanye West. Your single is a hit on the Internet."

"Yeah, well—there's one person I can thank for that."

"You can thank yourself for writing it."

"I should thank the inspiration," Billy said.

They shared another moment. One in a thousand.

This was the thing that Kayla didn't have with anybody else, including Ryan. This—this thing. Moments like this. Kindred, quiet moments.

And right before she could say anything else, the applause swelled and the lights went down. And the saga of the surreal was certainly what followed.

Kayla didn't know the new songs as well as the older ones, but it didn't keep her from raising her hands and singing along with the "ohhhh's" of the crowd. Any hesitation and resistance Billy had shown earlier seemed to have faded. He was loving this, enjoying the moment and the music and the experience.

During one song the sky rained glittering confetti butterflies as the band performed. It was magical and moving.

Another moment found the band running down a leg of the stage and performing in the middle of the crowd.

But it was when a security guy came up and spoke to Billy that she knew something bigger was up.

"What'd he ask?" she shouted in Billy's ear.

"He wondered what song they're singing."

Kayla thought it was an odd question.

One song later, Billy nudged her. He looked amused, his eyes big and the grin taking over. "Look at that," he mouthed as he pointed behind him toward the entryway that stood right behind their seats.

Several security people were working on a small stage that came off the ground by a couple of feet.

Kayla couldn't help hitting Billy in the arm. "No."

Billy only nodded.

She glanced at the men, who were setting up a microphone, security suddenly all around the stage. The band was finishing up a number, and the crowd was ecstatic.

"You don't think they're going to—"

Billy looked like a lottery winner. He nodded.

At the end of the song, with the crowd waving their hands and cheering and howling, the lights of the stadium lit up. The band sprinted off the stage and down an aisle in the middle of the crowd, then headed out one of the entryways.

Kayla grabbed Billy's hand.

And in moments, four sweaty young British guys appeared right in front of Kayla and Billy, stepping onto the stage, hearing the surprise and shock and amazement of the fans, especially those right in the area.

They were on a short stage, on the same level as Billy and Kayla, that barely fit the four musicians. They held up guitars and said a few words of thanks and welcome, then began playing a song.

Just any old song.

The same old song that had brought Billy and Kayla together, the song that had followed and stalked them, the song that had cemented its notes and lyrics onto their hearts.

And as the first few ordinary notes of that 'any old song' began to play, Kayla clutched Billy's arm.

The years dissolved and the paths faded and the decisions made crumbled away to these two sharing this moment.

The spotlight beamed on the band, with Billy and Kayla standing right in front of them. A snapshot showed the band and the two of them.

For several moments, that's all there was.

Nobody else.

No others out there.

No memory of parting and saying I'm sorry and crying and cursing and leaving. Tonight, it was just the two of them.

Kayla felt Billy's arm around her, holding on to her.

They looked at each other for a brief moment.

And then Billy leaned down and kissed her on the lips.

It was soft and warm and familiar. Most of all, it was comfortable, and it felt right.

But as she smiled and reached up to wipe a lone tear off her cheek, she noticed the glint of the ring on her left hand.

" 'Nobody said it was easy,' " Chris Martin sang. " 'No one ever said it would be this hard.' "

▶ 44. Mother

Well, that certainly didn't work.

Thomas turned up the stereo in his car as he drove. Once again, the thought came to his mind.

Music will prevail.

It never let him down, even when everything else in this world had.

The summer shower tiptoed against his windshield as he drove. He listened to songs by Sting that he had never heard before Kayla gave him this mix CD, songs that now were moving him with their emotion. The CD had given him the idea to make this journey today.

It was a few days after the Coldplay concert, and after seeing Billy for a few minutes, Thomas realized that the concert hadn't worked.

Once again, something he tried failed.

All Billy said was that, "it was a little too close for comfort." When Thomas probed him for more, the young man simply shook his head and gritted his teeth, saying, "I swear, I think fate is against us."

Thomas thought of his mission so far.

The sightseeing excursion that was meant to bring back memories of their falling in love during college nearly derailed the whole thing. The July Fourth event had been surprisingly uneventful. And at the Coldplay concert something had happened, Thomas knew. But it didn't have the results he had hoped for.

And now, as Billy's concert at Lollapalooza approached, Thomas knew that he had to strike fast. He needed to remind Kayla of who she was and where she came from. Perhaps she knew that the music was still in her heart and soul. But he needed to show her why.

As he drove, the song playing haunted him in its beauty. He couldn't believe that the same artist who had penned "Message in a Bottle" wrote this one. The maturity and the depth astounded him.

Thomas wished he could tell artists that you continued to play music and create songs in Heaven. And no, it wasn't all done on harps either.

He glanced again at the scrawled-out directions on the sheet of paper. He was almost there.

What he was going to do when he arrived was the question.

It was an attractive, two-story brick home in a south suburb of Chicago. The name of the owner was LaMotta; must be the guy Nicole was living with. So far, from everything Thomas had learned about Kayla's mother, she hadn't remarried. Thomas knew that she worked, and had tried to call several times today to see if anybody was home. Nobody answered, a good sign.

For fifteen minutes Thomas remained in his car watching the front of the house and the driveway for any sign of life.

He climbed out of the car and felt the slight drizzle on his forehead.

He knew he'd be breaking-and-entering, but he had to find something that he had created for Kayla years ago, and he couldn't exactly call Nicole and ask for it. But something told him that she might still have the tape. She surely hadn't given it to Kayla. She wouldn't have known about it unless she actually took the time to watch it. And time was something that Nicole had never seemed to have enough of.

Impatience, that's a trait Kayla got from her mother, he thought as he pressed the doorbell.

Nobody answered.

He went around back, casually stepped onto the wooden deck behind the house, and knelt down to reach underneath the large, stainless steel grill. He was counting on Nicole's still following the trick he'd taught her when they were living together.

Sure enough, there it was. A small, rectangular box the size of a pack of gum. He slid it to find a key inside.

Guess she listened to a few things I said, Thomas thought in amusement.

The key opened the back door. He entered a room that had a coat rack and an assortment of shoes on the floor as well as a washer and dryer.

He dried his shoes on the rug, then walked into the house.

He was quiet, listening for any sound he could hear.

The laundry room was attached to the kitchen, an open and airy room with a large stove and refrigerator. For a moment, Thomas thought of what a shame it was, having such a fabulous kitchen—he was sure Nicole didn't spend much time in it. He tiptoed over the wooden floor and rounded a hallway.

He still couldn't hear anybody.

He wasn't sure where to start, but he figured he would try the bedroom.

Anywhere that might have Nicole's "junk," stuff that she probably hadn't looked at in a couple of decades, but might be difficult for her to get rid of.

A large picture hung on the living room wall, Nicole cuddling up to a dark-haired guy who looked like a mobster. She looked older and harder, but she was still attractive.

It was strange, seeing her photo.

This woman was the mother of his only daughter, and for that reason alone there would always be a special place in his heart for her. Even if she had left the two of them on their own.

Thomas wouldn't have changed that if he could. He only wished that he could have been around longer for Kayla as she grew up.

He walked up the carpeted steps, still careful to be quiet, and found the master bedroom. He looked around the large, tidy room, completely missing the figure watching him from the bed until it shifted and moved—and started barking.

Thomas braced himself until he saw what kind of dog it was. A Lhasa-Apso, short and hairy and hysterical. It acted ferocious, but soon was licking his hand.

Thomas went into the bedroom closet, feeling not only nervous but also a little guilty for invading this couple's privacy. As he knelt to look through some boxes, he felt the dog pulling at his pant leg, wanting to play.

"Go on, get out of here," he said.

After a few minutes, he realized there was nothing of interest in here.

For half an hour he examined closets and storage places. The dog stayed with him, looking for opportunities to playfully take a bite of his pant leg.

LaMatta must be a neat-freak, Thomas decided, because the house was immaculate. There was no basement, so he checked to see if there was an attic. Sure enough, there was a small outline in the ceiling of the second-floor hallway. Thomas found a chair and pushed the panel up, revealing a small area that contained dozens of boxes.

Exactly what he was looking for.

He lifted himself up into the dusty attic and looked down at the dog, panting feverishly below him. By the light of two small windows, Thomas began opening boxes and going through them.

An hour passed. A second one began to fade away.

Still nothing.

And then, as he neared the last set of boxes, he saw one marked simply *TR*. His initials.

Sure enough, it contained a variety of items that belonged to him. For a brief moment, he wondered if he would find his old guitar, but then he realized that it had probably been sold. But he still found mementos of his life.

Not once did he feel sadness or regret.

But he did worry that he had made this trip for nothing.

Then he hit the jackpot.

45. Every Breath You Take

Thomas remembers.

Not long ago, he was a part of this life, taking breaths just like everyone else, not knowing that he would soon take his last and wake up to see something far more brilliant than he could have ever imagined. He wishes he could tell everybody here, all these strangers who pass by with time to kill and the future on hold. He watches the stage that Billy and his bandmates step on as they pick up their instruments and greet the crowd.

Thomas looks around and still doesn't see Kayla.

She's supposed to be here, meeting him near the oversized tree just next to the building where they were selling T-shirts and across from the stage where Song of the Day is performing.

He's already left her three messages detailing exactly where he is.

Maybe the plan hasn't worked.

In fact, he knows it hasn't.

Because Kayla needs to be here for this moment.

Billy begins to play. It's a small crowd since it's the last day of the three-day marathon and it's only three in the afternoon. Still, people are cheering, and as the music plays more people head toward the small stage located close to Buckingham Fountain.

Thomas glances at his cell phone.

He wonders if this is his last shot, and if so, what that means.

He closes his eyes for a moment, and remembers.

He doesn't want to leave, not yet.

Not with so much to tell her and so much left undone.

Billy sings.

They're playing well, as well as he could ever have hoped for, with Chad especially getting into it. They have a set list, mostly consisting of their songs with a few covers and a final song that was Thomas's suggestion.

A pretty damn good suggestion, too.

As Billy sings, he sees Thomas standing near the back of the crowd near a large tree, but he doesn't see Kayla.

Last time he spoke with her, she said she would be here.

Of course she would be here.

And even if the Coldplay concert had made things even stranger and more surreal, Billy still believed she would come to this.

This was the moment he'd been hoping for and that she had always said would come true.

Sure, they had kissed at the Coldplay concert as the band played *right in front of them.* He couldn't help himself. He couldn't *not* kiss her. And even though Kayla understood, she had said nothing about it except that she really needed to get home that night. She had driven him back to his apartment in complete silence. Billy tried asking her what she was thinking twice, but didn't get an answer. Maybe she was mad at him, or at herself, or maybe at Mr. Thomas. Maybe all three.

He hasn't seen or talked to her since.

And now as he plays and sings, he assumes that maybe she is there, hiding somewhere, not wanting to be noticed, not wanting to be seen.

With each song they play, the crowd gets into it more, applauding louder, singing along to their one (and only) hit that everybody seems to know.

It is exhilarating.

But it isn't the same, wondering if she's there.

The set list isn't long, and as they get to their last song, Billy scans the audience.

Still no Kayla.

It doesn't matter.

He plays the song anyway.

He plays it for himself.

It will certainly get the crowd going, playing one of the best-known songs from the eighties.

Billy sings into the microphone, the rest of the guys playing the music. He holds onto the mike and closes his eyes and imagines that he is singing to her, for her, about her.

Because he is.

Kayla trembles.

An hour away, in the suburb of St. Charles, in her aunt's empty house, Kayla watches the videotape that she has already memorized.

It haunts her.

It came in the mail yesterday. Just a simple VHS tape along with a typed note.

I found this and thought you might like to see it. You don't have to thank me, Kayla. I wished I could have given it to you years ago.

The note wasn't signed, but the only person it could be from is her mother.

She studies the tape again, feeling as if she's watching it for the first time.

A tall figure is standing there, putting on the record and then looking into the camera. And as the music starts, he dances with a tiny little girl.

She must be a year and a half, maybe two.

As the most popular song ever sung by The Police plays, Kayla holds her father's hands and sways to the music. She leans back, and he twirls her until she lands on her back on the carpet and laughs and jumps back up and says "More."

Her father looks so young, so carefree, so happy. And so does she.

He swoops her up in his arms, then takes one hand and dances as if they're ballroom dancing. The couple drifts in and out of the camera.

And Sting sings "I'll be watching you" over and over.

Every word you say and every step you take and every smile you make.

They dance and laugh and finally, as the song ends, they both cheer.

Her father looks into the camera and waves.

"Say hi, Kayla," he says.

And she follows suit, saying a big "hi!"

And Kayla, now twenty-six years old, can't keep herself from watching this over again, and having it break her heart one more time.

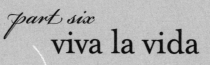

part six
viva la vida

What would I tell you now if I could? What wisdom would I share?

I would have told you this at two or twenty-two.

The world is busy, full of brokenness, and it's easy to be swept inside its maelstrom. Stay strong, Kayla. Be yourself. And never doubt this: your father watches over you.

You're going to fall. But stand up and get up on your feet again.

You're going to fear. But breathe in and believe. Fill your heart and soul with hope.

Because you're also going to fly.

I know your strength. It's one of the things you got from your father. Not every trait you inherited from me was good, but this was.

Keep your eyes wide open, looking up.

And Kayla. When the gray cloud of gloom moves across your blue skies, escape it.

Turn the volume up high.

Immerse yourself in something you love.

Battle the demons of doubt.

Wonder, but don't let that make you wait.

Life is a blink, a breath.

I blinked and you were in my arms.

I breathed and you were two.

And then I was gone.

Life will be mysterious, and magical, and miraculous.

So be you.

Mysterious, magical, and miraculous you.

"Hi."

For a moment she tried to collect the thoughts doing acrobatics in her head. There were so many things she wanted to say. But then again, there always had been and there always would be.

She smiled.

"Do you know in three weeks I'm getting married? Three weeks from today. And there's a part of me—several parts actually—that are unsure. But I knew it would be that way, right? I knew that's what would happen. I just didn't know—I didn't know that *you* would happen."

She waited and listened and watched. But she didn't see or hear anything.

"I have to do this. Now. Right now I have to do this before I spend my whole life spinning in circles and feeling some weight that's not mine to begin with. I hope you understand. It's time I said good-bye. And not good-bye in the way you say when you're coming back tomorrow or next week or next month. But good-bye as in farewell. Forever."

Kayla felt a slight breeze and glanced up into the sky. It was a clear, pretty day all around. She hoped that it would be like this on her wedding day.

There were so many things to think about.

And this—this was one thing she needed to put to rest.

She knelt down on the grass and touched the gravestone. Felt it the way she might feel her father's freshly shaved face if he were asleep.

"Why? Why can't I escape you? Why can't I ever let you go?" She cleared her voice, suddenly hoarse and weak. "Billy's not my problem. Or Mom. Or Ryan or the wedding or anything. It's you. It's here. It's this damned thing."

She pounded her palms against the stone.

"Why did God take you? Why? I just want to know why. Why

I'll never be able to have closure. I just wish—I just wish for once—God, I wish—that I could hear from you. That I could know you're watching over me."

For a long time she was quiet, waiting for something, though she didn't know what.

"I don't want to live my whole life haunted by ghosts of the past. I know you wouldn't want me to. I believe that you want me to be happy. I don't want to believe that the best times in my life are behind me. I want to believe that I can experience the happiness and the freedom and the joy I had when I was a child. I know I've had a good life, Dad. I know it. But seeing that video—hearing myself laugh. Perhaps that's just what being a child is. But I want that feeling again. I want that hope. I want to laugh and I don't want to think about all those what-ifs. And what-ifs plague me night and day."

Kayla swallowed. Her mouth felt dry, her head light. Her fingernails scraped the ground, digging into dirt. It felt good.

"I know that you hear me and always have. But I walk around as though—as if I have something to prove. To prove to a man I don't even know. A man that I'll never be able to know. I just—I need to escape your shadow. And this—coming here and talking and not hearing anything back. I feel as if it'll never happen if I keep doing this. And that's why—that's why I have to leave. I have to go on my own. And if you were here, you'd be giving me away three weeks from now anyway. So consider this a gift, Dad. I'm letting you give me away early. I'm letting you go. And I know—I know that you aren't going anywhere. It's just—it's just that I have places to go. So let me. Let me go to them."

She leaned over and kissed the gravestone.

At the light at the intersection in the shadow of the sleeping city, you wait.

The waiting kills you.

But waiting is all you do.

You walk into the red light ignoring any oncoming traffic, oblivious to everything around you.

You soon reach your destination, your sanctuary from the voices, your solace for the time being.

Once inside, you check your cell phone. You check it for any messages, for any signs of life, several times an hour, on every hour. But as usual, there's nothing.

It's sometime in August—you're not sure of the exact date—but you do know that in just around two weeks she will be getting married. The same girl you took to the concert and you kissed and you haven't heard from since.

Nothing.

No Lollapalooza, no apology for not being there, nothing.

Nothing but silence, just like the studio you enter that is yours for the next couple of weeks.

It's not much of a studio, but it's still a studio, one that someone is letting your band play in for a few weeks to record your first "official" album.

But something in this picture is wrong.

Someone's missing in this dream.

If this is the dream come true, you'd hate to see the nightmare.

There are so many songs you're writing and putting down, but only a few will make the cut.

You have big dreams, but they often sound like remnants from a C-level rock band.

But it doesn't matter. Right now you're here not because of obligations or duties, but because you have something you need to get out of you. Something that's burning inside that you to need to cool.

Something you need to say but don't exactly know how to articulate.

Behind the vintage piano, you can express yourself.

The keys feel alive underneath your fingertips. The sounds are oh so sweet to your ears. Nobody's around. Nobody's bothering you. Nobody's criticizing or complaining and you feel good.

With each note you are soothed, like the motion of a massage grinding out the knots in your soul.

This is where you belong.

This place. Right here. Doing this, doing what you're doing.

You play.

And you try to put things in perspective.

You're young.

How many years do you have in front of you?

God only knows.

But this is here and this is now and this is right and this is where you belong.

Don't ever forget it.

You've spent a lifetime saying no, hearing no, and living a life of no.

But today is a yes day. Tonight is a yes night. The rest of your life will be yes.

For however long you have.

You're alive. And you can do what you want.

Don't get bogged down.

Not just yet.

You've still got time, Billy Boy.

You can make something out of this, this misery, this heartache.

You can build something beautiful out of this.

So play away.

And in the words that you're singing now, do it.

Do it and do it now.

Let her go.

And you're close.

You're oh so close.

▶ 48. Life in Technicolor

Kayla stretched and opened her eyes. The window above her bed was cracked open and she could hear the birds singing to her, notes she wished she could look up the lyrics to. The morning breeze felt good, as did the pillows that surrounded her head. She looked around for a clock, then remembered that there wasn't an alarm clock in her room at Aunt Cynthia's. Yet another good thing about staying overnight here: not having to worry about the time in the morning.

And on this day, there was nothing planned. The rest of the week and the month and her entire life (it seemed) were all planned out, but there was nothing to do on this bright and sunny summer day.

And as she stared at the ceiling, Kayla had the strangest thought.

And the scary thing was that it made perfect sense.

⌒

"Is Billy working?"

The hostess at the front of the store was cute. She looked young enough to be in high school. She looked at her clipboard. "He came in—let's see—he was in today at 10:30. He's in the bar area."

Kayla thanked her and walked toward the bar, scouting out the restaurant and remembering when she was here a few months ago.

She couldn't believe how much time had passed.

She was less than two weeks away from getting married.

And right now, she couldn't believe that she was in Brewtown looking for Billy.

Who knows what he would do when he saw her this time.

She was going to sit down when a figure approaching caught her eye. Just by the way he walked she knew him. The saunter. The Billy saunter.

He slowed down as if he was nervous, as if she was an assassin and he was the victim. For a second, a crazy thought entered her mind. The sequel to *Mr. and Mr. Smith*, originally starring Brad Pitt and Angelina Jolie, now starring Billy Harris and Kayla Rowe.

"Hi," she said.

He nodded, looking wary, not speaking.

"Look—before you say anything—I just—I want to ask you a favor."

"A favor," Billy said, his voice suspicious and his eyes still not even slightly warm.

"Yes. And I swear—I swear, Billy—I'll never ask anything of you again. This will be the last thing I ever ask you to do for me."

"I can't be in your wedding, if that's what you want," he said, a slight smile on his face.

Good, she thought. *A joke is good.*

"I'm serious, Billy."

"Okay, fine. What's up?"

"I know this is going to sound crazy."

"Nothing is crazy. Not anymore. You could tell me you're pregnant with twins."

"How did you guess?" she joked.

"It's called being jaded."

"Listen—just—I want you do something for me, okay?"

"What is it? We have sales meeting in just a few minutes."

"Well—that's the problem."

"What?"

"Do you have a change of clothes?" she said.

And Billy couldn't help but laugh.

49. Strawberry Swing

Billy watched the figure in shorts and a Cubs jersey walking toward him carrying the tray. It was a beautiful sight. Not just the blonde hair up and the long legs and sunglasses and the smile on her face, but the fact that she was walking toward him.

He had suddenly found a pill and had been transported back in time, back to meeting her his junior year of college and back to being engaged for that oh-so-short period.

"Here you go," Kayla said as she sat next to him on the bleachers. "I loaded up the dog. Did I miss anything?"

"Still no score. Top of the third."

She handed him a beer.

"You got one for yourself?" Billy asked.

"Sure. Cubs game. Gotta have a beer, right?"

"I thought you hated beer," Billy said.

"Not always."

"So is this your day of making exceptions on the things you hate?"

She raised her eyebrows and took a sip. "Um—mm."

Billy had left Brewtown in less than five minutes after Kayla came into the place. He told Erika to tell the manager that he got ill. When she asked for more details, he just shook his head and told her to make something up. He wasn't about to miss this, whatever "this" was.

He still wasn't sure as he sat next to Kayla, eating a hot dog and drinking a beer and watching the Cubbies.

"So you think they're going to get to the World Series?" Kayla asked.

"This is the year," he said.

"Such confidence."

"No—this is the year, K. I'm telling you. They're pretty much the best team in the league. They have too many weapons. They won't choke, not this time, not this year."

"See, that's one of the differences between you and me."

"What? I'm an optimist and you're just a downer?"

"No, no," she corrected him. "I'm a realist. Not a pessimist, a realist."

"The reality is that the Cubs are the best team."

"And the reality is that they're the Cubs. You and I both know what that means."

"Debbie Downer," he said.

"Just wait and see."

Around the seventh inning, with the Cubs up by six and sitting comfortably, just like Billy was, he felt enough liquid courage to ask Kayla what this was all about.

"What do you mean? It's a Cubs game."

"I've tried hard to not ask the obvious since, well, just because. But I have to."

"And what is the obvious?" Kayla asked.

"You don't return any of my calls. You don't show up at Lollapalooza. And now almost a month after the Coldplay concert, you show up at work and we're just casually spending the day at a Cubs game."

The smile filled her face. "Any complaints?"

"Complaints? No. Just questions."

"I am sorry I wasn't at your concert. I heard you did great."

"From who?"

"Mr. Thomas."

"Yeah. Well—I don't know about that."

"I mean it, Billy. I'm sorry I didn't make it. I just—it would be hard to explain why."

"You can try."

"I'd rather buy you another beer."

"Trying to get me liquored up, are you?"

"No."

"I just—I don't get you."

"When have you *ever* gotten me?"

"I'd like to think I sorta get you."

"Sorta doesn't fully do the job, you know?" she said.

"So is this—are you going to tell me something?"

"Like what?"

"Like maybe—I don't know. Did you call off the wedding or something?"

"Of course not."

"Oh, sorry. Yes, of course not. How could I be so stupid? A month ago we were kissing at a concert and then—"

"You kissed me."

"I felt someone kissing me back."

"I might disagree."

"I'd take a replay," Billy said.

"No. Stop."

"See—this is what I'm just lost at. Where are we? What are we doing here?"

"I wanted to make up for not coming to see you perform."

"Okay. But you're still getting married in what—"

"Eleven days."

"But who's counting?" Billy joked.

"How about that beer?"

"You're changing the subject."

"No, I'm not. I'd like another beer."

"Are you sure you're going to come back?"

"I'm not going anywhere," Kayla said with assurance.

"Then stay by my side. Someone will be coming with another beer."

"I'm impatient," she said as she started to slide away.

⸺⸺

What Kayla really needed to do was check her phone. And on it were six messages. Shannen had been texting her, along with Ryan. Her aunt had called.

But there was no emergency or catastrophe. They all simply wondered where she was.

And she liked this, this feeling of freedom, the slight buzz from the beers and the rays and the afternoon.

There might not be many more glorious places to be than in Wrigley Field on an August afternoon.

She texted Ryan and Shannen back, saying she was by the lakefront taking some time for herself.

And that's exactly what she was doing.

She just happened to have a friend by her side to help out.

⁓

They continued to sit in the bleachers as the crowds left. The game ended in a lopsided win. Billy stared out onto the field.

"That was fun," he said. "Thanks."

Kayla glanced at him, studying him. "How did it feel, playing at Lolla?"

His gaze didn't change. "It felt good. It felt right, you know."

"I know."

"But it didn't feel complete."

"Why?"

He looked at her. "I don't need to answer that question."

"Yeah, okay. I'm sorry I wasn't there."

"You don't need to apologize ten times."

"I sorta do."

"I'll take nine."

"I'm sorry."

He nudged her. "Are you ready?"

"For what?" Kayla asked.

"Uh, maybe only one of the biggest days of your life. You know—the wedding. Hello?"

"Yes. And no. And maybe."

"Does your fiancée know we're—"

"Nope."

Billy shook his head. "Okay, then."

"Billy—can you take a walk with me?"

"Of course. Where?"

"Does it matter?"

He looked at her and leaned over to take off her sunglasses. The sun was fading in the background.

"No," he said. "You lead and I'll follow."

⁓

They make a good-looking couple, and they've always known

this. And as they walk down the lakefront path, most people think that's what they are. A couple. It's easy to imagine this. And in some ways, they are, and always will be a couple. There's a shared history there, a friendly disposition, a familiarity, a fondness. A fondness for each other's jokes and each other's faults and each other.

And they walk and keep walking and sometimes they talk and laugh but sometimes they just walk in silence.

As if both of them know.

There's no awkwardness, no apprehension, no anxiousness.

That's what both think, deep down, is the true definition of love. The ability to be free and open and yourself.

The sun tugs into the horizon and the lakefront begins to clear and the windy city prepares itself for a weekday night.

They sit on a wall overlooking the subdued light over Lake Michigan.

For a while they sit in silence, watching, waiting, wondering.

～

"It's such a perfect day," Kayla said.

"Yeah, it is."

"Did you have fun?"

"Still having it."

She looked over at his face, so handsome, so mysterious, so Billy. He was handsome in a warm, inviting way instead of an aloof, macho way. For a few moments, Kayla studied the outline of his face, his deep-set, sad eyes, his full lips.

"You know I love you, Billy Harris?"

His lips opened slightly in shock, as did his eyes. He shook his head gently and tried to speak, but he didn't know how or what to say.

"I know it sounds crazy. But I'm crazy. I'm the crazy person you fell in love with, right? But I do. I love you and I always will. But that doesn't mean we should be together."

"Yes, it does," he blurted out. "Of course it does."

"No, it doesn't."

"Then why—what—I don't understand."

"I don't either, Billy. How can I? Do I love Ryan? Of course I do. But in a different way."

"How different? I don't get it."

She reached over and held his hand, looking into eyes that were surprised and hurt and confused.

"I think this—well, I've thought this for a while, but I think this now more than ever. I think I was given the opportunity to meet you to see what my father might have been like. To prove to me something that I know deep in my heart now—that I would have truly admired and loved him for the man he was."

Billy still looked confused. "What's that mean for us—for me?"

"I don't know. I just—I needed you to know that."

"Damn it, K."

"What?"

"Why? Why now? Why after all this time?"

"What?"

"I keep getting around the fact that you're gone, but you're never gone. You're not and it keeps appearing as if you never will be."

"What do you want, Billy? What do you really want? You want me to call off this wedding right now? Is that what you want? You want to go to Vegas and elope?"

"I want you to be happy, Kayla. I want you to be whole."

She felt tears slowly running down her cheeks. "I don't think I ever can be."

"I can try to help."

"You *have* helped, don't you get it? That's what I'm trying to tell you. But it's just—it's just that I don't—"

"It's okay, all right?" He put his arm around her as she gently cried against his shoulder. He began to talk gently into her ear. "I never told you this, but before that winter interim, before we actually got a chance to meet, before seeing you at that U2 concert with your big boyfriend, before all that—I remember seeing you for the first time."

"What?" her choked voice asked. "When?"

"It was in a school building somewhere at college. I remember you coming out of the elevator—I was like 'who is this beautiful angel?' "

"Not an angel. Just a girl."

"Just a girl, huh?" Billy asked with his arm still around her, holding her as they both stared off into the horizon. "Just a girl, with the boy who will always love her."

▶ 50. Yes

"Okay. That's it. Enough already."

Billy stared at the figure standing in his apartment.

"What?"

"Turn this off!"

"Why?"

Chad strode over and clicked the blaring stereo off.

"What are you doing?"

"What are *you* doing?"

"Watching the news," Billy said.

"Watching heads talk, since you can't hear a single word over the music."

"So?"

"And what soundtrack are you swirling around to today?" Chad asked.

"Doesn't matter."

"Shut up. Of course it matters. It always matters."

"Jeff Buckley."

Chad shook his head.

"What?" Billy said.

"You poor, sad sap."

"I'm not a poor anything."

"The lady of your affections has been missing for how long?"

"Shut up."

"Ah, let me see. It's been since the Cubs date that 'wasn't a date.' "

"It wasn't."

For the first time since Chad had popped up unannounced, knowing where the key was and freely letting himself in like he always did, in a 'Kramer from *Seinfeld*' sort of way, Billy noticed how he looked.

"What's up with you? Going for a job interview?"

"You could say that," Chad said. "Perhaps you'd like to come?"

"And where would that be?"

"New York City."

Billy didn't say anything.

"I'm jetting out this afternoon."

Again, Billy didn't say anything. He knew that Chad wasn't making this up.

"I came by to bid you a fond farewell."

"And try to get me to come with?"

"Oh, no. You, my friend, are at the end of an alley, staring at a brick wall. You definitely are not going anywhere, though you love that wall so much, don't you?"

"Thanks."

"I speak the truth," Chad said. "When's the wedding?"

"A week from now."

"Yes. So you think that wallowing in misery listening to Jeff Buckley and dreaming about all the might-have-beens and could-have-beens is going to help?"

"Not necessarily."

"The momentum of Lollapalooza needs to continue."

"I agree."

"Then do something about it instead of sitting and dreaming and wasting away."

"So what are you going to do?"

Chad shrugged. "The inevitable question. One I can't answer. But I know I'm not sticking around here. I don't like staring at brick walls, Billy. The question is, when will you wake up and feel the same?"

"Every time I think that, there's another reason for me to stay behind."

"You are a toy on Christmas morning for her. But she always moves on to other toys and puts you on the shelf."

"Shut up. You have no idea."

"I'm wrong? How many songs have you penned about the two of you? How long have you been waiting around? Pining away? You're close to thirty years old, aren't you?"

"Four years from now."

"Yes. And then thirty will turn into forty and what are you going to do? Where are you going to end up?"

"You don't understand," Billy said.

"No, I don't. And at this point I don't want to understand. I just came by to give you a little present."

"What's that?"

"My bike."

"Really?"

"I can't take it with me. And who knows when I could sell that thing, you know? So I want you to take it."

"Why?"

"Because maybe—I don't know—maybe you'll change your mind and follow me to New York."

Billy shook his head. "You just don't—"

"I know I don't. There are many, many things that I 'don't.' But as for this—the keys are on the table. Billy, listen to me. Love is a ruse. A love song is a cliché, because it's never that way in real life."

"Sometimes it is."

"But this is not one of those times. And you are not one of *them*."

"What's that mean?"

"I think you know. Call me crazy or eccentric, but we're not part of that, part of it, part of them. And we never will be."

As his friend began to walk away, Billy wanted to say something.

He needed to say something.

But the lyrics weren't there. There was no stanza and no chorus, nothing.

The track was empty.

He heard the door shut and felt the silence sweep into the room.

▶ 51. Lost

"Hey—Mr. Thomas!"

The figure across the street stopped and glanced her way. It was evening and the brilliant day was dimming. Mr. Thomas waved at her and then waited a few moments to cross the busy street.

"What are you up to?" he asked.

"I'm glad I got here in time to see you."

"You all right?"

"Yeah, sure," she said, appreciating the gentle manner in which he asked the question. "I just said good-bye to Leona and wanted to do the same to you."

"I plan to be there on Saturday."

"Yeah, I know. But I'm sure that the day is going to be a big blur. That's what everybody tells me."

"I'm sure it will."

Kayla glanced at the leather briefcase he held. "Do you—are you busy now?"

"Oh, am I busy. The life of a jetsetter, that's me."

She laughed. "Would you like to have coffee somewhere?"

"I'd love to."

After walking a couple blocks to the nearest Starbucks and grabbing a couple of coffees, which Mr. Thomas paid for, Kayla wasn't sure how to start. She didn't exactly know why she was nervous. Perhaps because she knew what she wanted to ask but wasn't sure why she wanted to ask it. Or if she even should.

"How's Leona?"

"She's a dear," Kayla said. "I actually got all emotional when I told her good-bye. Good-bye for now. That's what I said to her. It's not like I'll never see her again. It's just—well, you never know. She's older and—I guess I've grown up knowing that anything can happen. Probably because I lost my father at such an early age."

"Anything can happen," Mr. Thomas said. "But I'm sure you'll see Leona again. She's a strong lady. She acts more like she's in her forties than her eighties."

Kayla chuckled as she shared a few funny stories about Leona, trying to avoid getting to the conversation she really wanted.

Mr. Thomas seemed to sense it as well. "Kayla, what's wrong?"

"What do you mean?"

"Well, it's the Wednesday evening before your wedding. I'm sure you've got a lot of things going on. But you act like something's on your mind."

"It is." She stared at her cup of coffee for a moment. "Have you seen Billy lately?"

"No," Mr. Thomas said. "And with the summer almost over, it doesn't look like I will."

She nodded, wishing she could know how he was doing. Or what he was doing. Or anything about Billy.

"And why are you thinking about Billy?"

"Oh, I'm always thinking about Billy. You know—sometimes I wonder about this summer. I don't think that everything happens for a reason. I try not to read into things too much. But why in the world would God put Billy and me together—this summer—the summer before my wedding—working together like this at Angel Hands? I don't believe that was coincidence. Do you?"

Mr. Thomas shook his head. "No, I don't think it was."

"But why? That's what I can't figure out."

"I know he's still crazy about you."

"When did he tell you that?" she asked.

"He didn't need to. But you know that, don't you?"

"It's like—it's like he's held up his dreams in order to wait for me."

"Maybe his dream is you."

Kayla looked at Mr. Thomas and felt a wave of confusion and hope and sadness. She was tired, sure, but she felt more than that.

She felt empty.

"Billy cares deeply for you. I know that."

"I just—there are so many things—so many things that I can't even articulate that make me scared. That make me worried. That make me wonder."

"About Billy?"

"Yes, about Billy. But also about Ryan. And marriage in general. And then I just think—I think that I must be crazy."

"You're not crazy," he told her. "Trust me. It's just a tough time for you right now."

"You have a daughter, right?"

Mr. Thomas nodded, but for the first time while talking with her, his eyes shifted down.

"You said she's my age, right?"

Again he nodded.

"Is she married?"

"No."

"What would you tell her regarding her 'boy troubles'?"

Mr. Thomas took a slight breath and thought for a moment. He seemed apprehensive. "I would—well—it depends on the situation."

"Let's say she's getting married in three days and she's marrying this great guy whom she loves. But then there's her first real true love, the one that got away, who's suddenly in her life again. The one that doesn't necessarily look the best on paper but that—for some crazy reason—she still loves and wonders about. What would you tell her to do?"

Mr. Thomas glanced at her and smiled a humble, sad smile. Kayla could only think that he was thinking of his daughter right now, at this very moment, because the look that filled his face was pure, unbridled love. That was the only way she could describe the glance she saw.

"I would tell her to follow her heart."

"But what if—what if she made the wrong decision?"

"That's life. That's what this life is all about. It's like when you're two years old. You stumble on the floor when you're running around. You fall and skin your knee and you cry. But you get up. That's what life is all about. You make mistakes. You fall. But your father is there to help you up and put you back on your feet."

"Yeah, but—well, in my case, I'm on my own. That's why—I don't know—I hope it's okay even asking you any of this."

"I'm honored that you even bring it up," he said. "And I know—I'm sure you'll make the right decision."

"What if there really isn't a 'right' decision?"

"There will be. Just—just follow your heart, Kayla."

She sits on a stone wall and faces the lake. The breeze feels good against her face. She stares out at boats sleeping in their docks, boats floating nearby, boats cruising out to the dark shadows beyond the city. Behind her Chicago buzzes. She glances to her right and looks at the round building lit with floodlights.

This was the place.

Five years ago, she thinks. *Five years ago in January. That's when we came here.*

She can still see them walking between the planets at the Planetarium. She can still see his boyish but confident smile. She can see the stars they watched. She can feel her hand taking his in the darkness.

It's close to midnight, and she should be back at her apartment, getting rest. Getting ready for the big day tomorrow. Or, depending on what time it is, *today.* But after the rehearsal dinner downtown ended she'd told Ryan and Shannen and Aunt Cynthia that she just wanted a little time to herself. That's all.

And this is where she ended up.

Maybe if this were a movie, she would see Billy walking this way, the place they first fell in love, the place where it all began. He might sit down next to her and put an arm around her and not say anything for a long time. What was there to say? Everything. And nothing. He would hold her and the minutes would stop and they would look out at the shadows of the lake falling asleep and they would dream. They would dream of a different life and a different time and a different outcome.

But Kayla finds herself here all alone, thinking.

Thinking and remembering.

And she hears Mr. Thomas's words.

Follow your heart.

But her heart says a myriad of things.

All along she's been trying to follow her heart.

All along, she's been trying to hear the voices deep down.

She prays that she's making the right decision.

But even as she prays, she isn't sure what that final decision will be.

She remembers the snippet of a conversation held not long ago.

Not long ago, yet an eternity.

— *I think it's so easy to know where you're going in life that you lose track of the places you could go.*

—*And where should I go, Mr. Billy Harris?*

—*I can't answer that. All I want to do is encourage you to look up. To see all that's out there.*

And with those words, and that memory, Kayla stands and looks back at the planetarium.

Time is so short, and I'm sure there must be something more. . . .

⌣

Not too far away from Kayla, at a party in a loft belonging to a friend of a friend of a friend, Billy dances in the middle of a room full of strangers. The lights blur and the paintings on the wall bounce and the music blares and the bottle in his hand suddenly seems to drop and break. But the music and the dancing and the night go on unhindered. And he wishes that the same could be said about his life and his soul and his heart.

He wants to give something new a try, but he's not sure he can.

Chad's gone and there are no more songs of the day to be sung. The album they were working on is unfinished. Undone. Just like so many damned things.

He wanders into a kitchen full of fun, happy, ha-ha people who seem to love life. They nauseate him. He finds something else to drink, though he probably shouldn't. He's already half blind but that's okay because he's half of everything. Half in love and half heartbroken and half a man and half a lover and half a person.

Half a person.

And half of everything might eventually add up to something whole. But only God knows what that will be.

A girl talks to him and she's attractive and if he were a normal human being he'd be interested but he's so not interested and he walks off before the conversation is over. Reuben should be somewhere in this place, but maybe his friend bailed. They all bail. They all eventually bail.

He circles the room and sees the clock and knows it's almost one.

The time ticks and nears and gets oh so close, oh so close.

The beer he's drinking doesn't even have a taste anymore.

For a moment, he falls asleep standing up.

He wants to erase the past two years. He wants to go back in time. He wants to correct something. His life, his heart, his soul.

Reuben appears and tells him they should go home but Billy doesn't want to go and doesn't need a babysitter and he shoves Reuben away and then wonders why he's doing so.

For a moment, he sits on a couch next to a girl who looks very goth and who looks like she might kill him. He smiles but she doesn't smile back and he shuts his eyes for just a moment and then he sees the sweet, sundrenched, soulful smile that he wants and that will always and forever belong to him but that never belonged to him and never will.

And then he's out.

What have I done?

Thomas stands up from his knees and finally walks toward his bedroom, knowing he needs to get some sleep.

Sometimes all the prayer in the world doesn't change the outcome.

And in this case, Thomas knows that the outcome might be because of something he said.

It's not about a dance. It was never just about a dance. And the dance isn't about two or three or four minutes in front of a room full of people looking and staring.

It's what that dance symbolizes.

Music, which was his passion, the bridge to Kayla's heart.

Dancing, which symbolized the bond that he shared with this tiny, precious creature in her first few months of life.

It was about a connection, a shared history, a dream, a hope.

It was never just about a simple dance.

This was all about Kayla being happy, being content, and making the right choice.

But Thomas knows that he said the right thing to her.

He still would say it now.

He wants her to follow his heart.

But now, on the eve of her following her heart, Thomas feels like he's failed.

Will I be able to go to the wedding?

Will I be able to dance?

Will I be able to say anything about her decision?

He feels like a ghost here in this place, on this planet.

He wants to leave. But what if he can't? What if he's stuck here? He's failed and the gates of Heaven are closed and he's stuck having to pick up the pieces of his failure.

Doubts. Insecurities. Fears. Anger. Frustration.

I hate this place, this world, this life.

But it's all because he has something else to compare it to.

As he prepares to get into his bed knowing that sleep won't come tonight, Thomas looks at the table and sees the notebook on top of it.

He sees the open page, the writing inside.

He's not sure how many pages he's written to her.

He sits down and continues writing.

Tomorrow, he will give this to Kayla. These words, these truths, these explanations.

Tomorrow he will follow *his* heart. Regardless of where that will take him or Kayla or Billy.

Regardless of the ramifications.

Thomas wasn't sure how this worked.

It was the big day, and yet he had failed. Did that mean he'd be getting his one-way ticket back to the big skies? Would James be showing up at his door soon? Or he would have to wait until it was official? Or wait a day from now, a week from now?

He walked down the sidewalk, early in the morning, the temperature warm and the sun peeking out between the high-rises. He sipped a coffee and walked to try to sort through his thoughts.

And after half an hour of this, he stopped and stared up at the skies.

This wasn't how it was supposed to go down.

Thomas, strolling through the awakening city, full of doubt and discouragement and despair.

Damn this world. Damn the demons filling it. He hated it. It was so easy to get down and get low.

But around him was life. Beautiful, sweet life. The breath of another day, the sun ablaze and the lake crystal clear. Another chance to do something, another opportunity to try something.

Thomas stared up at the sky and knew that his work wasn't done.

For a second, he closed his eyes.

And he pictured Kayla's bright blue eyes. Her little laugh. The way she used to say, "Come on, Daddy" when she wanted something. The way she would make him laugh with almost anything she would do. He could see a hundred mornings like this, sitting at the table, groggy and worried about the future and present, feeding her and seeing her get food all over herself. Watching a ridiculous show on television or lying on the carpet playing toys with her or cooking up imaginary food or taking her to the library or one of a thousand memories.

There should have been more, he thought. *There should have been so many more.*

But here he was, on this morning, and he still had a chance.

There was still one more chance.

She wasn't married yet, was she?

She was surely up and getting ready, but the ceremony wasn't until two in the afternoon.

Six hours from now.

He crossed the street and walked down the sidewalk, and the further he went, the more he believed it still wasn't over.

We only get one life and every day is another chance, another opportunity.

And if this was his last morning of his time in this place—this place full of doubt and dreariness and depression—so be it.

He would make the most of it.

Most people let their fears and frustrations seize their lives.

But he knew that he had one more chance.

He tossed his coffee cup into the garbage and starting running down the empty street.

He needed to get ready.

He had a wedding to go to.

And a groom to wake up.

54. Lovers in Japan

"Get up, Billy. Come on, rise and shine."

It took a minute simply to get his eyes open. He adjusted to the bright light and made out the figure hovering over him.

"Mr. Thomas?"

"You're a hard man to track down."

Billy continued blinking and then finally sat up. His head throbbed. His mouth was dry, his throat ragged. He glanced around the room. "Where am I? Where are we?"

"Know a guy named Anthony?"

Billy just shook his head. Mr. Thomas handed him a bottled water.

"I guess Anthony is a friend of Blake—who is the guy who had the party last night, right?"

"How do you know all this?"

"Well, I've spent the last couple hours tracking you down."

"What time is it?"

"About noon."

Billy moaned and yawned at the same time. His side hurt.

He glanced over at Mr. Thomas, who was staring at him and smiling. Billy noticed that he was wearing a dark suit and tie.

It took Billy a couple minutes to ask the obvious. "What are you doing here?"

"We've got a wedding to go to," Mr. Thomas said.

Billy laughed, then started coughing. "Yeah, right. The wedding's already happening."

"We've got a wedding to go," he repeated.

"Kayla's wedding?" Billy asked.

"Yes. And yours too."

Billy looked at Mr. Thomas. "Are you crazy?"

"Positively. But it's a glorious feeling, isn't it? Come on, stand up. We need to get you back to your apartment."

"For what?"

"I've got a plan."

"Oh boy."

Back at his apartment, Billy was a bit too hung over to realize what was happening.

Mr. Thomas told him to get into the shower and get dressed. Billy tried arguing but couldn't. He decided a shower would wake him up and clear his mind. Or at least clear his mind a little.

When he went to find some jeans, there was a coat and tie on the bed.

"You're not serious, are you?" Billy asked him, walking into the living room and hearing the song jamming on the stereo.

"I'm dead serious."

Billy listened for a second to the Coldplay song.

"What the hell is all of this? What's going on?"

Mr. Thomas looked at Billy, who was still dripping. "Tell me something."

"What?"

"Do you still love her?"

"She's getting married today. In a couple hours. Or less."

"Do you still love her?" Mr. Thomas asked again.

"That's besides the point."

"Answer the question."

"Yes," Billy answered, intimidated by Mr. Thomas's tone.

"Then fight."

"I've fought for four or five years. It's done."

"No, it's not."

"Yes, it is."

"Billy, get the suit on."

"What's your deal anyway? Why do you want us to be together so bad?"

"Because I know what you know—that you are *meant* to be together."

"But how do *you* know?"

"I just do," Mr. Thomas said. "You have to trust me."

Billy scratched his wet hair. "How are we even going to get there? I mean—I just got my license back but I sold my car. Do you have a car?"

Mr. Thomas shook his head. "Just get changed. And Billy—brush your teeth. A few times. You still smell like a brewery."

"I'm supposed to be working at a brewery today."

"Call in sick."

"For what? The morning shift?"

"Forever. Don't go back there. You've got a life to lead."

"You're like some motivational speaker from hell."

"I'm not from hell," Mr. Thomas said. "Trust me. You would know."

Billy strolled back into his bedroom, still hearing the sounds of Coldplay haunting him, still utterly confused but too tired to fight against any of this.

~

"This is crazy," Billy shouted.

"Yep."

"We're going to be late," Billy said.

"Just keep driving."

Billy guided the motorcycle through the city streets toward the expressway. Chad's bike wasn't one of those speed racers, nor was it a big Harley Davidson. Billy wasn't even sure how fast it could go, especially with the two of them riding on it.

Mr. Thomas clung to him. Strapped to his back was Billy's guitar. For some reason, Mr. Thomas wanted him to bring it.

Scary thoughts went through Billy's mind. What if he got there and Kayla told him to get out? Or what if—well, what if Mr. Thomas wanted him to serenade Kayla? That would be dreadful. It was tough enough playing to a small, uninterested crowd, but crashing a wedding to do a singalong?

As Billy drove the bike toward the suburbs, he knew that they wouldn't get there by two.

"Hurry up!" Mr. Thomas said.

On the Eisenhower, Billy got the bike close to a hundred miles an hour. But as they were coasting down the street, he heard something crack. He slowed the bike down and turned around briefly.

Mr. Thomas was saying something.

"What?" Billy asked.

"Keep driving."

"What was that sound?"

"Nothing."

Billy looked around and couldn't see his guitar. He guided the bike onto the side of the highway and stopped. "Where's my guitar?"

"About a mile back?"

"That's my only guitar! We need to go back and get it."

"It's in about twenty pieces."

Billy cursed. "The one time my guitar gets trashed into pieces, and I can't even say that I had the fun of doing it myself."

"I'll get you another guitar."

"What do I need a guitar for anyway? I'm not going to serenade Kayla or something like that. This isn't some Cameron Crowe movie."

"I'm hoping for something more like *The Graduate*," Mr. Thomas said.

"The what?"

"Dustin Hoffman? Come on, you've never seen that? The big finale where he rushes in to the wedding?"

"No."

Mr. Thomas shook his head. "Let's go. Come on."

The helmet on Mr. Thomas looked funny. Billy laughed and started the bike up again.

They exited the expressway right at two o'clock.

Right when Kayla was supposed to be walking down the aisle.

Billy didn't know what he was driving toward or what he was going to do when he got there. But maybe the madman on his back really did have a plan.

Maybe that plan would work.

Maybe.

Billy knew Aunt Cynthia's house well. It was in a pretty, affluent neighborhood, tucked away behind the trees. The secret was the amazing garden in the back, one that sprawled out in the shape of an upside-down triangle.

Billy drove the bike up to near the driveway. Cars were lined up and down the block and even other streets. More cars parked on the lawn. Billy and Mr. Thomas hopped off the bike and tossed their helmets to the side. Billy glanced at his watch.

2:18.

She's married. I know she's married. And if she's not then she's going to be in just a few moments.

"Come on," Mr. Thomas said.

"Where are we going?"

"Inside. To catch her before she walks."

"I don't think she's going to want—"

"Just go. Come on. Where's her room?"

"Why?"

"Trust me," Mr. Thomas said.

Billy felt a sense of euphoria as he opened the front door. There was nobody in the entrance. He could hear distant music coming from outside in the back garden.

"She's probably already—"

"Come on. Upstairs!"

Billy led Mr. Thomas up the stairs and he reached the top, pausing for a second.

It had been so long since he had been here.

So many memories.

So many hours spent inside this house.

He saw her door shut.

Maybe . . .

"Is that her room?" Mr. Thomas asked.

"I can't."

"Yes, you can."

"I shouldn't—it's not right."

"Billy, come on."

Billy went to the door and knocked. And knocked. And knocked again.

Mr. Thomas looked as if he was ready to leave if someone opened that door. But nobody was there.

"I told you."

"Open it," Mr. Thomas said.

"No," Billy said in a whisper.

"Go ahead. Go on."

Billy tipped it open with one finger and found a messy room full of clothes and bags and makeup and hair products.

But no Kayla.

"She's not here."

"Then come on," Mr. Thomas said, standing at the doorway, almost out of breath. "Let's get down there."

Billy moved to the window. He had been in this room and knew the view. He knew the view too well. As he stood at the window, he looked down and saw the most beautiful vision he'd ever seen.

Two rows of people stood, turned toward the house, turned toward her.

A long aisle of white rose petals, flanked by flower arrangements, seemed to stretch on forever.

And there she was.

Kayla Rowe, a waterfall of white, a picture of perfection.

"Come on, Billy!"

But Billy just stood there. He could see her outline, her profile, her tall form standing and facing the crowd.

The music played. Billy opened the window a little more to hear it. "Come here," he said.

Mr. Thomas rushed over. He looked pale as a ghost. "Come on, we need to get—"

"No," Billy said firmly.

"Billy, please. We can still get down there."

"No. Just—let's just watch."

"No."

"It's fine," Billy said. "And we're here. That's what matters."

And then Kayla began to walk down the aisle.

All by herself.

Billy felt his skin prickle over, his eyes glisten, his mouth tighten. She looked so amazing. So amazing in so many different ways.

But probably what looked most amazing was how content she appeared.

She looked radiant and happy. Not melancholy, not doubtful, not hesitant in the least.

And she walked strong and proud.

Billy couldn't help but wonder—wonder and hope—that her father watched her.

That he watched her and was unimaginably proud.

He didn't notice Mr. Thomas at his side. He was too enthralled watching Kayla walk up to the end of the aisle where the pastor and her fiancé and the wedding party awaited.

He sighed as the pastor began to talk, wiped the tears off his cheek. Then he glanced at Mr. Thomas, and suddenly what he saw made sense. Suddenly Billy understood something that had been pestering him since the beginning of the summer, something that had been nagging at him but that had been unexplained.

Until now.

Mr. Thomas looked moved. Not just moved to tears, but devastated with emotion. *Wrecked* might be the word. He didn't look despondent, nor did he look elated. He looked—

He looks like a father might look the day his little girl walks down the aisle.

And Billy knew.

He stared at Mr. Thomas and knew without a doubt. It was crazy, of course, but he suddenly saw Kayla in Mr. Thomas. And Mr. Thomas in Kayla. The resemblance . . .

Why haven't I seen it before?

Billy wanted to say something, but he couldn't.

He didn't want to deprive the father from his moment.

And it hit Billy.

If he is . . .

If Mr. Thomas *was* in fact Kayla's father, then that meant—

This whole summer had been about Mr. Thomas trying to get Billy and Kayla together.

All the things with Angel Hands. Getting Chad back in his band so he could play at Lollapalooza. The Coldplay tickets.

It was too much for Billy to comprehend. But he believed.

He believed it now without a shred of doubt.

"She's amazing, isn't she?" Billy said.

"Yes, she is," Mr. Thomas said as only a father could.

The pastor speaks to the bride and groom, who both look happy and hold hands and listen to his words. The rest of the wedding party listen as well, as do the two figures in the open window who watch in secret.

"Love is patient and kind," the pastor quotes.

Kayla looks at Ryan and knows this, can see it in his eyes, and believes this after the unexplainable journey she's put him through this summer.

"Love is not jealous or boastful or proud or rude," the pastor continues, and Billy and Thomas watch with wonder.

"Love never gives up, never loses faith, is always hopeful, and endures through every circumstance."

And as the pastor says these words, Thomas puts his arm around Billy.

"When I was a child, I spoke and thought and reasoned as a child. But when I grew up, I put away childish things."

Thomas thinks of his child and thinks of the ten thousand glorious pictures and memories he still has. He only had her for two years, but what a brilliant couple of years they were. To have had a day, or a month, or a year—all of those were a blessing.

And now his little baby has to put away childish things.

She's made her choice.

She's on her own.

"Three things will last forever," the pastor concludes. "Faith . . ."

And Kayla looks at Ryan and smiles.

". . . hope . . ."

Billy glances down. He still loves Kayla and knows that he always will.

". . . and love."

Thomas stares at his daughter and knows that if he is given nothing more than this, that all of this was an incredible, indescribable gift.

"And the greatest of these is love."

56. Clair de Lune (Moonlight)

God gives us moments such as this.

The man in his fifties enters the reception area in the yard in a suit and tie. He hears the music playing and sees the couple on the floor, dancing.

He has been there to see it all, the walk down the aisle, the spoken vows, the lighting of the candle, the kiss.

And now this amazing, wonderful gift he has been given is coming to a close.

She followed her heart.

And she picked someone else.

Yet Thomas couldn't be more proud, more happy, more full of life than at this moment.

She glows as she dances. She always has. And always will.

The crowd gathers around the dance floor, standing next to tables with remnants of dessert still on them. He isn't sure how this will work, but he strides toward the crowd knowing it will, knowing that he has doubted enough and that everything has happened as it should have.

Life moves on and works out even when they don't listen to you, even when they don't make the right decision. Life moves on and love remains.

Thomas takes a glass of champagne and has a sip, toasting Ryan and Kayla. He sees them dancing to the music, and he smiles at the song they selected.

Brilliant choice, he thinks to himself. But of course, he knows who surely chose.

For a second he feels a pang of regret, thinking about Billy.

He's a good man with a good heart. But Ryan is too, and he will take care of Kayla.

He is thankful to at least have seen and heard about this man who will stay with his daughter, who will protect her, who will guard her smile.

Tears already form in his eyes, and he knows it's far too soon for them to do so.

This was all I asked for, this moment.

He feels a wave of warmth wash over him. Goose bumps. Sadness. And joy.

The song stops, and instead of the father-daughter dance that would have come, Kayla does something that surprises him.

But why should it surprise you? Of course she's going to do this.

She leads Aunt Cynthia out onto the floor, and they dance together to "What a Wonderful World" by Louis Armstrong.

He can't help the grin that threatens to leap off his face. There is no regret, no thought that it should be him dancing right now. It is a gift to be here, to watch this, to remain a spectator.

Kayla looks so unbelievably happy.

And several songs pass, and he watches, smiling, his heart exploding, his mind racing.

And then she spots him. She is coming off the dance floor, and her face lights up. "Mr. Thomas!" And she gives him a hug. "I can't believe you made it! I was so hoping—I wasn't sure during the ceremony—I didn't see you."

"I wouldn't miss this for the world."

Even clichés can take on a whole new meaning.

"Where's Ryan—oh, I need to get Ryan—have you seen him?"

For a moment she looks around and can't see him. The DJ puts on an old classic.

"You look lovely tonight," Thomas tells his daughter.

"Thank you."

And then she seems to realize that she isn't going to find Ryan for the moment. "Mr. Thomas? Would it be forward of me to ask you for a dance?"

Of course. Just like that. She's the one that asks him.

He smiles and controls his emotions. "This is your day. Anyone who gets to dance with you is a very lucky person."

She smiles and they go out to the dance floor.

And suddenly it's not the DJ controlling the set list anymore.

There's somebody else at work here.

The music slows down, with the orchestra starting. It's a song he knows, and he knows well.

"I love this song," she says to Thomas. "I told them to play this sometime."

And some famous orchestra plays Debussy's classic for the hundredth time. But to Thomas, the music feels brand-new, as though just performed for the very first time.

It washes over him. And he holds the bride of white, his daughter, his beloved, in his arms.

And he remembers.

A man with a broken spirit dancing with a sweet, precious soul. The dance hall disappears and he finds himself in that old, tiny apartment on that New Year's Eve, the baby girl nestled in his arms, moving and rocking her to sleep as the music plays.

He remembers every moment of every day of the time he was given.

And that, just like this dance tonight, is a gift.

Life is a gift and love is a gift and there is so much—so much—to be thankful for.

The world floats away.

This is not imagined, this is real, and there is more, Kayla, there is so much more.

He doesn't think of saying good-bye. He can't think of anything. He is proud, full of love, full.

"This song reminds me of my childhood," Kayla says, breaking his heart.

He nods and tries not to let her see his eyes. The tears are as real as this floor and this music and this beautiful bride dancing with him.

"What's wrong?" she asks.

"I'm just thinking of my daughter. And how much I love her."

"She's very lucky."

"So is Ryan."

And as the song crescendos, he closes those eyes, and he prays.

God, give her a long, happy life. Watch over her and give her joy, the joy she has given me.

And he sees himself as a younger man but just a second ago, embracing Kayla, finishing the dance and kissing her on a soft head with fresh hair. Telling her words that he knew she heard even though she didn't understand, words that were imprinted on her soul.

I will always be your father. And I will never let you go.

And as the song softly comes to an end, Kayla looks up at Thomas with tears in her eyes. "I'm sorry," she says.

"No, it's fine."

"I've been on an emotional roller coaster today," she says with a laugh, wiping her eyes. "Thank God for tear-proof eyeliner."

"Yes, thank God," he says with a smile. "It's okay."

She's about to say something else, but she doesn't have to. He knows what she feels. Missing her father, wishing he were there, wondering what it would be like to have known him, wanting to have shared a dance the way they shared this one.

But then she does speak her heart. "I . . . miss my dad."

And he says without hesitation, "He's watching, Kayla, and he's proud."

She smiles and wipes her eyes and looks down at the floor. "Thank you," she says.

He nods, and he thinks of the letter in his coat pocket, the thick letter that sums up everything he's wanted to tell her and more, that sums up everything he's thinking and feeling right now.

"Stay happy," he says. "And don't ever forget the music in your soul."

She beams a smile and nods.

And it will be the last smile of hers he will see for some time.

And as the masses take her and the music changes and he sees the princess of white swallowed in a sea of black, Thomas sighs and wonders if he can even move.

Thank you, Father, thank you for this gift.

The smile is still on his lips.

And as he walks out of the reception area underneath a clear sky opening up to a sea of stars, he looks at the gift table with its presents and cards. His hand finds its way into his coat pocket, grabs the letter, then pauses.

He turns and can see her strolling onto the dance floor.

His little baby girl.

In his hand is everything he wants to tell her, all the words he wishes she could hear.

He smiles as he places the letter onto the table. Then he pauses for a second, picks it back up, and heads toward the moonlight.

57. The Escapist

It's Sunday afternoon, and Billy has everything he needs.

It's amazing how little that is when you really think of it.

He straps the backpack on, then starts the bike. He hopes it will make it all the way to New York so he can give it back to Chad, with one caveat.

He not only wants to keep working with Chad, he needs him. Eccentric, moody, unpredictable—all of those things are what make Chad the crazy person he is. And Billy wants to keep playing music with his friend.

He'll also need a place to live for a while.

But the future will come.

It will come in one way or another.

It takes him a few moments to get out of the city streets and onto the highway.

He's listening to his iPod. The ride to New York will be a long one.

Billy is excited and anxious and knows that it took this—this heartache—to finally get him moving on.

Moving on is hard but so many people in life don't ever do it and they get stuck.

Billy never wants to get stuck again.

On the highway, with the music coursing through him and the lanes open and free, he sees a plane high above him.

And he smiles, knowing that somewhere Kayla is moving on too.

And he hopes that she stays happy.

He loves her and he always will.

my love and my pride and my hope—you embody them. But you don't need to hear this because you live this out. Day after day.

You don't need my words. And as much as I might want you to hear them—even as much as you might want to hear them too—they are words that must wait.

Life in this world is not easy, and it is not always happy. Life is tough. Love is tough. And you will be hurt and let down. You'll let yourself down.

And I can't say that I know your future, just as I didn't know my own. There will be heartache and tragedy. That is life.

But there is more beyond this life. And to see it and know it with my own eyes—it is like nothing else.

Beautiful, yes. Moving, yes. Miraculous, certainly.

And to have left you for a second time might break a man's heart, though I know I leave you in good hands. And I know that I will see you again.

Being a parent, I know now, is not just about loving, but it's about letting go.

This letter—these words and memories and emotions— they will be waiting.

I'll be waiting.

And I promise.

We will dance again.

acknowledgements

With thanks to the following people:

Sharon, for showing me that love is indeed patient and kind. And also very necessary when you're living with a moody writer.

Kylie, my beautiful little girl, who this book is dedicated to, for allowing me to discover a whole new meaning to love and life.

My parents, for continuing to encourage me in this writing journey, especially with this little story.

My in-laws, for continuing to help and support our family in big and small ways.

Claudia, for believing in this story and working hard with me on it.

LB, for partnering again with me on another one.

Karen Watson, for saying no to a mediocre project I pitched to you years ago, thus forcing me to try and come up with a great hook. This story is a result of that.

All my fans and readers out there who help me realize I must be doing a few things right.

For the artists who provided the soundtrack to this story, especially the blokes from Coldplay.

And for anybody gracious enough to pick up a copy of this story: don't ever forget the music in your soul.

Postcards from Far Away
An author note

There's a wild wind blowing down the corner of my street. No, seriously. I know that's a Coldplay lyric, but there *is* a wild wind blowing outside today. Halloween weather is here a day early. But the good news is that I'm wrapping up this pretty little journey, so the dark clouds outside won't get me down.

I have a love/hate relationship with author notes in novels. Sometimes I love them—for instance, when Stephen King does one of his notes to his "constant readers," I usually find them quite interesting, as if he's sitting across the table talking to me. That's what I'm going for with this note.

My hope is that you enjoyed *Every Breath You Take*. More than anything else, it's a snapshot of my first few years as a father.

I want to explain a little why I self-published this story.

When I left my full-time job at a publishing house in September 2007—the one with the biweekly check and the benefits and all that wonderful stuff—I held in my proverbial creative pocket this idea. I felt the hook was a strong one, so I spent a good chunk of 2008 working on this with my agent. I had to rewrite over half of it before she sent it out in early 2009. By then, several things had changed in my publishing universe. That's what you have to deal with if you're a writer—the ever-changing world of publishing. One of the things was that I was in the "supernatural suspense" genre, quite different from this tale. It didn't quite make sense publishing a story like this in the midst of my other works. Then again, my publishing career has never made sense to anybody except me and maybe my friend Andy Bilyeu, who's a bit on the crazy side.

The publishers my agent sent it to rejected it. Some of the rejections were quite encouraging, but no still means no. By the end of this summer, I realized that *Every Breath You Take* was going to end up where some of my other stories have gone: to the closet to be forgotten.

This story is different for many reasons, but here are a few. First, I feel that it's strong enough to sit alongside my other books. Second, as I mentioned before, it's a snapshot of my first few years as a father. If I never released it and then suddenly became the next J.K.

Rowling five years from now and publishers start asking to publish my grocery list, I don't think I'd want to release this because it reflects Travis Thrasher in 2008-2009 (the Rock Bottom years, as I will call them). I had fun with this story, but I doubt I would write it like this years down the road.

For the last five or six Christmases, I've thought of self-publishing a Christmas story. I've written a couple (pretty dreadful stories if you ask me). I've always wanted to go through the process of publishing something myself to see how it goes. Do I recoup the money spent? Do I sell a boatload? Will it become the next phenomenon in the world of self-publishing?

All I care about is being able to pay for the costs of this book and, even more importantly, that I'll hopefully hear from readers that they were moved by the story.

My daughter turns three on November 12. She is a blessing from God, and she is so loved by her mother and me. The first few nuggets of this story came from the love I have for her. I hope that some of the feelings I have for Kylie were transposed onto these pages. And I hope that this little story will remind you of your loved ones, of the love you have for them, and of the fact that every day is a gift.

This book in many ways is a gift. A gift that was given to me. I wish I had the ability to give it out free to all my readers and acquaintances. Maybe one day I'll be able to do something like that. We'll see.

Okay, I've probably already failed the Author Note test. Oh well, I'll try to get it right the next time. In the meantime, crank your favorite song next time you're driving and think of this story. Tell someone you love about it.

Better yet, just remind that someone that you love them.

October 30, 2009

Also by Travis Thrasher

The Promise Remains (2000)
"Driven by authentic characters . . . Sara and Ethan are two of the most real and sensitive lovers to grace the genre, and readers will find themselves moved."--*Publishers Weekly*

The Watermark (2001)
"A beautiful, sometimes whimsical journey to faith as a man grapples with feelings of unworthiness while learning that God has been there all along. A highly recommended work."--*Library Journal*

The Second Thief (2003)
"The end of Thrasher's tale has an unusual twist that will surprise the reader."--*Publishers Weekly*

Three Roads Home (2003)
"Thrasher writes stories that are deeply touching . . . His style is edgy and imaginative, and he creates characters that are fully-dimensional and thoroughly believable"--*The Romance Reader's Connection*

Gun Lake (2004)
"Ambitious suspense novel . . . with redemption themes"
--*Publishers Weekly*

Admission (2006)
"This is Thrasher's best novel to date, with a nifty, airtight plot; a love story; and a serious theme about how some of us reform, and some of us don't."--*Booklist*

Blinded (2006)
"Fast-paced, it's full of twists and turns with an ending that I never saw coming."--*Infuze Mag*

Sky Blue (2007)
"Travis Thrasher weaves a powerful tale of sorrow and grace in this work. The ending is so powerful the reader literally leans forward through the last pages, as if in some way trying to help the story along."--*OnceUponARomance.net*

Out of the Devil's Mouth (2008)

"Thrasher's unique writing voice brings a level of freshness to a familiar genre. No adventure story would be complete without a hint of romance and Thrasher doesn't disappoint in this area."
--*FictionAddict.com*

Isolation (2008)

"Like Stephen King, Thrasher pits flawed but likable characters against evil forces that at first seem escapable but gradually take on a terrifying ubiquity."--*Publishers Weekly*

Ghostwriter (2009)

"There's a deep love story between the author character and his late wife interleaved with lots of cinematically creepy scenes played out at ordinary places in upscale suburbia . . . An emotional wallop of a book. Thrasher just keeps getting better."--*Publishers Weekly*

Travis Thrasher lives with his wife and daughter in a Chicago suburb. For more information on Travis, visit www.travisthrasher.com.